TORN APART

Also by Marta Sprout

Never Text a Stranger
Tobacco Field Boy
Fall Line
Mea Culpa: Guilt
I Will Make Her Dead

◆

Coming 2013
Twitterbe
Torn Apart 2: Finding Ryan

◆

Coming 2014
Furious
Torn Apart 3: Back with a Vengeance
All The Bishops Men

TORN APART

The Abduction of Gillian Curtis

A Novel

MARTA SPROUT

Marta Sprout

StormRider Publishing

Copyright © 2013 by Marta Sprout.
All rights reserved.

TORN APART: The Abduction of Gillian Curtis is a work of fiction. Names, characters, locales, and incidents either are the product of the author's imagination or are used fictitiously. Any resemblance to actual persons, living or dead, events, or locales is entirely coincidental.

No part of this publication may be reproduced, distributed, or transmitted in any form or by any means, or stored in a database or retrieval system, without the prior written permission of the publisher.

Published 2013 by StormRider Publishing
www.stormriderpublishing.com

Cover Photography by:
Serhiy Kyrychenko/Fotolia
yellowj/Fotolia
used with permission
Cover design copyright © 2013 StormRider Publishing

ISBN: 978-0-9857973-0-0

Printed in the United States of America

First Edition

To Ron
because every girl needs a big brother

EVENING - DAY ONE
Wednesday, October 10

One

The Curtis House, 7:25 p.m.

GILLIAN CURTIS GLANCED out the kitchen window at an unfamiliar white van parked down the street and then went back to bobbing her head to the beat of a tune blaring through her ear-buds. Twirling in a circle, she threw down some rock moves and pretended to sing into a microphone that was actually an ice cream scooper.

Her eyes went wide the moment she heard footsteps stomping toward the kitchen. "What the hell are you doing?" The voice of the mighty Dr. Michael Curtis, her one and only father, bellowed at her as he wrung out a sponge at his custom-made kitchen sink.

Gillian licked her sticky fingers and returned to concocting a volcano of a sundae made with layers of mint chocolate chip ice cream, chocolate syrup, and Oreo cookies. "I'm getting dessert."

Her father scowled at her and the rivulets of melting ice cream spreading over his precious granite countertop. "What about your homework?"

"I did it already." Gillie brushed cookie crumbs off her neon orange top with the back of her hand. It was only seven-thirty and already her efforts to avoid hacking him off weren't working.

"I'll bet you did. That's why you are doing *so well* in geometry," he said while staring at her chocolate covered hands. Gillie thought her paranoid dad worried more about what she'd contaminate next in his stupid mansion than her feelings.

She watched him through her tousled blonde bangs. His eyes shifted to the underside of her left wrist where red lacerations ripped across the white flesh. Her collection of friendship bracelets – the ones she wore to cover the wounds and to remember the people she missed – had shifted. He jerked her arm up into the air as if to embarrass her in front of some invisible audience. She hated the way his eyes bulged when he got really pissed.

"What are these? For God's sake, are you cutting yourself?"

Gillie tore her arm out of his grasp – even though it hurt. Any hope of compromise died and was replaced by a thunderclap of angst. "I can't even get a stupid bowl of ice cream without you jumping my case. Well, excuse me for breathing, but I never asked to move in with you. The school here sucks. I want to go back to *my* school and be with *my* friends."

He was all puffed up and indignant like he really expected her to jump at his every command.

Think again, Bucko.

Of course, he didn't get it. He never did. "Come on Dad. Can't you understand that I miss my friends? Can I at least go to the dance at my old school? *Please.* It's on Friday."

"Your life is here now. Get used to it."

As usual, it was his way or nothing. What a douche. Gillie crossed her arms, hoping he'd give in. "I'm calling Mom. I want to go home."

"Non negotiable. You're not living with that woman."

Gillie watched him sopping up the mess on the counter and wondered if he knew how stupid he looked as he contorted his body to stay as far away from the chocolate swirls as possible. God forbid anything get on his perfectly-pressed shirt.

"*That woman* is my mother. And I love her, even if you don't."

Gillie pushed the sundae away, causing more to slosh over the edges of the bowl. "You don't get to decide what I feel. You can't just order people to be all happy." She knew this would hack him off. It did. A red blotch flared over the skin behind his ear.

He pointed the soggy sponge at her. "Watch your tongue with me, young lady."

"What's here for me? Not you. And if this is *my life* – " Gillie made quotes in the air with her fingers, " – did you ever consider asking *me* how I felt about moving?"

"That is enough."

Gillie ignored his raised voice. "Why worry about me? It's always about what you want anyway. I'm sick of being alone all the time. I wanna go home and walk my dog and hang out with my friends."

By now red blotches had taken over his whole neck. "You will shut your mouth and do as I tell you." Her father threw the sponge into the sink.

"Get the memo: I'm not another object in your art collection. What am I supposed to do here? I can't touch anything without you having a stroke about it."

"You're getting to be a real pain in the ass. This discussion is over." He turned his back on her and washed his hands at the sink.

"I hate you!" Gillie impaled her melting sundae with the ice cream scooper and bolted from the kitchen. Her feet stamped up the steps to her room while her father continued hollering in the background. "Get back down here – this minute."

Blow it out your ass, old man.

After slamming her bedroom door shut, Gillie curled up in the one piece of furniture she had been allowed to keep from her old room – her papasan chair. It was the only place in the whole house where she felt comfortable. Gillie rubbed the remaining chocolate off her fingers and called her friend, Kip.

"Hey, Gillie. What's up?"

The sound of his voice felt like summer vacation. "My dad is ruining my life. I can't stand it anymore." She sniffled when sloppy wet streaks began trickling down her face. "Everything is such a wreck, I just need to talk to someone who cares."

"Remember in eighth-grade English how I'd bring you gummy bears?"

She tried to laugh as she snagged a Kleenex but it came out sounding pathetically desperate. "I wish you were here now. I could use a hug."

"The last time I tried that your dad threatened to shove a restraining order up my ass."

Gillie winced at the memory. "I hate it here. Even the sheets have so much starch in them it's like sleeping on cardboard." She tried to keep her voice from trembling, but it didn't work. "I should just slit my wrists and be done with it."

"My God. Gillie, *please* don't do that!"

"Kip, he won't even let me see my dog. If I could just take Cody for a walk, I know I'd feel better." Her eyes overflowed again. "My life sucks so bad, it just doesn't matter anymore."

"It matters to me. In a year and a half you'll be eighteen and you can tell him to shove it. Besides, if you kill yourself, I'm gonna come over and kick your ass."

She started to laugh. "But I'd be dead, you idiot."

"Gillie, please, you're scaring me."

"I used to be an honor-roll student. Now I'm just the *emo* girl who's flunking Geometry. The kid's here are so hung up on how rich they are they don't have time to be nice to anybody. I feel like a guppy in a shark tank."

"But I like guppies. So, why cut yourself?"

Gillie swung her legs, kicking her backpack with each swing. "I guess it's like dipping your toe into the pool before jumping in.

Offing yourself is harder than I thought – it's kinda gross too. Maybe I should just run away."

"Where would you go?"

"To my mom's, *duh*."

"I'll bring the gummy bears. Maybe we could meet up?"

Gillie felt a slight tingle of hope and promised she'd text him if she felt like hurting herself again.

After ending the call, she turned up the volume of the music playing through her laptop and flopped on the bed. One day she had been a regular teenager hanging out with her friends and the next felt like she'd been abandoned on a planet of aliens who wanted no part of her.

As of late, every day was just another reminder that she didn't belong here. It killed her that she could only listen to the sound of her friend's voice on the phone or see if he'd cut his hair on Facebook. It wasn't the same as seeing him in person.

She rubbed her sore wrist. She hadn't cut herself to get attention. It was never about that. Gillie had been serious about killing herself until the thought of running away had popped into her brain. Maybe running wasn't such a bad idea after all.

Thinking about how great it would be to go home, her eyes scanned her room and landed on the lame painting on the wall by some stupid Dutch dude. Out of spite, Gillie had envisioned using a few Sharpies to decorate the painted vase of flowers, but she'd never done it. Her father would have gone nuclear. Definitely not worth it, unless she wasn't coming back.

Nothing here felt like home, especially her room. She hated the bed with the huge headboard and the big dresser her father told her had been hand-carved in Italy. Who gave a shit? It was still butt-ugly.

One of the weird things about living with him was all of his stupid rules. Everything had to be put away so the maids could dust and vacuum. No clothes on the floor. No posters on the walls. And God forbid if a bracelet or sunglasses were left on the dresser, the world as we know it would come to a freakin' end.

Who lived like that? Gillie blew her bangs out of the way and stared at the ceiling. The thought of going home sounded better by the minute.

She rolled over with her head and arms dangling off the edge of the mattress, searching for a small wallet she kept under her bed. Opening it, she pulled out a photo of her mother and turned onto her back to look at it more closely.

The only things that had stopped her from committing suicide were friends like Kip and her mom's expression in that one little picture. The thought of what would happen to that smile if she really went through with it had prevented her from cutting deeper.

Gillie popped a stick of cinnamon gum in her mouth and started thinking of a new plan. She knew all too well how paranoid her dad was about security. If she left the house, she would set off the motion-sensor lights around the property. On the other hand, the local cats had been doing that for the last week. Her father was used to it. Last night he didn't even get up to look.

The risks no longer seemed so foreboding. Things with Dad couldn't be any worse, even if she did get caught running away. The taunting faces of the preppy kids faded. In their place her mind focused on the welcoming arms of her mother and her friends.

Gillie sat on the side of the bed with her Aéropostale sweatshirt held next to her nose. It still faintly smelled like her real home where her mom and dog lived. Even a few of Cody's hairs were still stuck inside the pockets.

I've had enough of this crap. It's time to go home.

She emptied the textbooks and papers from her backpack into the bottom drawer of the Italian monstrosity. Then refilled it with her laptop, phone, and a few necessities. At the last minute she collected the little things that meant something, like her mom's picture and the silly plastic gecko Kip had given her that stuck its tongue out when you pinched its belly.

She walked across the gloomy bedroom for what she hoped was the last time. Opening the door, Gillie listened for any sounds downstairs. A clock faintly ticked away. The tingle of nerves turned her gut into a knot. It grumbled. She held her stomach and remembered that she hadn't eaten dinner and never got to finish her sundae, but there was no time for that now. It was time to get out of there. If she were lucky she wouldn't see anymore of Dad eagerly waiting for another round of "Gillie Smackdown."

She took one last glance at her bedroom. The thought of never having to see this place again made her smile until worry set in. Was there anything else she'd forgotten?

Crap. I almost forgot the key.

She scurried back in and grabbed it from the nightstand. *Dad would shit if he knew I had this.*

As she passed the TV stand she stopped and pulled a happy-face sticker out of the drawer and slapped it on the oil painting. Gillie flipped off the light and slunk down the stairs like a cat tracking its next meal.

◆

Gillie scanned the kitchen and briefly thought of taking the carton of mint chocolate chip ice cream with her, but that would have been way too messy. Instead she snagged a bottle of water and shoved a box of Girl Scout cookies into her backpack.

Fortunately, the back door was right off the kitchen where her father couldn't hear her. From the looks of it, her all-too-important dad was back upstairs in his all-too-important office.

Within seconds Gillie had turned off the alarm and slipped outside into the fresh air. She tried to quiet her breathing as she closed the door ever so gently on the warm interior lights.

The smell of grass and the darkness surrounded her. The cool night air turned her fears into excitement as she tiptoed around to the side yard with the intention of hiding in the shadows.

Gillie counted each step like when she was a kid playing hide and seek. *Don't make a mistake*, she reminded herself, hoping she could get as far away as possible before Dad discovered that she'd left.

When she came around the corner her feet slowed to a standstill. Something didn't feel right. She swiveled her head and her eyes struggled to adjust to the darkness. The yard was never *this* dark.

Gillie's arms waved big swooping circles in the air. Nothing happened. Everything was still bathed in Halloween black. Where were the lights? Why weren't they coming on?

She licked her lips and remembered the white van parked up the street.

In the moonlight, lined up on both sides of her, the huge bushes took on the appearance of faceless ghouls towering over her with long-reaching tendrils. If the moon hadn't been so bright, she would have had to feel her way out to the road. That was a disgusting thought. Gillie hated spiders and spiders lived in bushes. She wasn't a big fan of gardening for that reason.

The faint fragrance of her mother's shampoo and powdery makeup floated through Gillie's memory. What she'd give to feel her mom's arms hugging her right now. She took a deep breath and edged her way forward.

A rustling noise from one of the bigger bushes slowed her down. Gillie stopped breathing and listened.

It's probably just a cat, right?

"Hey, Riley, didn't you jack enough from the trash cans?" On a normal night, Riley would have come out of hiding and done a figure eight around her legs, to elicit a good back scratch. But not tonight.

Gillie's shoulders tensed.

She tried to calm her bounding pulse.

For the first time she wished New Hampshire could see the sense in having at least a few neighborhood street lights. In a hurry to get to the safety of the road and in view of passing traffic, she picked up her pace through the grass.

The lawn was dry. Goosebumps rose on her arms.

The sprinkler system always went on between seven and eight. Dry leaves from a low branch swiped her calf. Gillie jumped. Everything should be wet – but it wasn't.

She drew closer to the last big bush. Up ahead were the sounds of a vehicle in idle.

Good. People are out on the road.

Then she heard a grunt as someone came up behind her.

Before she could react, big arms engulfed her like a wave pulling her under. A warm, meaty hand covered her mouth. The other dragged her toward the street with surprising strength.

Let go of me, asshole!

She felt the bulk of the big man behind her. Gillie twisted and kicked. Out on the grass near the road she dug her heels in – hard.

Great, can anything else in my life go wrong?

She took a deep breath and tried again, but her thrashing was of no use. Something in her snapped. Her jaw locked. The bristling anger from the argument came back. In a flash she pumped her elbow into the solid torso of her captor. Totally against her will, her body was still being thrust forward.

I can't believe this.

She flapped her arms trying to get free, but the big shoulders only tightened their grip and pulled her hair. *Ow-ow-ow. Shit. I swear I'm gonna smack you.*

The idling sound was getting louder. Within seconds Gillie saw the same white van up ahead with the engine running.

She felt a puff of hot moist breath on her neck as her abductor tried to open the van's door.

Gross.
He grunted again.
Double gross. Clearly this guy was big.
Great, I'm being abducted by a reject from *"The Biggest Loser."*

Two

Outside The Curtis House, 8:05 p.m.

WALTER LOVETT HAD HIS HANDS FULL.

At first he had thought it was his lucky day when he didn't have to trigger a diversion or set off an alarm to get the girl to come out of the house. However, he had been caught completely off guard when she marched into the side yard before he'd been ready.

Of course, he'd thought of contingencies, but her sudden appearance had forced him to dive into the bushes. That was his first inkling that this wasn't going to be a typical extraction.

His years in Nam had taught him to think ahead. He'd run through every step of his plan maybe a hundred times or more, but it had never occurred to him just how strong teenage girls could be. He'd expected her to be so shocked and scared that taking control wouldn't be too difficult. So much for that idea.

Faced with the flailing arms and legs of this spitfire, Walter wished he was about twenty years younger and in a hell of a lot better shape. Sweat poured down the middle of his back as he tried to keep his wits about him.

"Knock it off," he said in a gravelly voice.

Walter used the most imposing tone he could muster, but it only brought another elbow to his ribcage. Before he could get her to the van, she'd pummeled both of his shins and he could feel his lip swelling where she'd hit him with her head.

Now he had a hell of a dilemma. He had to open the van's door. If he let go of her mouth with one hand she would scream; if he let go with the other she would wiggle away. *Mother of God.*

Finally, he just used his weight to pin her to the side of the van while he slid the door open. Getting her inside became simple when he stumbled over her pumping feet and they both tumbled to the floor.

"Shit," he said.

He was just glad he'd secured all of his handyman tools or her head might have landed on the big pipe wrench that was usually there. Pinning her to the floor, Walter reached for his trusty duct tape. Her continuing protest was muffled by the thickness of his hand over her mouth.

"Mmet, Mmoff, Mmee," she said.

He cupped his hand to keep her from biting his fingers. A nice big piece of duct tape took care of that crap.

Walter wiped his hand and reached for the zip ties. Working around her backpack without hurting her and holding her still long enough to secure her hands proved to be a workout in and of itself. The pulse at the base of his neck pounded like a fullback running a sixty-yard dash to the end zone. Finally he just pulled the backpack off her shoulders and chucked it aside.

As soon as he sat back, after neatly securing the flinging limbs and gnashing teeth, the girl rolled over and flipped into a sitting position with her back against the tool shelf.

Walter saw the eyes of Miss Gillian Curtis for the first time.

She looked like a raccoon with all the black smoky streaks of makeup running down her face. Even so, her eyes were pretty – a deep hazel. Her oval face had that unfinished look, somewhere between that of a woman and a child.

Walter squirmed under the fierce glare leveled at him. A sizzle of guilt shamed his sense of honor. He'd once given his all to protect the innocent and rescue people just like this kid. Sure he had served his country and done his share of manhunts too, but only to root out ruthless monsters who had been bent on hurting others. Tonight was a huge departure from anything he'd ever done before.

The knot in Walter's gut relaxed when he reminded himself of the real target – the girl's father. Walter's wife had died because of that inhumane bastard's protocols. He figured he'd deal with his conscience later, for now he had a job to do. Reverting back to his training, he did what he'd always done on missions. He stayed doggedly focused.

Walter's voice returned to a more fatherly tone. "This will be over soon. Just quit fighting it."

Her ferocious eyes glared at him. Each exhalation through her nose blew tufts of blonde hair from her face.

"I am sorry about this," he said as he hauled her petite body over to a flip down seat on the wall next to a shelf of small tools and strapped her in with the seatbelt.

Walter dropped into the driver's seat. His heart raced and his hands trembled just enough to make it more difficult to put on his own seatbelt. Finally, he checked the mirror for oncoming traffic and drove away.

As he left, he glanced up at the second floor of the Curtis house. The light was on upstairs. Walter had hoped there wouldn't be a confrontation, but had expected it might come to that. He'd envisioned the doctor charging toward him to save his daughter. Fortunately, that didn't happen. Damn good thing because handling her was enough for one night. If they'd met back in Vietnam, it would have been a different story. Then he could have taken them both with one hand and eaten his lunch with the other, but not today. Walter watched the traffic on I-93 and continued south onto the Everett Turnpike toward his home in Hudson, New Hampshire. He'd seen enough of Concord for one night. He tooled off the highway and took his favorite backroads. The traffic on 3A was lighter at this hour of the night, making for an easy drive provided a deer or a moose didn't jump out in front of him. Walter had just begun to calm down when a blonde head lurched over his shoulder into the front cabin. *What the hell? Where's the duct tape and zip ties?*

"I'm gonna hurl if you don't let me sit up front. I get carsick real bad if I have to sit in the back."

Walter swerved the van to the side of the road, slammed it to a stop, and jumped in the back. She wiggled away and threw tools at him. He slipped on a crowbar as he grabbed her wrist. The girl latched onto an extension cord hanging neatly on a hook. Walter pulled his arm away, just before she bit him. "That's it. I'm done with this crap."

Walter pulled out his old Colt pistol from his days in the army. He hadn't bothered to clean it nor check to see if it still worked. The damned thing hadn't been loaded in over thirty years, but she didn't know that. He still knew how to hold the weapon and act like he meant business.

"Cooperate or I'll blow your head off. Your choice." He hoped frustration had given his words a convincing edge.

Much to his surprise, she didn't even look at the barrel pointed at her nose and screamed right back at him. "Go ahead, asshole! Do it! I was planning on killing myself anyway."

The girl stood there defiant as all get out with his screwdriver still in hand.

What the hell? This wasn't at all what he'd expected.

There in the back of his old van, he and the girl were huffing and puffing and waiting for the other to do or say something.

Due to the limited head space, Walter's six-foot-three frame was forced into a very uncomfortable crouch, which only made him feel even more ridiculous.

"If you don't want to get hurt, you've got to listen to me," he said.

"Okay, I get it. Just let me sit up front. *Puleeease?*" She let go of the extension cord and started to chuck the red-handled screwdriver back on the shelf.

"Put it back gently. It's my favorite one," he said.

He stowed his pistol in his vest pocket. If Walter hadn't been so flummoxed, he probably wouldn't have given in. "Okay, but if you do anything I don't like it's back you go. Clear?"

"Clear."

As the girl climbed into the front seat Walter could see that her tights were torn. "Miss Curtis, I'm truly sorry about your stockings, I didn't intend to tear up your outfit."

She snickered. "I bought them this way. They are supposed to be torn. And you can call me Gillie. 'Miss Curtis' sounds like a math teacher."

Walter wasn't sure what to make of this girl. He seated his hat down low on his head, pulled back into traffic, and headed toward the house while trying to wrap his brain around why anyone would pay good money for clothing that was already ruined.

"What happened to the duct tape and how in the hell did you get free?"

"You've got a shitload of tools back there. Right next to me was a pair of wire snips. It didn't take a rocket scientist to figure that one out. You new at this or something?"

"It certainly isn't a habit of mine."

"I've never been kidnapped before, so it's my first time too." A big grin busted out all over the girl's face. "Hey! I don't have to go to school tomorrow. Sweet."

Walter was halfway between wanting to get out of the van and run – or just shoot himself.

"What do I call you?" she asked.

"Walter."

"That must be your real name. No one makes up a name like that."

His head pivoted between the road and the girl.

As he made it closer to the house he couldn't help staring at her. What an odd creature. Her blonde hair wasn't messed up from their struggle as he had first assumed. It was the style, if you could call it that. If his daughter had worn her hair like that he'd have sent her back into the house with a hair brush. But no, this one wore hers cut in random lengths with one lock running along the side of her face that was tinted pink. He could see dyeing hair brown, blonde, auburn, but pink?

Kids. What can you say? It sure was a different world these days.

Out of nowhere Gillie punched him in the right biceps. "Yellow punch buggy, no punch buggy back."

"What the hell was that for?"

"Are you kidding me? That's what you hafta do when you see a VW bug. Or you can just say *green one* or *silver one*. See?"

Walter glanced blankly back. He was at a loss for words. The girl just sighed, shook her head, and looked out the window. After a few seconds she brightened up. "I'm starving. Let's get a burger."

Walter knew there was a Wendy's across the river, but he wasn't going there. "I can't."

"Oh, right. You've got a kidnapping vic and someone might report us. Right?"

He took off his hat, threw it on the dash between them, and shook his head.

"Aw, come on. How about the drive-thru? *Please.* I'm having french fry withdrawal."

"No. I can't eat fast food. Doc says I have to stay away from saturated fats and too many carbs."

"*Seriously?*" Gillie put on his hat, slumped down in the seat, and started to cackle. "So, you always wear your seatbelt, you obey the speed limit, and follow your doctor's orders. Oh, and by the way –" A fit of giggles filled the van. "– you do a little kidnapping on the side. *Hello?*"

Walter scowled at the road up ahead. This sure as hell wasn't going as planned.

◆

WALTER PULLED INTO THE DRIVEWAY next to his little white house with the green shutters. "Don't give me any more trouble. I'm warning you. And I'll take my hat back now, thank you."

As they emerged from the van, Gillie caught sight of a woman next door peeking at them through the drapes on a second-floor window. "Who's that?"

"That's my snoopy neighbor, Mrs. Jacober. She's the neighborhood busybody."

"Mrs. Goober," said Gillie with a giggle.

"No. Not goober – *Jacober*," said Walter as he unlocked the side door.

Once inside, Walter showed Gillie to her room, where he had carefully secured the window with a new sheet of plywood. Of course, he'd put a new lock on the door. And, just to be on the safe side, he'd added an extra smoke detector and a quilt in case she got cold. "You can stay in here."

Walter watched the girl looking around the sunny yellow room. She set her backpack down, flopped on the bed, and stroked her hand over the blue comforter. "It's better than where I sleep at my dad's house."

The sadness in her comment tweaked Walter's conscience. He sat down heavily in the old oak rocking chair that he'd once used to rock his own children to sleep. They'd grown up a long time ago, but it was still handy when his back pain flared up. It was somehow soothing to rock away his sore spots and remember the good times.

"I need you to empty everything out of your backpack and your pockets. Please."

Gillie rolled her eyes and dumped everything on the bed. The array of things that tumbled out told him something important. She was running away. That's why she had left the house.

Now the makeup, deodorant, and the extra clothes made sense – it was the other things that puzzled him: stickers, plastic bracelets, and what the hell was she going to do with a toy gecko? Walter picked it up and frowned when the damn thing stuck its tongue out at him.

"Hey, Kip gave me that for my birthday."

Walter carefully put down the gecko and scooped up her cellphone, computer, and then checked to make sure she didn't have anything that could hurt either of them.

"Thank you. You'll get these back."

"Whatever. I get it."

Walter studied the girl on his guest bed. He thought that if you looked beyond all the makeup and wild colors of her clothing, she was a pretty little thing with a feisty but pleasant disposition that seemed at odds with the leering skull printed on her shirt. If he were to pick out something he thought suited her, it would be a dress in a pastel pink or soft blue.

Neither one of them seemed to know what to do.

Those eyes were staring at him again.

Walter laughed at himself. He had comfortably stared down many men who, if given the chance, would have taken his head off and yet with this girl, the silence was becoming awkward.

Gillie sat up and toyed with a lock of her hair.

Walter cleared his throat. "So, why would a young girl like you want to kill herself?"

"It's a long story."

"It can't be that long. I have underwear older than you."

"Whitey-tighties or boxers?"

If Walter had been a younger man he would have blushed the color of summer cherries, instead he just gave out a hoarse harrumph to dismiss the question.

Gillie crinkled up her nose. "My life is a disaster." She fell back into the pile of pillows as if she'd been shot. "My dad and I fight all the time."

"Adolescence is tough. I don't know if it's worse for the kids or their parents, but it's not an easy time for anyone. You have a lot to figure out. My kids and I fought then too."

"Yeah, well, you didn't see the fight we had tonight."

Walter wondered what the real story was between her and her father. He already knew Dr. Curtis was a cold bastard. It didn't really surprise him that the guy didn't get along with his kid.

"So, you still hungry?"

Three

The Curtis House, 8:50 p.m.

Lyn rang her soon to be ex-husband's doorbell. No one answered. Her wristwatch said it was nearly nine. Michael's car was parked in the driveway. She knew they were home.

Her thumb pressed the button again. She waited for what seemed like forever. This time Lyn heard Michael yelling at their daughter. "Gillian, get the damn door."

Lyn had always hated how he barked at Gillie.

When their daughter didn't respond, a light went off in a second floor window and he stomped down the stairs loudly enough that Lyn could hear his steps and his grumbling. Through the front door's beveled-glass, she watched Michael descending the grand staircase as if it were beneath him to do something so mundane as to answer a doorbell. *Some things never change.*

The front door finally opened. Even at this hour, Lyn wasn't surprised to see Michael dressed in one of his fancy shirts with the sleeves rolled up, and a pair of pressed jeans. They must have set him back a few Benjamin Franklins. The other thing he always wore around her was that damn smug expression.

By now it didn't even surprise her how quickly he'd forgotten that she was the one that supported him through medical school and his boards until he'd found his niche, which in his case was a mission to never lay hands on a single patient. His position as medical director of New England's largest health insurance company allowed him to do things more in line with his temperament, like bossing people around. At YorkCare he decided who got their claims paid and who didn't.

Finally the porch light came on. She braced herself for the first insult.

"What are *you* doing here?"

Lyn decided to ignore his emphasis on the word "you" that made it sound as if she were some kind of foul-smelling deadbeat who had crawled out of a gutter to scam him out of a few bucks.

"Is Gillie ready?"

Michael just stared at her.

"I told you I'd pick her up tonight. Didn't you tell her? She has a dentist appointment tomorrow afternoon. I'm the responsible parent who is going to take her while you're off schmoozing with your big-time buddies, remember?"

"So I forgot. You don't have to make a federal case out of it."

While Michael went to call up the stairs for their daughter, Lyn stood at the breakfast bar next to the kitchen. Judging by the streaks on the counter, Gillie had made her mark. A devious smirk stretched across Lyn's face until she realized how much she missed that kid.

The thought left her biting her lower lip and hoping one day Gillie could come home.

She had known she would miss her girl desperately, but she'd never thought she would miss the trail of socks, half-empty soda bottles, plates by the TV, and the endless messes in the kitchen, but she did. She missed every goofy grin and late-night chat. Even the mornings when she had to pry her complaining daughter out of bed to go to school, she missed that too – every single second of it.

"Gillian, your mother is here. Come down – *now*."

There was no answer. Lyn brushed past Michael, who stood there stiff as a drum major. As usual he wasn't going out of his way to find out why Gillie wasn't answering. Lyn glared at him and shook her head.

Whatever you do, don't exert yourself.

"Gillie, sweetie, it's Mom," said Lyn as she went up the stairs to the east wing. She noticed traces of what looked like chocolate on the wall. Gillie wasn't that careless, unless she was really mad about something. And the only person who pissed her off that badly was Michael.

"Gillie?" It wasn't just that there was no answer. There was nothing. No music. No TV. No water running in the bathroom. *Where is she?*

Lyn knocked on the door, which opened just a crack.

She tried not to overreact when her mother mode went on full alert. The hair stood on Lyn's arms, even before she turned on the lights. Something was wrong. Her fingers flipped the switch. "Sweetie, where are you?"

The lights only proved what Lyn already knew. Gillie wasn't there. More than that, it didn't even look like she'd ever been there, save for the rumpled bedding.

"Michael. Where's Gillie?" Lyn turned and demanded an answer as she hurried back down the stairs.

"What do you mean?"

She hated how Michael looked at her as if she were speaking Mandarin Chinese. It was truly amazing how such a handsome man could look so stupid.

"It's not a trick question. Where the hell is our daughter? You know, she's about five foot one, blonde, always has earbuds stuck in her head."

Michael just stood there.

In complete frustration, she gave up on his obstructionist bent and started to look for Gillie herself.

"How the hell should I know?" he said while trailing behind her.

Lyn stopped and turned back to look at him. "Excuse me, but aren't you the one who is demanding sole custody and claiming that you are the better parent – 'the one most able to meet her needs' – isn't that what you said? If you're so much better, then why in the hell don't you know where she is? You're her goddamn father. She lives here. It's your job to know where she is."

Michael continued to stand there with his hands in his pockets, while she began a room to room search. As Lyn frantically investigated every cupboard and corner it quickly became painfully obvious that her little girl was missing. Lyn kept swallowing and taking deep breaths to try and bat down the fear that was making it harder and harder to breathe.

"Maybe she went out."

"With whom?" asked Lyn, teetering on the edge of panic.

"I don't know. She's a kid, they all have friends."

"That's really vague." Lyn was staring right into his blue eyes. "Who, Michael? Who are her friends?"

"How the hell am I supposed to know that?"

"It's called listening to your child. It's what good parents do. Maybe, if you paid as much attention to her as you do about having your shirts starched, you might have a clue."

"Look, we had a fight."

"Jesus, Michael."

Lyn was so upset she went outside for a few minutes to calm down. It was that or give into her urge to smack him.

She stared up at the night sky. It looked like smoky blue velvet covered in twinkling white Christmas lights. It was one of the charms of living in New Hampshire where you could actually see the stars.

Scanning the vacant street and wondering what had happened to her girl only made it worse. *I just can't believe this is happening.*

Every fiber of Lyn's maternal being wanted to see that kid leaning against her car, popping her gum, and waiting to go. Where was her little girl?

◆

WALTER GLANCED UP at Gillie stretched over his breakfast bar. He listened to her chattering away as she watched him search for his special frying pan.

"Walter, what are you making?"

"My famous grilled-cheese sandwiches, if I can find the damn pan."

Walter had been getting by on things he could microwave, but knowing he was going to have "company," he'd stocked up on things he didn't normally eat. Like snacks kids her age liked and real food that had to be cooked on the stove. His wife had been the family chef. Helen knew where everything from the mellon baller to the measuring cups were located. But for Walter it was still a hunt-and-peck operation.

"Helen, my dear, where is that damn pan?" He still had the habit of talking to her even though his wife's death was still bitterly etched in the front of his every thought. They had been married for more than forty-five years and it was a hard habit to break.

"Who's Helen?"

Walter just handed Gillie a sack of potato chips and hoped that would keep her quiet for a while. After the night he'd just had, he wasn't in the mood for chitchat and he'd already gotten closer to this hostage than he'd intended.

Finally he spotted the pan and set to work.

As soon as he fired up the blue flame of the gas burner it was like old times when he used to make these for Helen. They were a family tradition on Monday nights when he was home early and she had been so tired from taking care of the kids and her own part-time job at the pharmacy. *God, I miss those days.*

Walter pulled open the freezer door, causing a billowy mist to condense in front of his eyes. He snagged one of those ready-to-steam bags of vegetables and flopped it into the microwave. After all, Gillie was a growing girl who needed her vitamins. If he was going to detain her, the least he could do was keep her healthy.

The sandwiches had reached the glory of golden goodness on both sides when he lovingly slid them onto the plates. "Let's sit at the table," he said with just a smidgen of pride.

Dang, they really do look good.

Gillie took both plates to the table. Damn if she didn't sit down right in the very spot where Helen used to sit.

Every morning he used to find his wife right there by the window, looking out at the birds and the marauding gray squirrels plundering the bird feeders. Helen would laugh at their antics while sipping her coffee. He was never sure if it was the coffee or the critters that she loved so much. Probably it was both.

He shook off the memory and soon joined Gillie with a bowl heaped high with brussels sprouts and butter – actually in this case it was a butter substitute.

"What's that smell?" Gillie had her hand over her nose.

"They're brussels sprouts. It's called a vegetable."

"That's just gross. I don't eat green things that stink."

"Haven't you heard that you need to eat foods in a wide variety of colors like yellow peaches, green beans, blueberries, and – "

"Skittles?"

Walter put his napkin to his mouth. One look at her raised eyebrows and bright eyes and he just couldn't help himself. A chuckle boiled up from deep inside that he simply couldn't hold back.

"That was a good one. Oh, what now?" Gillie was doing a seated dance and pumping her fists around in a circle in the air.

Walter found himself enthralled by this quirky kid, who was now going after the sandwich as if she hadn't eaten in a week. "Don't they feed you?"

"I get wha I can gwap," she said around the hot mouthful. Gillie wiped her chin and swallowed. "Sorry. I get what I can grab or make in the microwave myself. My dad doesn't cook and he won't let me use the stove – doesn't want to risk getting it dirty. But my mom is a great cook."

Walter watched the girl's face turn pensive. "I miss her like crazy. I haven't had anyone make me something to eat in a long time."

"What happened to your mom?"

"Divorce. My dad insists I live with him. I don't know why, it's not like he spends any time with me."

"I'm sorry to hear that. I haven't had someone make me a meal in a long while either. It's nice when it happens, don't cha think?"

"Yeah. This is wicked good." Gillie continued to gobble down her grilled cheese with gusto. Apparently all of life was a full body experience for this kid. At least it seemed so to Walter as he watched her string the melted cheese all over. She wiped her face on the napkin and went back for more. The gleam in her eyes showed she was enjoying herself, which Walter thought odd, considering their circumstances.

"You have any soda. Coke? Dr. Pepper?"

"I have milk, OJ, and water. Anyone of them are good for you."

"You sound just like a parent." Gillie sounded annoyed, but Walter made sure he showed no signs of giving in.

"You win, the milk will have to do," she said with a sigh.

Walter started to get up, but Gillie beat him to it. She rummaged around for a glass and got it herself.

"It's nice to have someone to eat with for a change," he said. It was the ordinary little things that he missed so much – like the way Helen would hold his hand while they watched TV programs, how she used to walk next to him at the grocery store, or even how she had insisted on folding his skivvies when she did the laundry. Most of all he missed having someone to talk to.

Walter rubbed his hand over his chest. His fingers found nothing out of the ordinary, but to him it felt as if a hole bigger than his heart had been blown away. By far, the worst was not being able to kiss the love of his life goodnight before going to sleep, and then the horrible reminder every morning when he awoke and rolled over to face her empty pillow.

Gillie's voice snapped him out of his mournful thoughts.

"Thank you. This is really good."

Walter smiled and they both laughed. "It does hit the spot."

"I get tired of eating by myself too," said Gillie. "Even at school, I always end up eating alone. It sucks."

"Where are your friends? A girl like you must have lots of them."

Gillie grimaced at the brussels sprouts and pushed the bowl away. "Thanks. I do have friends, but they are all back at my old school. I don't get to see them much anymore."

"I understand. I don't do well by myself either. It just – " Walter shook his head.

"It rots?"

"Yeah." Walter had to agree. "It does."

This goofy girl was growing on him. Walter wondered if her father knew what a great kid she was – then again – he was Michael J. Curtis, M.D. Enough said.

"So, why did you kidnap me?"

Walter sat back in his chair and scratched the back of his head. "I've been wondering that myself. Listen, I've got to use the facilities, I'll be right back."

"Facilities?" Gillie's face scrunched up into a frown. "Oh! Gotcha."

Down the hall Walter went.

Once in the bathroom, he wrestled with more than his zipper as he sat down on the commode. He rested his face in his hands. His conscience was eating him alive.

I should just take her back to her mother.

He knew how to disappear and wasn't worried about the police pursuing him, but what if her mother wasn't home? Who would take care of Gillie then? He couldn't just leave the girl alone and he sure as hell wasn't going to take her back to that bastard father of her's. Besides, he and Dr. Curtis still had a score to settle.

After washing his hands and checking his blood sugar, he took his insulin. Walter decided he would have to think long and hard about this one. His thoughts were interrupted. He cocked his head and stilled his breathing. Water was running in the kitchen.

Four

The Curtis House, 9:40 p.m.

MIKE CURTIS PACED BACK AND FORTH in his living room, stopping only to turn his Steuben glass sculpture so that the light gleamed through it at just the right angle.

To him it was a remarkable miniature universe captured in clean, clear glass. That he owned one of only ten pieces in existence was noteworthy, but it was the piece itself that Mike loved so much. Art was a noble world, set apart, untouched by the tainted hands of society. Such things were made by people who were on a higher plane than the bumbling hordes that choked city streets.

He went back to pacing. Mike had already lost his patience and was fed up with both Lyn and Gillian. He didn't have time to deal with their crap. Not now – not so close to winning the contract.

Mike was standing on the precipice of something huge. Not only would this make him wildly wealthy, he was going to change the face of health care in this country. His groin tightened at the prospects. Mike was wielding the kind of power he'd always dreamt of – and then some.

It almost made him giddy.

Much of this plan was already in place, like lowering payments to doctors while quietly buying up struggling hospitals. The plan was one of control, which was gradually proceeding right on schedule.

Two major things were in his favor: a complacent public and a congress who didn't need to worry about their own medical needs. Washington was so distracted by political gamesmanship, by the time they figured out what was happening, it would be too late. His plan would be solidly infused into the infrastructure of medical care management.

He loved the unfunded mandates and the privacy laws that increased physicians' already bloated paperwork loads. The sum of these bills ensured even more pressure on practices that were already over stretched. By far the best one was the abundance of seemingly innocuous regulations that had been tacked onto other bills sliding through the legislature for years. Together they would tie the hands of anyone who wanted to stop it later.

He still had so much to do and precious minutes were dribbling away.

Looking at his Rolex, he realized his whole evening was turning to shit quickly and the mother-daughter duo wasn't helping. Friday night was only two days away. That was the pivotal moment where he planned to win the veterans' contract for all of New England.

The problem now was that Lyn had overreacted and called the police. Why in hell did that woman have to have an emotional response to everything?

He halfway hoped that Gillian *was* lost and that it scared the crap out of her. It would serve her right. How dare she ignore his authority. When he got her back, things were going to be different. If she didn't like things before, just wait until she got a load of what was coming next.

In the meantime, he needed a plan to extricate himself as efficiently as possible from this circus. The cops would arrive any minute with a lot of prying questions to suck up even more of his precious time.

It was already nine forty-five when he looked down at Lyn's red hair. Of course, she had no concept that there were more important things at stake and that he had better things to do with his time. As if the way she nervously picked at her nails wasn't enough to drive him nuts, she had this stupid expectation that the whole goddamn world had to come to a standstill just because she was worried about Gillian. What was the big deal? The girl was sixteen; hell, by the time he was twelve he'd been on his own.

"You know you're overreacting. She probably went off with that boy – what's his name? – just to get even with me."

Lyn turned her head away from him and shifted in her seat on the couch.

Mike was about to pressure Lyn into giving Gillie more time to return on her own when he saw the lights flashing in the front yard. *KNOCK – KNOCK*. That was just bitchen, this was going to be a PR nightmare when the news got its hands on this one.

Lyn started for the door, but he signaled her to stay put. "This is my house, I'll handle it."

Lyn stood but didn't say a word.

Mike escorted a detective Andrew Determan from the foyer into the dining room while slipping the cop's business card into his pocket. The detective was only slightly shorter than himself and also dark haired. His clothes were nothing more than off-the-rack, but this Determan seemed like a no-baloney kind of guy. At least Mike could respect that. He liked men who were all business. Saves time.

The guy wore his gun in a holster on his left shoulder like they were old friends, comfortable with each other. Most of the time it was hidden by the man's overcoat, which told Mike this cop was sure of himself. He didn't need to show off his weapon to get respect. For now he armed himself with a pen and a notepad.

Mike braced himself for a battery of none-of-your-damn-business questions that surely were coming next.

"I understand you have a missing daughter," said Determan in a polite but to the point tone.

They sat at the dining room table. Lyn joined them in a seat across from Mike. While she bent the detective's ear with her twaddle, Mike rotated his foot around in a circle under the banquet-sized table and kept an eye on the time until he realized Determan was speaking to him.

"Was she upset about anything?" Determan asked.

Lyn turned and glared at Mike.

He cleared his throat. It was time to give the detective a morsel of truth to chew on. "She's pretty miffed at me right now."

"What about?"

"The usual stuff: doing homework, cleaning up after herself, and talking to her parents with respect – she's not highly skilled at that one."

Lyn's lips tightened into a slit as she looked away, but Mike took pride in himself for having the presence of mind to use the plural *parents*. It sounded so much more cooperative and he was able to undercut Gillian's credibility at the same time.

Mike watched Determan nod as he took in the data. The man didn't react openly. Mike thought this guy played his cards pretty close to the vest.

Predictably, Lyn continued to keep the detective busy writing notes as she poured out an excessive description of Gillian and a bunch of unnecessary details the guy didn't need to know. She just had to tell him that Gillian was such a good kid. *Horse shit. She's a mouthy pain in the ass.*

"What was she wearing, the last time you saw her?" the detective asked.

Lyn looked down at her hands. "I haven't seen her today."

"Don't you live here?"

"No. We are in the middle of a rather challenging divorce. I live in our old house over in Goffstown and Michael just moved here with Gillie about six months ago."

Mike felt the pulse in his neck rise like the sap of a maple tree. That was none of the cop's damn business.

Mike tried to give Lyn one of those shut-your-face looks, but she just turned away and blabbered on like she always did. He hated her for that.

He hated her for everything – especially for all the trivial little jobs she did as if any of them mattered. To hear her talk, making lattes was an art form and teaching a few lowlifes to read was some noble achievement.

"I see," said the detective still eyeing his notes. "Dr. Curtis, you've been here all evening?"

"Yes, of course," said Mike as he sat back in his chair.

The detective flipped to yet another new sheet of paper. Mike wanted to scream.

"What was your daughter wearing when you had the argument?"

Mike looked up at the ceiling and stretched his neck. His first thought was *how the shit should I know?* But he dared not say that to the detective.

"Let me see. She had on…" Never having paid any attention to her clothing, he stalled for time. "She had on a black T-shirt and black jeans. And those high topped sneakers. Pink or blue, I think."

"They're called Converses and they are red. I should know, I gave them to her for her birthday," said Lyn as she shot Mike another one of her looks.

He ignored her.

"So her parents are getting a divorce, she has had to move, leave friends behind, and transfer to a new school. It sounds like she's a kid who's pretty stressed out."

Mike stood and looked at his watch. It was time to wrap this up before the detective started prying further. "You are right, of course, but we are working through the adjustments. And that's not the point. I need to know where my daughter is and I don't. So, if you don't mind, can we get on to the part about finding her?"

Determan stood eyeing him closely. "It would help if we had some idea if she ran away or was abducted."

Lyn gasped and held a hand over her mouth.

That's just great. Now we have to suck up more time dealing with her water works.

While the detective attentively comforted Lyn, the man's partner stuck his head in the door. "Hey, Deter. You better come look at this."

Determan slipped the notepad back into a pocket and followed his partner outside to the front of the house. Mike trailed behind trying to ignore the irritating presence of his wife.

"Folks, stay back," one of the cops warned them. "This is a crime scene."

Lyn instantly melted back into her sloppy tears. *Christ, she looks like a busted sprinkler head.*

Mike turned away from her. He'd expected a robust response based on his stature in the community, but even he couldn't believe the spectacle on his front lawn.

Yellow tape and flood lights blanketed the side of his house. A team was examining something near the road while others armed with everything from lights and cameras to plastic bags and tweezers combed the side yard. Two more cars arrived with sirens blaring.

The street in front of his house was filled with a caravan of emergency vehicles. It was only a matter of minutes before the press would catch wind of this. Even though the homes in the area were secluded in the woods, anything happening in such an exclusive neighborhood would draw attention.

While the cops tiptoed through his yard, Mike set his mind on a more useful purpose – how to handle the press. Perhaps there was an opportunity in this after all.

Mike straightened his tie and brushed one hand through his dark wavy hair.

Five

Lovett House, 10:15 p.m.

GILLIE PLAYED WITH THE BUBBLES in the sink and enjoyed the warm water bathing her hands. This was so weird. Tonight had actually been nice. And it was way better than her dad's house.

Walter obviously didn't want to hurt her. He'd made grilled-cheese and had hung out laughing with her. He even tried to make her eat healthy stuff. Walter was definitely harmless. She figured she could get away any time she wanted to, but for now she cleared the table and started doing the dishes. That's what she and her mom used to do. One cooked and the other cleaned up.

Maybe this Walter guy would take her home to her mom.

Gillie doubted her dad even knew she was missing and wondered how long it would take him to realize she was gone. He probably wouldn't figure it out until the school called – that could be days. As soon as Mom found out about the kidnapping she would freak. Gillie hoped her mother wouldn't hear the news for at least a day or two. Maybe by then Walter would help her get back home.

Finding the dish soap and kitchen towels had been pretty easy. It was the brussels sprouts that hung her up. She had no idea what to do with them.

Walter walked back into the room with his head cocked. She couldn't help smiling. He looked kinda cute when he was surprised. She felt proud of herself for pitching in. "What do you want me to do with those disgusting green things?"

Walter glanced over at the bowl on the counter. "They give me gas. I don't have a disposal. We could put them in the flower beds."

"I think even the skunks would revolt. Can't say I'd blame them."

Walter chuckled and handed her a few plastic bags. "How about we recycle these?"

Gillie double bagged the offending brussels sprouts and tossed them into the trash. Turning back to finish up she reached into the soapy water. "Shit!"

Walter rushed to the sink. When she pulled up her hand, red immediately mingled with the soap bubbles and ran down her arm. She gasped. He grabbed a wad of paper towels and her finger.

"Ow. I think I found the knife."

"Take a deep breath. Water always makes it look worse than it is. You're gonna be fine." His voice was so calm she believed him. Walter wrapped more of the paper towel around her bleeding finger. "Hold pressure on it and come with me."

Together they hurried down the hall to the bathroom. He ran water over the cut and then as she sat on the counter he put more pressure on the wound. "Hold your hand up higher," he told her. "It needs to be above your heart."

While they waited for the bleeding to stop, Gillie looked around at the tidy bathroom. It was decorated in powdery soft hues of pink. Wait a minute. Pink wasn't a color a guy would use. A pair of women's slippers were by the tub and a second toothbrush stood in the holder. A brown wig sat on a faceless stand. Helen was his wife, that had to be it.

Was – that was the key word.

Gillie just hoped Helen hadn't been some cold witch who had taken off and left Walter. He was too sweet for someone to just dump him like that. She imagined that this Helen loved him, probably for a long time. If that were true, she must have died. That would explain why Walter seemed so sad. Gillie hoped it wasn't twenty years ago, because that would be just plain creepy, like that old movie where the motel guy kept his mom around after she was long dead and talked to her.

The horror-flick images leaping from her vivid imagination clicked off when Walter gently pulled back the paper towel to check the cut. She watched as he put antibiotic ointment on a BandAid and carefully covered the wound, putting just a slight amount of pressure as he wrapped it around her finger.

"If the tip of your finger turns anything but pink or it starts to tingle, loosen up the BandAid."

His hands fascinated her. They were rough like those that had seen a lot of hard work. They had a few old scars, one deep, and were slightly swollen, especially around his knuckles. Gillie would have given anything to find him last year when she was doing her photo project for class. She had done hers on hands because she thought that everyone's hands told a story. His were epic.

"There you go," said Walter.

"I'm sorry I got blood on your sleeve."

He looked down at his plaid shirt and shrugged. "It's washable."

Walter checked her fingertip and took the balled-up paper towel out of her hand. Gillie tensed when he saw the cuts on her left wrist. To her amazement, Walter never looked her in the eye. She knew he'd seen them, but he never said a word. Yet there was something in the softness of his eyes that made her feel as if he understood her pain. Instead of grilling her like her father had done, he just turned her hand over and patted it gently.

Gillie blew her bangs back with a heavy sigh and examined the bandage. She remembered how nice it was back when her mother did things for her like this. As Walter helped her off the counter she wondered how long it had been since someone had taken care of him.

◆

DETERMAN RAKED THE BEAM of light from his flashlight across the tortured grass in front of the Curtis house. The rest of the lawn was meticulously groomed, which made the skid marks and clumps of displaced sod even more out of place.

He ran his light down a path of divots – each one layered over the other – and was glad the ground wasn't too dry nor too soggy. His eyes scanned for patterns. According to what he saw, they were either dancing or in one hell of a scuffle.

One set appeared to be that of a smaller person, maybe a little over a hundred pounds; the other weighed in at twice that. It sure looked like the girl had put up no small amount of resistance. Deter contemplated the torn-up turf and wondered what had played itself out on this lawn.

A few things were already off kilter about this case. Kidnappers typically lay in wait for their victims as they follow their usual routes – like jogging paths and bus stops – but this time the footprints showed the probable perp as running away from the victim and into the bushes. Toward the front of the house it looked like a kidnapping. But how did the perp know she was going to leave the house just then? And why did she take the longer route around the back instead of just coming out of the front door? Part of this scenario looked more and more like a runaway.

Deter played with his mustache and mulled over the facts. Finding the truth took careful analysis. He didn't like jumping to conclusions. A few rookies at the station were prone to running in, balls to the wall, to handcuff the first plausible suspect they could find. He'd rather let the facts speak for themselves, circle around, and let the perp hang himself.

Deter's right knee popped as he stood. He shook it off and slowly ambled around the vehicles in the circular drive and back to the front door. Up ahead the silhouette of Dr. Curtis stood there looking like a page torn out of *GQ*. Lots of things about that doctor bothered him.

That old annoying buzzer in the back of his brain sounded. Something was a little off like milk not yet spoiled but damn close. In some ways, it didn't matter. The only thing now that really counted was finding that girl. He needed to know more about her and that was starting right here on this stoop.

"Dr. Curtis, does she have a pattern of leaving the house around this time?"

"No. She was *supposed* to be in her room doing her homework," said Curtis.

Deter wasn't about to tell the doctor that his habit of belittling his daughter wasn't helpful – at least not until he could determine the doctor's role in this situation. "Do you have a picture of Gillian?"

"I um…I don't have one handy, but I could get one…" Deter watched Dr. Curtis half-heartedly patting his pockets, while his blue eyes stayed focused on the processing team.

"I do," said Mrs. Curtis as she pulled Gillian's school picture from the wallet-sized purse slung over her shoulder.

"Can I see her room, please?"

"Sure," said Dr. Curtis pointing over his shoulder toward the front door. "It's in the east wing at the top of the stairs on the left. Help yourself."

The doctor's eyes remained glued on the latest wave of arriving vehicles. Deter's brow went up. Curtis had given him free rein to explore the house. The guilty were always extremely interested in his findings, but not this guy. He looked as if he couldn't care less. Dr. Curtis stayed outside while Deter walked through the house. The man might not be very fond of his daughter, but so far, he wasn't acting like a suspect either. Deter reminded himself that such acts could be deceiving. He'd seen that before too.

Curtis was right about not having a picture. Oddly, he didn't have any family photographs – not in the living room nor anywhere else in the entire house. Deter couldn't even find a school picture stuck on the fridge.

Upstairs, Deter almost missed the girl's room. It sure wasn't like his own girls' bedrooms nor any he'd seen. The bedding was a little messed up, but beyond that it looked like a guest room. The colors were dark and muted, mostly browns and golds. Again, not what he'd expect in an adolescent girl's room.

The closet had a modest array of clothing that took up less than a quarter of the space. He saw mostly typical teenager things, except the clothing was either all black or vibrant colors. A pair of red high-topped Converse sneakers were lying on top of a sweatshirt.

It was rapidly becoming clear that Gillian wasn't wearing her black jeans – they were still in the dresser – nor the high-tops. The dad was way off base. Either the guy was clueless or he was trying to throw him off. Time would tell which one it was.

As interesting as it was to see what was in a vic's room, Deter often learned more from what was missing. There wasn't a laptop nor a cellphone.

Across the hall, the bathroom drawers were nearly empty: no hair brush, no makeup. Teenage girls were rarely separated from any of these. Since when did a vic pack her makeup to prepare for being abducted?

Determan retraced his steps. There had to be something else he wasn't picking up on.

He looked further and found the books and papers in the bottom drawer of the massive dresser. Obviously, she wasn't planning on going to school tomorrow.

Most of the drawers were empty. Unless she ran away with a U-Haul, her possessions were very few. This girl lived very simply compared to her pampered father. She certainly wasn't being spoiled by her dad's obvious wealth.

She could be a runaway, but that wouldn't explain the scuffle in the grass. It was the evidence of an abduction that bothered him. Being a father himself, the possibilities were chilling. The cases with kidnapped kids were always the toughest, especially when they turned out badly. So far this one wasn't looking too promising, but he reminded himself that it was still early in the game.

Something prodded him that he couldn't quite put his finger on. It had to be right in front of him. He could taste it. Determan sat on the edge of her bed, looked in the nightstand, felt around the edges of the headboard, and smelled the pillow casing. No drugs. No notes. Nothing.

As he sat there lost in thought, he noticed a subtle bump in the linen mat on the nightstand. A water bottle had dampened the fabric and left an imprint of a key that had been kept underneath it. *What is so important about this key to make her want to hide it?* Deter raised up a corner of the mat with his pencil tip, the key was gone.

This girl had thought carefully about the things she took with her. Maybe she didn't intend to come back.

Runaway or kidnapped, either way, he had to find her. He looked around the room one more time. A crumpled ball of tissues was on the carpet next to the papasan chair. He flipped it over with his pencil. It was still damp and stained with eye makeup. She'd been crying.

Deter stood. On the wall next to him hung an oil painting that appeared to be old and expensive. His eyebrows went up. Stuck right in the middle of it was a brand new smiley-face sticker. He chuckled. This kid had a sense of humor.

He had a routine of taking something of the victim's with him and keeping it close for good luck until he found the missing person. He carefully peeled off the sticker and pressed it to a page in his notebook opposite the girl's photograph. *I will find you. I promise.*

Deter walked over to the bedroom window, trying to make sense of the oddities of this case. Below him on the lawn, the press was turning the whole scene into a sideshow.

He pulled out his phone and called down to his partner. "Hey Carl, back up that perimeter. No one goes near our evidence until we process everything and get what we need. I don't want this turning into a media clusterfuck."

"Roger."

Goddamn it. The press was already talking to Dr. Curtis, who had put on a somber face – a striking contrast to earlier in the evening. Deter watched Curtis trying to put his arm around his wife, which was strange considering the nonverbal sparring match between them earlier.

Mrs. Curtis pulled away and put her hand up to shield her eyes from the lights. Deter felt sorry for her. She rocked back and forth with her arms wrapped around her sides as if trying to keep herself from shattering into a million pieces.

It made him sad that a poor kid had gotten caught in the middle of their domestic warfare. Then again, a crisis like this had a way of righting a parent's priorities. The mom was clearly devastated by the loss of her daughter, while the doctor appeared to be more annoyed by the interruption than anything else. Judging by the interactions between the couple it was too late to salvage that relationship. He just hoped that it wasn't too late to save the kid.

Deter galloped down the stairs and ordered a team up to the bedroom. "Secure the room. Take pictures. Bag and tag anything that might be important. And look for her damn cellphone, computer, and any keys you might find."

While a string of scene specialist trooped up to the girl's bedroom, Carl charged in looking excited. "Someone tampered with the motion sensors for the exterior lights and the timers for the sprinklers were turned off. Looks like a kidnapping. And there were no prints – this guy was good."

It was going to be another long night. The area had to be canvassed and surveillance had to be set up on the house and phone. This had to be an abduction, the question was *why this girl?*

Typically, people who abduct teens do it for sexual gratification, for money in the form of ransom or selling them into the sex trade, or simply the age-old motive of revenge. This one could be for any of those motives, but from what he'd seen of Curtis, Deter's money was on revenge. Somewhere along the line Curtis must have crossed the wrong person. He'd bet his badge on it.

When Deter marched out into the cool night air, the glare of the press strobes nearly blinded him. He caught sight of a reporter, Janice Winslow, wielding a microphone as if it were a Geiger counter sniffing out the latest greatest story with sizzle and pop. As usual, she was busily whipping any shred of information into a hyped-up human interest story of epic proportions. She probably had a deadline looming.

Deter pressed down the hairs of his mustache with his thumb and watched the show. Her first target, Mrs. Curtis, was so upset she couldn't even talk. Her refusal to allow them to powder her face or to cry in front of the camera was met with Winslow throwing her hands up in the air.

When Mrs. Curtis turned her back on the cameraman it made Deter laugh. *Good for you.* The disaster hounds weren't getting their ration of tasty soundbites.

However, when it came to Dr. Curtis's response, the interview took on a whole new tenor. That man was made for prime time. Not only did he willingly submit to a few touch ups from their makeup technician, he seemed so genuine. Curtis appeared as any dad would if his little girl were missing. Deter almost felt bad for doubting him. Almost.

Deter stayed out of the lights and monitored the progress of the processing team. The reporter wisely never tried to interview him. Hell, she didn't even bother to look in his direction. Winslow knew better. Their paths had crossed many times before on crime scenes. At least for now they had a truce. She stayed on one side of the yellow tape and out of his way.

For hungry reporters, there was nothing like getting the drop on a story before the rest of the stations picked up on it. Deter expected Winslow to do a snatch-and-run to get back with their exclusive footage. He was right. As soon as they'd gotten the dewy emotions on film, their oozing compassion was packed up along with the rest of their gear as they headed out at a dead run. Deter guessed the eleven o'clock news would get their BREAKING NEWS story – if they could transmit it in time.

Six

Lovett House, 10:55 p.m.

WALTER SAT AT THE TABLE sharing some ginger ale with Gillie. After all these years he was surely getting soft. He'd given in to her pleas for a soda and pulled out a couple of cans he had stashed away. "Weren't you scared?" he asked.

"Of you?" Gillie shook her head. "No. I was mad."

"A stranger jumps out of the darkness, ties you up, and points a gun at your face – hell, I'd be scared, but you weren't. Why not?"

"Seriously. Have you looked in the mirror lately? No offense, but that's like being afraid of Mister Rogers or Elmo."

"I thought Mister Rogers was before your time."

"I used to watch reruns when I was little. Hey, it's almost eleven. *NCIS* is on, you wanna watch it?"

Walter checked his watch. They went into the living room where he tossed Gillie the remote control. At least it was something to do. He'd never thought about entertaining her. He assumed she'd stay in her room and want nothing to do with him. *So much for that idea.*

"Seems like you're hooked on this show."

"Abby is my hero. I want to have a job like hers when I grow up."

They relaxed and watched the *NCIS* crew's fast-paced charge to find a killer. Over looking what he thought were a few procedural screw ups, Walter had to admit he was enjoying the character

Gibbs until the words *BREAKING NEWS* flashed across the screen. When the anchor displayed a picture of Gillie and reported that she was missing, they both sat up.

"Oh, God. I hate that picture. Why couldn't they have used a good one?"

Walter felt his palms begin to sweat. He probably would have jumped off the couch if it weren't for Gillie patting him on the leg and telling him to "listen to this" as she pointed excitedly to the screen.

Cops filed back and forth in the background. The reporter identified as Janice Winslow eagerly interviewed Dr. Curtis as he dabbed his misty blue eyes and pleaded for the safe return of his daughter. The final shot was a close up of him looking stoic and heartbroken as he slowly turned away from the camera.

Walter watched Gillie launch herself off the couch. "Oh, please. What a bunch of crap." She was furiously waving her hands in the air. "He never cries. *Ever*. Even when Nana died, he didn't cry – and she was his own mother. He should just go to Hollywood and become a freakin' actor."

"Gillie, calm down. Maybe he does care about you."

"No. You don't know him the way I do. He's putting on a show for the camera. Trust me, this is all about his image. It's always about him and his stupid image."

Walter looked at the time. "Speaking of your dad. I've got to send him an email."

Gillie went pale. "Don't tell me you are going to email a ransom note to him."

Walter felt rather sheepish. "It isn't about the money. It's something else."

"I don't care about his stupid money. That's not what I mean. You can't send him an email from your computer cuz they'll trace it right back to you."

Even though he'd set up a new email without using his name in the address, Walter hadn't thought about it being traced back to him. Modern technology with all its apps and downloads and widgets – whatever the hell they were – was getting way too complicated for him.

Gillie's eyebrows went up. "We could use my laptop. I know a few tricks that will make it harder to find us. And we could send it from my email address. Then who cares? They won't find us, especially if I don't use your network."

Walter was stunned. This was getting stranger by the moment. He surely hadn't expected his hostage to help him send the ransom note. What the hell? This was crazy, but she was right. He was going to need her help to do this.

He retrieved her laptop from his bedroom.

Gillie booted it up and began to type. "You don't even have a password on your wireless. Walter, we are going to have to talk about security."

He watched over her shoulder as she found another open network named "GasAndGo" for a convenience store up the street. Then she handed "the beast" as she called it over to Walter.

"I think I'll do better with this if I'm sitting at a table."

Back at the eating area, Walter began to type slowly and deliberately. His hands were still strong, but his arthritic fingers didn't move as fast as they once had.

His carefully written missive was to the point: "*Since you seem to feel that you have card blanch to destroy the lives of others, it's about time you get a taste of your own medicine, doctor. Get one million dollars ready in unmarked bills if you want to see your daughter again.*"

Looking over his shoulder, Gillie read the words. "If you want to see your daughter again?"

Walter just shrugged. It sounded like something out of a movie, but it was the best he could come up with on the fly.

She brushed the bangs out of her eyes and continued squinting at the screen. "No way, one mil is nothing. Make it three."

Walter changed it to two.

"Hold it. Carte blanche isn't spelled like that."

"What are you, Daniel Webster's evil twin? Who cares? He'll get the point."

Gillie put up her hands. "Sorry. It's fine. Send it."

Walter did, but his hand was shaking when he hit the enter key.

Gillie was still staring at the screen. "My mom is going to be crazy worried when she watches the news. Can I send her an email too? Please? It kills me when she's upset."

Walter had been so focused on Dr. Curtis, he hadn't thought about the girl's mother. He scratched the short hair behind his ear. "Gillie, I understand. Let me think about it – I'll figure out a way to let her know you're okay, but for now I've had enough for one day. It's bedtime."

"But I always stay up at least until one."

"Not tonight."

Gillie stuck out her tongue.

"What have you got in your mouth?"

She was trying to talk and point to her tongue at the same time. "Th-thisth?"

"It looks like you have a BB stuck on your tongue."

"It's a tongue piercing, kind of like an earring."

Walter recoiled. "That's disgusting. Doesn't it hurt?"

"It was awful at first. If I'd known how painful it was going to be, I'd never have done it. But now it's okay unless it gets infected. I guess you just get used to it."

"There are somethings, dear girl, that no one is meant to get used to. Let's go."

Walter escorted her down the hall to her room. "I'm going to leave the door unlocked for a while in case you need to use the bathroom. There are towels, toothpaste, and a new toothbrush in the cabinet. Help yourself." Before leaving he checked the tip of her finger. The circulation was fine and the cut had stopped bleeding.

Walter went back to the kitchen to get a glass of milk and to keep an eye on her just in case. Her laptop was still on the kitchen table. It pinged with a new incoming message.

Gillie poked her head into the kitchen. "Can I see it?"

Together they opened the email. "When and where?" was the curt reply.

Walter took a deep breath and typed, "You have forty-eight hours to get the money. Will advice." Then he looked at Gillie, who shook her head. She reached over his big shoulders and changed *advice* to *advise*. She nodded and he hit send.

◆

GILLIE SAT ON THE BED in Walter's guest room with the lamp turned off. Light still poured in from the hall through the small space between the door and floor making it easy to see the shadow from Walter's feet as he padded up and down the hall.

After a few minutes she tested the door. He wasn't kidding. Incredibly, it was unlocked. If this had been her dad, the promise of an open door would have been a trick to manipulate her. But not Walter. *How sad is that? I can trust my abductor more than my own father.*

Across the hall in the bathroom, she found the toothbrush just as he had promised. *A considerate kidnapper too. That's a twist they should put on NCIS.*

While brushing she stood in the doorway. The photographs that covered the walls of the hall drew her attention. Some were really old. Others looked like they had been taken only a couple of years ago.

She was intrigued by the pictures of a slimmer, younger Walter and two happy looking kids. But most of all there were photos of a woman who was always smiling. Gillie thought the only thing prettier than her smile was her eyes. They were gentle and trusting. When they looked directly at the camera they softened in a way that said she loved the man behind the camera's lens.

The photographs told the story of a couple who obviously adored each other. Gillie bet they were like the people she'd seen who'd been together so long they could finish each others sentences. *That's sweet.*

Gillie studied several of the photos. There on these walls she watched Walter teach his son to fish and help his daughter off a big red horse. There were birthday parties. And by the look of it, Walter had been there in all of them, even the pink glittery ones for his young daughter.

By far, her favorite picture was of the one where Walter had fallen asleep after reading to his kids. One sleeping child was under each arm with their heads resting on his chest. Walter's mouth and the book in his lap were both wide open. Gillie giggled. She recognized the book. *Cat in the Hat.*

She bent a bit closer, her brows pulling into a slight frown as she clinched the toothbrush in her teeth. If she had one secret wish, it had been for a father like that, but she'd given up on that concept a long time ago. Gently wiping the dust from the frame, she then straightened the picture.

About to choke on the toothpaste, Gillie rushed back to the sink, washed out her mouth, and returned once again to follow the photos down the hall toward what she assumed was Walter's room.

The last photograph on the left had turned yellow from age. In it the smiling young woman wore a simple white high-waisted dress that stopped just above the knees and a wreath of delicate flowers in her long brown hair. The handsome young man next to her was in uniform with what looked like a pair of silver wings on his chest. She didn't recognize either the uniform or the distinctive hat he was wearing, but she was mesmerized. This was a wedding picture. She stared at the muscled arms and trim abs, but it was the intense brown eyes that gave it up.

That's Walter. Oh my God – he was hot.

Gillie was about to return to her bedroom when Walter's low voice softly drifted down the hallway. It almost sounded as if he were talking to someone. She edged closer. His words became more distinct. Peering around the open door, she could see a dresser covered in more photographs, all in frames and lined up in neat rows. Walter sat on the edge of his bed with his big back to the door. His head shook slowly back and forth. Gillie wasn't sure if he was in pain or trying to shake a thought out of his head until she heard him speaking to the pictures.

"Helen, my dear, I've tried so hard, but I fear I've made a mess of things. I just wanted Curtis to pay for taking you away. I'm so sorry."

Walter wiped his eyes on the back of his sleeve and put down his glass of milk. "I don't know what to do anymore. If only you were here. Old girl, I do miss you." His voice broke. "It's lonely here without you."

Gillie had heard enough. For just a moment she leaned against the wall and closed her eyes, but no matter how hard she bit her lip the tears still seeped through her lashes. After wiping her face, she somberly returned to her room, hoping that Walter would be able to sleep tonight.

The bed was soft and comforting, but she couldn't help thinking about him and about how awful it was to be lonely.

◆

WALTER FINISHED his glass of milk and nightly "talk" with Helen. He put on his slippers and shuffled down to the kitchen to put his glass in the sink. Being a tidy man of habit, he filled it with water so it would be easier to clean in the morning.

On the way back to his room he realized that he'd forgotten to lock the door to what he was already thinking of as "Gillie's room." Never had he allowed himself to get so close to a hostage nor had he ever been so forgetful. *Christ, I'm too old for this crap.*

Walter poked his head into the room, half expecting her to be long gone, but she wasn't. There on top of the covers was Gillie, fast asleep. Walter took the quilt off the back of the rocking chair and covered her up. This time as he left the room, he remembered to lock the door.

MORNING – DAY TWO
Thursday, October 11

Seven

The Coffee Shop, 6:00 a.m.

Andrew Determan sat at a small table in the corner of the popular Java Gourmet Coffee Shop.

A few minutes earlier he had shown his badge to a friendly man in a white apron who had let him in a bit early and who had been nice enough to pour him a hot cup of coffee. When Deter had pulled out his wallet to pay, the dark haired man waved for him to put it away. "This one's on the house, you drop in anytime," he'd said.

The digital clock on the wall showed it was barely past six a.m. and already the morning crowd was filtering in.

The years of being a detective had taught him patience, but when a kid was missing time was a luxury he didn't have. He itched to find the answers sooner rather than later.

His adrenaline had waned after being up all night canvassing the neighborhood. Caffeine was now his only hope for pulling through the rest of his day. Sipping at his steamy cup of black coffee, he waited for Lyn Curtis to show up for work.

Deter, as the guys at the station had dubbed him years ago, didn't mind the long hours. It was losing a case that he found intolerable. Each one was like staring down the devil and he didn't intend to be the one that blinked.

He doodled on his notepad and looked at the bright yellow happy-face sticker. In some ways, this case was typical of two adults who were so busy fighting with each other they had forgotten about the poor kids who always ended up caught in the middle. Often these children get fed up with all the hate and discontent and run to get away from the pain.

All of his instincts told him there was more to this case than what was obvious at first blush. For starters kidnappers move quickly. They typically want to offload their vic as fast as possible and waste no time in communicating their demands. But they hadn't heard a word out of this one, unless Dr. Curtis was being less than forthright and was trying to do an end run.

Deter had seen that before too. It never turned out well. Perps always tell their marks not to call the police. They comply out of fear and the misguided hope that everything will turn out all right if they just cooperate. It's hard to convince distraught parents that the kind of people who do this sort of thing aren't the kind of people who are going to leave loose ends – like a kid who could identify them.

The faces of frantic parents from previous cases did a slideshow in Deter's brain. Parents of missing kids get so emotional they just can't think straight. He knew what that felt like, which made him realize the significance of the anomalies in this case. Michael Curtis didn't appear to be either emotional or incapable of thinking straight. With Deter's suspicions on high alert, he put a question mark next to the name of the girl's father in his notepad.

Curtis had proven that he was anything but desperate. Instead of looking to Deter for answers, the doctor had kept checking his watch. Behind that polished exterior was a man who was used to having his own way.

The doctor's touching display in front of the camera didn't jibe with his inability to come up with even one photo of his only kid. Everyone has at least a few scattered around the house or in a wallet. Deter checked his own wallet. The photos might be a little dog eared, but he had ones of his own two girls, even if they did live with his ex-wife. Why didn't Dr. Curtis have at least a wallet photo? Deter put down another question mark.

He tugged at the corner of another image. His fingers teased it from its plastic sleeve. Every year his ex sent him new school pictures of the girls. However, this one couldn't be updated. It was his son's kindergarten picture. It had been nine years and two months since he had last seen Ryan. The boy's smile still shot an agonizing dart through Deter's heart every time he was brave enough to look at it.

When he got too tired or it seemed that a case was getting the better of him, he'd pull out Ryan's picture and stare at the freckled face and mischievous grin that made his own fatigue seem irrelevant. Deter was going to make damn sure that the picture in Lyn Curtis's wallet was not the last one she'd ever have of her daughter.

Deter rubbed his tired eyes and took a couple more slurps of his coffee. It was a hell of a lot better than the station's swill. He felt it burn down his throat and thought about Gillian's room.

It suddenly hit him why that room had sent up a red flare. Of course, the things that were missing once again told the tale. In any teenager's room he'd expect to find laundry, magazines, bracelets, posters, packets of gum, basketballs, DVDs, and other teenage whatnots scattered around, but Gillian's room was just the opposite. It was unnaturally neat for a teenager and nearly bare. Her room was like I-93 suddenly void of traffic – that just never happened unless there was a major problem down the pike.

The room he'd seen was so clean it had been hard to get a fix on who this girl was or what she cared about. Deter wondered if

Gillian's room at her mother's house was as sterile. He was betting it wasn't. That was something he intended to find out and soon.

"Detective, I'm surprised to see you here. Do you have any news?," said Lyn Curtis.

Deter looked up to see the puffy face of a mother who had obviously spent most of the night in tears. Mrs. Curtis stood next to his table pale and drawn, but hopeful in that sad sort of desperate way parents get when their child is missing.

"How are you doing?" Deter couldn't help but ask. Unfortunately, he knew what she was feeling all too well. The night Ryan turned up missing was, without a doubt, the worst day of his life. Looking at Mrs. Curtis's face brought it all back. "Can you sit down and talk with me for a minute?"

She looked over at her boss, the friendly man in the apron, who kindly motioned to her to go ahead.

"I couldn't work with better people. We all cover for each other. And no, I'm not fine. But falling apart isn't going to get her home any faster." She looked away. "After her dentist appointment, we were going to have a mother-daughter day out today." She put a trembling hand over her mouth and stared blankly at the table top.

Deter did his damnedest to stow his own emotions as he flipped open his notebook. "Did Gillian have a boyfriend?"

"We call her Gillie, or at least the people who love her do, and no. She has a lot of friends, but not a steady boyfriend. All of her friends are at her old school."

"Do you think she ran away?"

"I thought about that. She and her dad have never gotten along. She isn't at all happy about moving in with him. At first I thought she might have run, until I saw the marks in the grass. Besides, if she had run anywhere it would have been to come back home to me. We are really close. Always have been."

"Then why isn't she with you?"

"Careful, detective. I have to watch what I say. Michael is a very powerful man and not one you want to cross."

"Why is he so determined to control you? If you don't mind my asking. You seem like a great mom to me."

"You've seen his house and the way he dresses. Do the math. I work in a coffee shop and volunteer at the Goffstown Public Library to teach reading classes to underprivileged children. My students have seen the worst sides of our society and never had someone take the time to help them learn. Does that sound like the kind of woman Michael wants on his arm at his highfalutin galas where he rubs elbows with Senators and CEOs of major corporations? I'm too plain-jane for his taste."

"I see your point. I'd like to come over and take a look at Gillie's room."

Mrs. Curtis said, "Excuse me just a minute." She went over to the man behind the counter and spoke with him briefly. He nodded his head and she came back to the table.

"Let's go."

♦

GILLIE YAWNED and stretched. One eye peeked over the fluffy pillow. The fleecy fabric against her cheek made it seem as if she were floating in a cloud.

The sheets that had been washed until they were velvety soft made her feel snug and secure. Still half asleep, her mind played through the events of last night almost in disbelief. It all seemed so surreal.

As she rolled over it became obvious that it wasn't a dream at all. The clock said it was six thirty-two. Even in the dim light from the hall, she could see that she was still in the yellow room that smelled like sunshine and fresh-cut wood. That wasn't so bad. It was a lot better than being back in that gloomy room at her dad's house with those stiff sheets he insisted be starched and ironed at the cleaners. In Gillie's opinion, the room had looked like something out of Dracula's castle.

Last night had turned out wildly different than anything she could have imagined, but at least she was away from her father. Now the trick was finding a way to get back to her mom. Gillie reached out and slipped her mom's photograph off the pillow next to her. She'd slept with it. A corner was crimped, but her mother's soft brown eyes were still visible. Gillie put the picture against her chest and wondered what her mom was doing this morning. Home seemed a million miles away.

So far Walter had been a man of his word. It wasn't exactly a promise, but he'd said he would find a way to contact Mom. Gillie thought he probably would help her as soon as he could, but patience was never an easy thing.

In her opinion all she did was wait. Wait until you're thirteen to pierce your ears. Wait until you're sixteen to drive. Wait until you make varsity before you get the good uniforms and the letterman jacket. Now it was waiting until she could see her friends, her mom, and sleep in her own bed.

She wondered if Cody was sitting in his spot behind the love seat and staring out the front window and waiting for her too. He was such a good dog. Gillie toyed with a loose thread on the pillow case. She was sick and tired of waiting. She wanted to do something now.

Images of her father pointing that soggy sponge at her and yelling at her to shut her mouth and *"do as I tell you"* still made her boiling mad. Being away from him and all his put-downs was like a vacation. Gillie shook her head at the irony of being held hostage and having it be an improvement.

Living with Dad was just one insult after another. At least Walter listened to her. He didn't yell at her or make her feel stupid. He even cooked for her.

The picture in her brain of her dad coldly turning his back on her at the sink was so like him, but after meeting Walter she feared there was more to this than her father's mean streak. Last night Walter had said her dad had taken Helen away. Was he really responsible for Helen's death? He must have been because Walter was too nice of a man to do something like kidnapping if her dad wasn't guilty as hell. In an unsettling way it didn't surprise her at all.

She thought about the wig in the bathroom and all the medicines in the drawer. Helen must have been sick. That her dad was a big shot in a health insurance company couldn't be a coincidence. Then it hit her. Dad was the one who decided who was approved for care and who wasn't.

Gillie remembered all the files her dad had been working on. They had to be important because he'd spent so much time on them. Night after night he was on the phone and up late in his study working on flow charts. There was that one special spreadsheet and his endless notes on what he called "strategic parameters." A bitter taste rose in her throat. Those numbers weren't about research or a database to improve their services like he'd said. They were about real people – like Helen.

Now she got it. Helen had died because of something in that spreadsheet and the choices her dad had made. Helen had fallen into the category of people too sick and too old for him to care about. Gillie wanted to hide her head under the pillow.

She'd seen what her dad was working on, but only now were the pieces fitting together and starting to make sense. She dug deep to remember the details. Something about green, yellow, and the worst category – the reds. Her father's words played through her head. He'd said something about *only a fool would fuel a sinking ship.*

The color red toyed with Gillie's mind. Helen was a red. Helen was dead. How many others had her dad put into his red category? Just when she'd thought she couldn't hate him any more than she already did, it all got worse.

If she was ever going to be able to live with her mom again, she had to prove how bad he was so that no court would allow a kid to live with a guy like that. She had to do something to stop him before he hurt anyone else.

Gillie wanted to call the police, but they weren't going to believe her. *Nobody listens to teenagers.* They'd just arrest Walter and send her back to her dad. That was a cold thought. She needed proof about what had happened to Helen – not just for Walter, but to protect herself.

If only she could get at that spreadsheet, she could prove everything. There was no way to get into Dad's smartphone without him knowing about it, but she'd bet anything he had emails with some of his colleagues that would spell out their plan.

As for Dad's documents, they were in his computer. Thankfully, she had remembered to bring the office key. But to get access to his computer she would need the passwords from her notebook – getting to it was the tricky part. The notebook was back under her bed at her mom's house. That might be a problem.

All this worry was making her tired. Gillie shifted and felt the comforting soft quilt securely around her shoulders. Wait a minute. Walter must have tucked her in because she had fallen asleep on top of the covers. What bad guy did stuff like that? The old man was growing on her.

Her eyelids grew heavy. Maybe after some more sleep she could get Walter to help her figure out what to do. Until then, having an opportunity to miss school and sleep in was the bomb and not an opportunity she was going to pass up. Those cushy pillows were just too inviting. She took a deep breath of the wood-scented air and drifted back to sleep.

Eight

Lyn's House, 7:30 a.m.

DETER SPOTTED LYN CURTIS'S HOUSE on 2nd Street with the gravel driveway and cozy wrap-around porch. It was at the opposite end of the spectrum from Dr. Curtis's mansion on Shenandoah Drive. Not that it was a dump. It wasn't. It was simply a nice but modest home nestled in an ordinary neighborhood where friendly folks waved to each other.

He scanned his surroundings. The first room he entered was a tidy kitchen that smelled of cinnamon and apples. A golden retriever named Cody sprawled on the floor under a ceiling fan. Next came a homy, lived-in room that told him almost everything he needed to know.

Unlike Curtis's living room, which felt more like an art gallery than a living space, this room was a place where a family had spent time together. The pillow and a blanket draped over one end of a love seat next to the phone told him that Mrs. Curtis had slept there last night.

Photographs of Gillie at all ages were on every ledge, shelf, and table top. He was getting the big picture quickly. Books were packed in every nook. A clumsily made vase, with a child's fingerprints still embedded in the clay, proudly sat in the middle of a mantle as if it were a priceless relic. This was home. Gillie's real home.

He passed through a small room and almost ran into a tiny table.

"Sorry, I put that there to keep people from walking on those loose floorboards. The house was built in the 1890s. The floor is original and has always been a problem. It sags so badly, I had to put shims under the bookshelves to keep them from falling forward. One of these days, I've got to get that fixed," said Lyn. Her voice trailed off as if such things had suddenly lost their significance.

Down the hall on the right, Deter opened a door that was covered in a Bob Marley sticker, a sign that said, "If you can't play nice, play field hockey," and a yellow plastic triangle that read "Caution: Gillie's Room."

Inside, nearly every inch of the pink walls were covered in posters and pictures of Gillie with her friends. Photo albums and magazines were piled in the corners. A dresser was littered with beads, candles, a signed baseball, and sunglasses that were neon green.

In one panoramic view he saw a fun-loving girl with a quirky sense of style who loved the Red Sox, bright colors, music, her dog, and had earned awards for her poetry in English class. She also liked gummy bears, based on the number of wrappers on the floor. Now he had a clearer picture of Gillie. Sadly, it made her situation at her father's house even more bleak.

Mrs. Curtis came in the room. "Sorry about the trash." She picked up some of the wrappers. "These made me feel like she was still here. I guess I wanted to believe that Micheal would send her back home." Mrs. Curtis sat on the bed and hugged the big pink hippo that was propped up by the pillow. She watched Deter through eyes that were raw and ringed in red.

"Let me guess, you've cried so much there aren't any tears left."

She nodded. "God, I love that kid. Where the hell is she? She always calls me. Always."

"You saw the news last night?"

"Yup." Her hands rubbed her tired face.

Deter sat across from her on a stool. "Mrs. Curtis – "

"Please don't call me that. It's Lyn."

"Lyn, I will find her. Now I need to look deeper. Do you know if she had a diary or a personal notebook or a drawing pad?"

"Not that I know about, but I haven't looked at all the stuff she shoved under her bed. You're a brave soul if you venture under there," said Lyn, half laughing and half crying.

As she left the room, Deter carefully knelt down on the floor. Once he got beyond the stray socks and empty soda bottles, he found a shoebox. Inside were some notes that looked like something passed back in forth in class, usual kid stuff. The rest of the box was a disappointing array of movie-ticket stubs and other souvenirs.

Deter put the box back, but then the sleeve of his coat snagged something tucked up into the underside of the boxed springs. A small notepad fell to the floor.

Sitting on the bed with the hippo blankly staring over his shoulder, he started to read. There were dates and a few email addresses, but the rest were a series of numbers. Codes of some sort? Maybe passwords? At the back was a list of what looked like file names. Obviously she was keeping track of something. *What* was the question.

"You find something?" Lyn asked from the doorway.

"Maybe. I'd like to borrow this." Deter held up the notebook that had stars drawn on the cover.

"Knock yourself out."

Deter thanked her for taking the time to let him look around. His next stop would be paying a visit to Dr. Michael Curtis. On the way out the door, Lyn stopped him. Her face was the color of plaster. "Detective, when you corner an alligator, it's likely to take your leg off. Watch where you step."

"You can call me Deter and I always do."

Deter waved as he jumped back into his car and drove away.

On the way to the YorkCare Building, Deter chomped down a potato bagel from Einstein's while it was still warm and thought about her warning.

Her eyes were deep wells of worry and regret. But behind the obvious pain lurked fear. The real kind that could change a person's life. She'd kept looking away whenever he mentioned Dr. Curtis. He was sure Lyn knew more than she was willing to tell. What was she so damn scared of?

♦

WALTER STOOD IN HIS KITCHEN and wondered how long it would take for the smell of hot-off-the-griddle pancakes to waft down the hallway and wake Gillie.

Her door creaked open. "Walter?"

After a couple of seconds of silence, he heard her voice again. *"Oh my gosh, pancakes!"*

He smiled at her enthusiasm for such simple things and listened to the footsteps rushing toward the kitchen. He'd unlocked her door about an hour ago when she was still sleeping. Now he was clean shaven and flipping pancakes like a pro. "Good morning, sleepyhead. I hope you like blueberries."

"Are you kidding, they're my favorite, unless you tried to put something gross in there like shredded zucchini. My mom tried that once, it was like totally disgusting."

Walter set a couple of plates and a big stack of hot fluffy pancakes in front of her. "Not a *zuke* nor a brussels sprout in sight." He pulled up a chair and was surprised how hungry he was this morning. They were just about finished with their last pancake when a strange *THUMP* came from the living room. It sounded as if a bird had flown into the front window. They both stopped and looked at each other.

Walter was worried that someone was at the front of the house trying to break in. There had been some punks a few months back who had hit a few of the houses in the neighborhood south of his. His hand lightly touched Gillie's arm. With a finger to his mouth, he gestured to be quiet and silently motioned for her to stay in the kitchen.

Walter pressed his shoulders tightly against the wall and peered around the corner – it was just his neighbor Mrs. Jacober. Walter exhaled loudly and marched toward the front door.

She'd had her eyes on him ever since Helen passed. She was more of a pest than anything else, but he didn't take it all too seriously. Not only was she a ditzy old girl, she had done the same thing with another widower down the road about four years back.

When Walter opened the front door he found Mrs. J in the flowerbed with her nose pressed to the glass of the living room window. Meanwhile, her rat dog, Pookie, was taking a dump in the middle of his lawn.

"Mrs. Jacober, is there something I can help you with?" Walter noted the bits of ferns stuck to her support hose and the smudge of dirt on the tip of her nose.

She jumped and smoothed down her hair with one hand. "Oh dear, Walter, I was just checking to see if you were home. I made these for you." She handed him a plate of what she called cookies and he called hockey pucks.

"Oh my, have you heard the news? A girl is missing and I saw you come in with someone last night." Mrs. J was whispering as if they had some big secret between them. Pookie had finished contaminating his front yard and had now moved on to using his doormat as a chew toy. "Do you think the girl who was with you knows anything? I couldn't see her clearly. It was so dark last night, but she looked to be around the same age."

Mother of God.

Mrs. J had always been suspicious of everyone. Last year she called the police on the cable guy. There were times when Walter suspected she was sipping on more than her Geritol. The last thing he needed was for her to go off on one of her phone calling campaigns to authorities, especially now.

Before Walter could muster a good reply, he felt Gillie's arm go around his shoulders. Much to his surprise, she had tucked her blonde hair up under one of Helen's wigs. With shoulder length brown hair and without makeup, he had to admit she looked like a different person. "Sad stuff about that poor girl who was abducted, huh? Come on, Gramps, please, let's finish the checkers game."

"I didn't know you had a granddaughter visiting. What a charming girl."

"I better go finish that game, I'll see you later." As Walter was closing the door Mrs. J was still craning her neck trying to see as much as possible.

"Damned snoop," said Walter under his breath after the door was closed.

Gillie looked pleased with herself and took the plate of cookies. She should be pleased, she did a damn find job with that disguise. This girl had an odd knack for thinking on her feet.

Walter pointed to the suspect cookies. "I wouldn't touch those if I were you. If you didn't like zucchini pancakes, trust me you will regret eating those. I swear she gets her castor oil and cooking oil mixed up. I tried them once. Had the runs for three days."

Gillie's giggling blew past the last thread of Walters defenses and made him laugh too. He enjoyed watching her take charge and toss the chocolate-chip hockey pucks into the trash.

Their laughter died when they heard another noise outside, this time it wasn't Mrs. J.

Nine

YorkCare Building, 9:00 a.m.

Medical Director Michael J. Curtis loved making a show of his entrance at work – only today it had an important purpose. He needed the time of his arrival to be well noted.

The doors opened and he blew by his staff with the pace of a man too important to walk slowly. Here at YorkCare they treated him like a deity and he played into every delectable moment of it. All eyes looked up.

Mike didn't kid himself or read too much into it. The staff's attentiveness was more about not aggravating him than any sort of sympathy they might have about his missing daughter. He'd fire anyone of them without a second thought, and they all knew it.

Beverly, his hand-selected secretary, was waiting at his desk with an icy cold Red Bull, his messages, and a copy of the *New York Times*. Mike cracked open the Red Bull. Anxious to get on with his own plans for the morning, he dismissed her as quickly as possible. On her way out of the door he said, "I'm hungry. Call doctors MacAbee and Hollister. Move our meeting up. Tell them I want to meet for brunch in about an hour."

Beverly stepped out of the way and closed the door as Gerald W. Blakely, his boss, waltzed in to congratulate Mike on the latest numbers. As usual Gerry was in his own little world and hadn't heard last nights news about Gillian.

"Fine job, Mike. Damn fine job. You have single handedly turned this company around. The board is going to dance on the table tops when they see last quarter's P&L."

"Gerry. We just need to stay the course."

"I understand lowering payments to physicians. It saves us money. However, I'm not completely certain why we are pushing to buy up hospitals. However, considering what I'm seeing, I hope everything keeps working the way it has so far."

"Our lobbyist will make sure we get what we need. And if we keep slowly reducing payments to doctors, they will have no choice but to close their private practices and come work as hospitalists in facilities we just happen to own."

Gerry paced back and forth while rubbing the back of his neck. "Now I get it. It'll be harder for them to advocate for their patients knowing we sign their paychecks." He was anxious, but clearly on board. "Genius. Mike, this is brilliant."

"Thanks, but I think it's been a team effort." Wearing his most sincere smile, Michael Curtis was indeed pleased at how his tone sounded so much like the humble golden boy. He knew how this game was played.

As his satisfied boss drifted on to other duties, Mike closed his door and called a number on his cellphone.

"Did you guys find the address I gave you?" he asked.

"We found it. Walter Lovett is inside. Haven't seen the girl, yet," said the voice on the other end of the line.

"Just monitor his movements until you hear from me. Do not do anything without my orders." Mike checked his Rolex. While the staff would swear he had come in at nine, he knew the time he'd put in last night and in the wee hours this morning had dealt him cards that were quickly adding up in his favor.

Mike pondered the details that had led to his change of fortune. As he remembered it, he'd received the email just before midnight. Mike gleefully replayed the satisfying moments in his head.

◆

LAST NIGHT, after the cops and Lyn had left, Mike had returned to his study, cracked open a beer, and settled down to get some work done.

The glow of his computer screen welcomed him back into his world where he was the master. While it linked with Wi-Fi he put a coaster under his drink and adjusted his seat. He could feel it all coming together. A hardback copy of *The Godfather* sat on the bookshelf. Mike imagined himself a *don*. *Don* Michael Curtis, the Czar of the health insurance industry. It wasn't as sexy as a mafioso, but damn, it had its perks. The computer chimed, alerting him to a new email.

The unexpected message caused him to sit up in his chair. He guzzled some of his drink and read the bluntly worded demand for two-million dollars for the safe return of his daughter. "Like hell – for that much you can keep her," he said to the screen.

Why would he comply with such an absurd demand when laying out good money for her college wasn't even in his plans? Instead he'd expected her to get a scholarship through the academy. If her mother wanted to slave away and sacrifice so her darling daughter could go off and fart around in philosophy classes and party with her pals, so be it, but not him.

Two million, for what? This idiot had to be kidding. Mike hated being bilked and he sure as hell wasn't going to send most of this year's bonus down the river without a fight. He'd earned it and by God he was going to keep it.

He suddenly realized the message was sent from Gillian or at least someone with access to her computer. Mike's surprise quickly gave way to studying the ransom demand as if it were a chessboard. He wondered about this mystery man who was now his opponent. That he'd used Gillian's computer only confirmed she was with him – maybe even conspiring with him. Fools. *I'm not one to be toyed with.*

Then something vaguely familiar drew him in. The words "Card Blanch" awoke his curiosity. Gillian always had high marks in spelling. This definitely wasn't some joke from her. Then it hit him, like a fragment of an old melody it tugged at something deep in his memory. He knew he'd seen that misspelling before. The question was *where?*

The part about having the money ready in forty-eight hours irked him. If the cops found out about this, they would take charge and stomp all over his life right in the middle of the gala. At all costs, he couldn't let that happen. Forty-eight hours from now on Friday night would be the moment when he'd seal the deal at their big event. He had to find Gillian himself and wrap up this situation before then.

The next two days were critical. It was time to call his discreet network for help. He dialed his phone, knowing that for the right price, someone would be eager to assist him with delicate matters that needed to stay under the radar.

"This is Curtis. I need a team."

"Twenty-five per day for surveillance. Fifty each for hits, unless the mark is a high visibility target," said the voice on the other end.

"No, nothing like that. I want them to bring back my daughter and pop the asshole with her. But your guys need to be fast and good because the cops are already involved."

"I see. That makes it fifty per day and seventy-five per hit or retrieval, your choice."

"Done."

His sources assured him that the team he was about to employ were some of the best in the business. Mike knew they were talking about thousands of dollars. Of course, that was a lot of money; even so, it was certainly cheaper than the damn ransom or the repercussions of losing the contract.

Men like these could work around the cops who were monitoring his house and home phone. But finding Gillian and shutting this down was the type of job more suited to hired help.

Mike ran his thumb over his manicured nails. His skills were strategic planning and influencing others.

He didn't do hands-on wet work, but the ones who did would be getting into position tonight and a man named Brock would be checking with him in the morning for instructions.

Mike appreciated such professionals as if they were all part of some elite team. There was a necessary niche in the world for people like him when corporations and governments were too hamstrung by their own short-sighted regulations and queasy consciences to do what was needed.

The dazzling products and services of big business were like the neat shrink-wrapped packages of meat in the grocery store. Everyone wanted their steaks, clean and tidy, they just didn't want to know what went on behind the scenes to get them there.

The business world survived because of a handful of men like himself – men who had the brains and the teeth to break trail and clean up anything that got in the way.

Mike set to work.

He opened an app on his phone to make it easier to track Gillian's whereabouts. Knowing where she'd gone and dealing with her when he got her back was only a minor part of the problem. The real matter at hand was figuring out how to snag the man behind the email.

Mike sat back in his chair, stiff from another long night. His beer can was empty. And it still annoyed the crap out of him that he'd had to waste precious time on his pain-in-the-ass daughter.

After a catnap, the puzzle of the misspelling drove him into the office long before Beverly or any of the others showed up for work. By four a.m. Mike was rummaging through the file cabinet in his dark office for what he called *the troublemakers*.

He preferred doing this without Beverly's assistance. It wasn't that he mistrusted her or disliked her; it was just that he had "projects" she didn't need to know about – and this was only one of them.

Mike felt it was probably a good thing that she barely had enough synapses to manage his schedule and take messages or she would have picked up on a few patterns he'd preferred no one notice. As for his boss and the board, they had pelted him with a plethora of questions when he'd first signed on, but it became amusing how their questions dropped to nil the moment their bottom line rose. Even Gerry and a few hand selected executives zealously joined in the game when they realized what was in it for them.

Mike admitted to himself that his techniques were a little unorthodox, but they had gotten what they wanted – profits – and he had earned a position of real power. In his mind, everyone won. And he had no intention of giving that up now.

Beverly did excel at filing, which came in handy as he thumbed through the neat folders and tried to remember where he'd seen that odd spelling. After scanning through a raft of them with no luck, he pressed-on.

The name Helen *Somebody* came to mind. Two files later the name Lovett jolted his memory. He pulled out the hefty file and almost dropped it.

The Lovett case was such a pain in his side, he'd been glad when the patient finally croaked. After the fifth letter, he'd been forced to take over the matter personally to keep it from spinning out of control.

Mike flipped through the bulk of documents in his lap. Most of the time their customers, especially the ones he labeled as "reds," were too sick and too frail to complain this much, but he remembered how this one had her husband's help.

He reached to the back of the file for one of the first letters. It was all coming back. Walter Lovett, of course – persistent son of a bitch.

There on the paper in front of him was the same odd misspelling. He sat back in his chair with a smirk. *This bastard should learn to play a better game of chess. He just gave up his knights.*

When a man named Brock checked in, as promised, Mike had passed on Lovett's address. Although it was nice not having a squirrelly teenager around, he had to get her back. She was the leverage that ensured his soon to be ex-wife's cooperation. Gillie was his trump card that would force Lyn to accept of the terms he wanted in the divorce.

Mike had to keep the Lovett file from coming to the attention of the wrong person. His voracious shredder tore into the bulk of documents forced through its blades. It was time to bury Walter Lovett and that damn file.

He shoved the nearly empty folder into the "send to archive section." After deleting some of the memos and records in the computer system, he forwarded a message to Determan with a list of Gillian's old friends that Lyn had emailed over. That would make Mike appear cooperative and, more importantly, he hoped it would buy him a little more time.

◆

Beverly's voice on the intercom confirming his brunch meeting interrupted Mike's reminiscing about last night and brought him back to the present. Gillian's whereabouts took on new meaning when he realized the real problem was getting to

Walter Lovett and his kid before that damned detective found them. Lovett's letters and actions had proven he was a stubborn son of a bitch. This guy just didn't give up. Mike suspected that this Determan would turn out to be cut from the same cloth. It was just a matter of time before they found each other, unless Mike stopped them.

In the meantime he had to devise a way to get Gillian back under his control, silence Lovett, and make himself look like a hero in the process. He could see the headlines now – "Dad saves daughter in daring rescue." The press and the public ate up heroes like they were Snicker's bars. That's how it had to be.

He had to find her first and on his terms.

Ten

Lovett House, 9:30 a.m.

WALTER PERKED UP when Gillie waved at him to come look through the front window. "That dude looks scary." Walter gently scooted her out of the way and scanned the yard. A man was indeed in his driveway and heading toward the side of the house.

Walter crept down the hall to the side door. Sure enough, through the window, he could see a short, stocky man checking out his van. He was packing a serious piece too – obviously this wasn't a cop or a private eye. He had to be ex-military. Walter had seen dozens just like him and knew a misfit turned mercenary when he saw one. He had been trained in Special Ops a long time ago, but once the knowledge is learned it was like sex – somethings you just don't forget.

The hired gun left his driveway. By the time Walter was back at the front window, the stranger had crossed the road and was getting into a blue muscle car parked down the street. The driver had a pair of binoculars focused on Walter's front door. At least it was just surveillance – for now.

Walter reached over and squeezed Gillie's hand. It was so soft it felt almost childlike. He didn't care if these bastards came after him, but he sure as hell cared if they came after her. He took Gillie by the wrist and pulled her into his room where the blinds were drawn.

"Stay away from the windows," he said.

She did as requested and sat in the armchair. He caught her double take when she realized her electronics were charging on the top of the dresser next to her.

Walter opened his closet, knowing her eyes were watching his every move. Pushing aside his uniforms – still clean, pressed, and neatly hung in full view – he hauled out a footlocker and his M16 rifle bag from the back corner.

Laying the weapons on the bed, Walter started inspecting "Old Faithful," his Colt Combat Commander. With one thumb he fondly rubbed a spot off the grip's rosewood stock. This pistol had once gone with him more places than his toothbrush. Even his buddies used to tease him because he could tell exactly how many 9mm bullets it held just by the weight of it in the palm of his hand. Currently, his Colt was empty, but not for long.

With an old towel spread out on the bed, he took apart and cleaned his pistol. "I think it is about time you tell me more about your dad."

His normally chatty guest had suddenly become quiet.

"Walter, you're scaring me."

"Sweetie, I'm protecting you. It's the guys outside you should be scared of. But they aren't going to get to you. At least not as long as I'm breathing."

Gillie jumped out of the chair and engulfed him in a bear hug. Walter was startled until he felt the weight of her head on his shoulder and her soft blonde hair against his cheek. As if comforting one of his own kids, he patted her head.

Her attention shifted. The girl stood with her hand still resting on his shoulder while she studied his closet. As she moved closer to the uniforms she said, "You tell me about Helen and these and I'll tell you anything you want to know."

Walter checked his Timex. It was nine-forty. "Which one do you want to talk about first?"

"It looks like you're about to throw a belt with a gazillion bullets across your chest and go Rambo. So, I guess you should tell me about these uniforms."

It was a fair enough question. "Did you study about the Vietnam War in school?" He looked up and she nodded. "Well, I was there, you just couldn't see me. Most of the time I was out of uniform and making myself invisible. Pull down that hat on the top shelf – carefully. That is called a beret and it is a lot more than an old hat. I was what you call a Green Beret. And I saw more than anyone should – " He stopped himself. She didn't need to hear about that. "Never mind. That's a story for another day. Anyway, what I did was called Special Ops. And I was damn good at it."

"Why did you stop? Did Helen make you?"

"No, I was retired by a slug, a seven point six-two *NATO*, that went through one of my kidneys." He watched her looking at him with wide eyes and then turning her attention back to the uniforms. Her fingers were gently examining the buttons and pockets of his first dress uniform.

"Was this the one in your wedding picture?"

"Yup. Obviously it doesn't fit anymore, but it has been a lot of places with me. I keep it to remember. The other one, I had made for a reunion with my buddies a while back. There are a few of us old farts still around."

"When did you meet Helen?"

Walter looked over at the dresser and switched to cleaning his M16 rifle. "We were married in 1963, just a few months before JFK was shot. We'd met the year before at a barbecue."

Gillie sat on the floor close to him with her back against the wall. Little did she know it was the safest spot in the room.

"So what happened to her?"

Walter braced himself. "We had a great life up to the end: two great kids, several good dogs over the years, and fun vacations. We were like a pair of bookends with a couple of great kids wedged in between. Then she got that damn breast cancer. At first, the two masses were small and containable.

"The doctor's office tried to get preauthorization for treating the aggressive type of cancer she had. Every time I called I was told 'your case is pending review.' Paperwork and phone calls went back and forth for months between Dr. MacAbee, the insurance company, and me. Meanwhile –" Walter took a deep breath. "– one of the lumps quietly got bigger and spread to her lymph nodes and her bone marrow. I wanted the hospital to go ahead and do the surgery, but they had some new protocols. As it turned out, the hospital was owned by a division of the insurance company. They said they couldn't do the treatment without their approval or prepayment in full – it was corporate policy."

Talking about it wasn't much different from being disemboweled all over again. The muscles in his neck hardened until they felt like a pair of hydraulic cylinders. "She died in my arms, right here in our bed. Just before she said goodbye, she…" His mouth opened, but no sound would come out. After a few seconds, he swallowed hard. "She thanked me for such a wonderful life."

His eyes burned. The memories of how cold she felt and how he'd stayed awake all night with her in his arms just listening to her agonal breathing were still so horribly fresh. "She said I was the best thing that ever happened to her."

Using his sleeve, Walter swiped at the salty tears blurring his vision and went back to cleaning. "Just before the sun came up, her breathing stopped. I laid there in the dark with my entire world imploding around me. Everything I cared about had left me behind to pick through the rubble of what had been my life and wonder what the hell I was supposed to do next. It was the loneliest day of my life. The kids were grown and off living their lives. Even old Duke, my golden mix, passed just before Helen had gotten sick."

Emotion took hold of his voice as he slammed the butt of his rifle on the floor. "It shouldn't have happened." Walter felt his fingers starting to tremble. "Not to her. Helen never hurt anyone. She should still be here."

Gillie scooted over to lean against his leg. What a sweet kid. He patted the top of her head and then pulled out a wrinkled handkerchief and blew his nose.

"I've thought a lot about all those letters I sent pleading for their help. I demanded that I get the services we had paid for – damn it all – it said right in my policy that she was covered for cancer treatment. Finally, they agreed, but it was too late for Helen. They didn't care. Their high-and-mighty medical director didn't have to watch her fight to take her last breath."

Walter shook his head. "He wasn't the one who had to let the ambulance crew in. He didn't have to watch the gurney go down the hall with the big black bag neatly folded on top. I'd seen enough body bags in my time to know what that was."

He gripped his knees and held on as if the wrongness of it all was about to knock him over. He blinked and tried to refocus on cleaning his rifle and to let go of the memory of life fading from her beautiful eyes and him left holding a shell ravaged by a heartless disease. She was like a broken doll in his arms.

Gillie's face had lost it's color. "That's what this is all about. My dad is the medical director."

"I owe you a huge apology. I should never have dragged you into this mess. This is between your dad and me. I was never going to hurt you. Hell, I have no intention of picking up the ransom, even if he does come up with it. I guess I just wanted to take something away from him – just for a little bit – so he'd feel at least some of the pain he had put us through."

Still sitting on the floor, Gillie wrapped her arms around his leg and rested her head against his knee. He felt the dampness of her tears seeping through his pant leg.

"Please don't cry. I'm so sorry I put you through this. That was my mistake."

"No. You don't get it. I should have known something bad was going to happen. Walter, I'm the one that's sorry."

Walter brushed some of the bangs out of her eyes. "Gillie, what happened to Helen wasn't your fault." He looked down at her, puzzled by what she'd said. "What did you mean by 'something bad was going to happen'?"

"My dad!" She shrieked as if it was all so obvious. "You're right about him and about everything. I've been fighting with him because he's just such a control freak. He always has to have everyone under his thumb. It's like this: I went with him to one of his big deal art auctions and he bought this ugly painting he didn't even like, just so the other guy who was bidding couldn't have it. The stupid thing hangs in my room. Anyway, he is like that with everyone. The only reason he wants me to live with him is so that my mom can't be with me. It's the same at work. He controls people. The thing with Helen is his fault. And she isn't the only one he hurt."

"How do you know he did this to others?"

"I've been in his office and seen what he was working on a bunch of times. Until this morning, I didn't realize what it all meant." She hesitated and picked at the carpet next to her bare foot. "You aren't going to like what I found."

◆

GILLIE WATCHED WALTER set his rifle down. It killed her to see the grief that twisted his expression, but she couldn't help watching when his eyes locked on to hers. They were now connected by more than loneliness. They each knew, first hand, the kind of damage her father was capable of inflicting. She was sure that telling Walter the rest of the story was going to hurt even more, but what choice did she have? He deserved the truth.

"So, last year my dad had gotten a big bonus: one million dollars. Every Friday afternoon, my mom used to drop me off after school at his office before she went to work. I had to wait around for him to finish his big-deal meetings. Last time I was there everyone in the office acted like he was *the bomb*. They were all like 'you should be so proud of him' and they endlessly talked about how he'd turned the company around. The stocks were up. Blah, blah, blah.

"Anyway, he was in some big meeting and his secretary had gone home sick. So I decided to look around. There was a memo in his drawer saying that if he kept the numbers on track and they got *the contract* he would be up for a bonus of three million dollars this year."

Gillie could see Walter was paying close attention.

"And I remember my dad spending a lot of time making this one spreadsheet. I even showed him some tricks on how to use Excel. He was like always on the phone with a Dr. Hollister and a Dr. MacAbee talking about *the sheet*."

"Wait a minute, Daniel MacAbee?"

"That was Helen's doctor, right?"

Walter nodded.

"He and my dad were talking about *cost containment* and something he called *controlled expenditures*. I didn't really pay too much attention at the time – it sounded like a bunch of boring yackety-yak until I saw the finished spreadsheet. It calculated ages and percentages of positive outcomes based on what they called a claims history. The sheet was sort of like one we did in my Math Models class. Dad said it was only research. He lied. It makes me sick now that I've got a clue what the numbers really meant."

"How was he using those numbers?"

"People who were young and were probably gonna get better were color coded in green. All the ones over fifty or anyone who had serious stuff were tagged in red."

Walter turned his head away. After a big long exhale he spoke. "What you are telling me is that they use this system to approve care to those who would recover quickly to keep their statistics looking good and delayed or limited care for other patients, in order to save money."

"I can't believe I helped him do something like that."

"You couldn't have known what he was going to do with his chart."

"I'm sure he did it for the bonus. Dad likes being a big shot. I know MacAbee was helping him. I heard Dad tell MacAbee how he would be 'compensated for his cooperation' if everything went through. And he warned him they couldn't deny care, only delay it."

Walter picked up his rifle and rubbed the barrel. "That's right. If they generate a barrage of paper work, it slows down the system of approvals under the guise of 'care management.' What he is really doing is rationing care. And in some cases by the time things finally do get approved, the patient is either dead or soon to be dead and their costs are dramatically reduced."

"That has to be what happened to Helen."

Walter stared at a picture of his wife. "Do you know what he meant by *the contract*?"

"Maybe. I heard him talking on the phone to someone about winning the veterans' care contract for the northeast region."

"Mother of God. Killing off civilians wasn't enough. Now he wants our vets too?" Walter's fist was so tightly wrapped around his rifle, Gillie thought that either his knuckles or the barrel would crack any minute.

"I think we can stop him."

"How?"

"I can prove what he's done. At least, I think I can. I know how to get to the spreadsheet."

Gillie thought he'd be eager to go after the proof. Instead he just scratched his forehead and stared at the floor.

"We have a bigger problem." Walter was slowly nodding as if he was sure of something important. "You and I just became a huge liability."

Eleven

YorkCare Building, 10:08 a.m.

Detective Determan planted himself in Mike Curtis's office and waited. He'd hoped to catch Curtis at work. It was only ten o'clock, but the doctor had already left for a meeting.

That wasn't so bad. Snatching a good look at Curtis returning from his little get together might reap additional rewards. Deter repositioned his chair at just the right angle so he could get a candid look at the doctor before the man realized he was being watched. It was one of a slew of tricks Carl had dubbed a *Deter Classic*.

His friends said he was like an old hound dog – once he got the scent of something, he just wouldn't stop until he found the source. Deter chuckled at the truth of it. He was going to keep a close eye on Dr. Curtis. Observing the unaware often spoke volumes. Sometimes two seconds was all he needed to get down to paydirt.

Curtis's secretary could see him through the glass walls. The situation called for caution; he definitely didn't want to annoy her. Secretaries and receptionists were the gatekeepers. It was always smart to keep them on your side. He stretched his stiff neck and scanned the room. The executive's circular desk with ebony inlays must have set the firm back, either that or they had really deep pockets.

Deter caught sight of a pen lying on the blotter. Normally that would be inconsequential except this one wasn't a Bic. It was a Montblanc with a fourteen-carat gold nib and platinum-plated rings. The only reason he knew this was because the guys at the station had looked into getting the outgoing captain just such a pen, but the pricetag forced them to consider other options.

Out of his coat pocket, he pulled his own pen and chuckled. His was a plastic ballpoint left behind by his plumber. He'd kept it because it had the phone number printed on the side. Deter put it away and continued to glean what he could from the room.

Everything about this guy's office screamed money. Even his file cabinets were faced in exotic woods that matched the desk.

The odd thing Deter had noticed in his years of investigations was that the really wealthy rarely flaunted it. Sure they enjoyed nice things, but for them it was about practical matters like comfort and efficiency. At airports, they wore blue jeans and T-shirts like everyone else – except for their shoes that were typically high end or custom made. The shoes always told the tale. Then there were the nouveau riche like Curtis whose surroundings became a billboard to display their look-at-me success. He'd played chess with men like him. They were often reckless and so taken with themselves that they made mistakes. Deter smiled at that thought.

The detective took in the display of wealth and wondered how many prescriptions for life-saving medications could be filled for the staggering amount of money that had been spent to decorate this one office. The overhead on this operation had to be mind boggling.

Deter popped out of his rumination to look at his Timex. Curtis's brunch meeting was taking longer than he'd expected.

He winced as he bent forward to stand. "Damn that knee," he said under his breath.

"Detective?" asked Beverly, poking her head through the doorway. "Would you like some coffee, a bottle of water, or I think we have Coke in the lunch room?"

"That is very thoughtful of you, but no, thank you. However, you can perhaps tell me how much longer it might be."

"Oh, it's always a long one when he meets up with those two."

"Those who?" Deter jumped on the opportunity to gather more info.

Beverly bent closer and whispered. "Hollister and MacAbee, but you didn't hear it from me. Oh my, that rhymed." She giggled in a ditzy sort of way that seemed at odds with her professional appearance. The years had thickened her waist, but with her neat graying hair and gabardine suit the color of fine Merlot, she carried the aura of one who knew her way around an office.

"I bet you are a real asset to Dr. Curtis. You seem to make this place purr like a well-tuned machine."

Beverly was smiling now. "Most people don't appreciate what a hard job this is. I can file like nobody's business, but they just take it for granted." She threw her hands up and shrugged. "They told me my job was the *executive administrative assistant*. I thought I'd made it big until I realized that was just corporate-speak for a secretary."

Already she had delivered more valuable information than Deter had expected. He now knew who Curtis was spending his time with, but one never knew when another innocent slip would break a case wide open. He decided this conversation was worth pursuing. "I bet your files are perfectly in order."

"Usually that's true, but not today."

"What happened?" he asked, hoping his voice carried the right amount of sympathy. The funny thing was that it wasn't all an act.

This woman seemed like a sweet lady who deserved better. She was just trying to make a living like everyone else.

"I had spent an entire weekend getting his files in order and was about to archive a batch, but when I came in this morning the files were a mess – well at least some of them were out of order. I knew Dr. Curtis had been in there because – here I'll show you. Look at this."

Deter couldn't believe his luck and played along.

She opened a drawer and pulled out a file. "What does this say?" Beverly pointed to the tab.

"It says 'Helen and Walter Lovett.'"

"Exactly. This morning I found it stuffed in the middle of the "Ms" in our send to archive section. When he puts files in there it means it's time to put them in storage. But this file isn't due to archive for another eight months – how crazy is that? Normally, Dr. Curtis only goes into these when there is a legal issue, which is a good thing because I think he must be dyslexic."

Deter let out a whistle. "You certainly have your hands full."

Beverly's expression changed to a frown. "That's odd. This file was filled with letters and documents. See?"

Deter could see the manila jacket was deformed at the spine. It obviously had held at least two inches of paper until recently. Now there were only a few pages of odd documents. Out of the corner of his eye, Deter caught sight of a few shreds of white on the carpet next to a paper shredder.

As Beverly searched the cabinet, Deter said, "That must have been an important file for you to remember such details. How do you keep all of that in your head?"

"I don't. Dr. Curtis and his committee review more than I could ever remember, but I couldn't forget this one," said Beverly as she continued to rummage through the file cabinet. "It was a sad case. The poor woman died of some kind of cancer. There were so many documents coming and going they wouldn't all fit in one file. So, I bent the rules a bit and started a second folder at my desk that I could just drop the papers into – it saved so much time. It's still in my desk, but where in the heck are the documents that are supposed to be in here?"

Deter glanced back at the paper shredder. In all likelihood, the missing records were already buried in its belly. Now he really wanted a look at that other file before it was gone too. "I'm impressed with all you do."

Beverly's head perked up when her phone rang. "It never ends." She snapped up the file and scurried back to her desk and the ringing phone. A few seconds later she leaned in and informed Deter that Dr. Curtis was on his way up.

While Beverly went to the back lunch room with her empty water bottle, Deter ducked behind the wall of her cubicle and opened the file drawer. There he found a folder labeled "Lovett 2" and pulled out a document. It was a letter from a Mr. Walter Lovett of Hudson, New Hampshire. Deter wanted to read the whole thing, but there was no time for that now. Instead he memorized as much as he could and carefully put it back *exactly* in the same slot where he'd found it.

Deter wrote down the name Walter Lovett in his notebook and returned to his lookout chair in Curtis's office. Just as he sat down, voices could be heard in the hallway and Dr. Michael Curtis strolled in the front door, looking like a man who was pleased with himself. The way he sailed past his secretary's desk, as if he had not a care in the world, wasn't exactly the picture of a distraught parent pining away to hear news about his missing child. His bright eyes were a stark contrast to his wife's that were all puffy and red.

When Curtis realized Deter was watching, his entire body language changed. Deter was starting to wonder about Lyn's warning and just how deep the deception ran in this guy.

"Detective Determan. Right?" Dr. Curtis reached out to offer a handshake.

"Yes, I thought I'd stop by and see if you'd heard from the kidnapper." Deter took his hand and was surprised how cold it felt.

Even chillier was the lack of correspondence from the kidnapper. According to the surveillance on Curtis's home phone, there hadn't been any demands for money nor calls taking responsibility for the abduction.

"Any request for ransom yet?" Deter asked.

"Nope. I was hoping *you* had some news."

Deter studied Curtis's frozen smile. He looked like a man who was running for office – or lying.

"Your wife is devastated. You don't seem very upset, if you don't mind me saying."

"I do mind. Of course I'm upset. She is my kid – *mine*." Curtis gently straightened a painting on the back wall. "Lyn is always emotional about everything. She calls it passion." Curtis dismissed the question with a wave of his hand and returned to his desk.

"So why did you insist that Gillie live with you?"

"What the hell does that have to do with this case?"

"Maybe nothing, maybe everything."

"I can't have her…" Curtis adjusted his Rolex and lowered his voice. "Gillian is now in one of the finest private schools in the state, not that she appreciates what a great opportunity it is for her." Curtis checked the time again. "I have a meeting in a few minutes. Sorry, but I have to get ready."

"You will let me know if you hear from the kidnapper?"

Curtis was already on the phone and twirling that pen around. Deter doubted the man even heard him.

On the way out of the office Beverly gave Deter a friendly nod.

Twelve

Lovett House, 10:45 a.m.

Walter stared at Gillie who was now on her feet and pacing the room with her hands out at her sides. "What do you mean we're a *liability*?"

"We know too much. What he's doing is more than unethical – it's downright illegal. If my file were to land on the right person's desk, the information in it could be a very big problem for your father. And if you think you can prove he has done this to others, he will want to keep you quiet and get rid of anything that could incriminate him. That means that we are a huge threat. My guess is that the reason those men are out there is because he doesn't want the truth to get out."

Gillie looked as if she'd swallowed a bug. "I'm so stupid. All this time I thought he was keeping me close because he hated Mom and liked making me miserable. I'll bet Dad is really pissed at me now. How did they even find us?"

"Doesn't matter. I'm more worried about keeping them at a distance. They aren't the local security types who think they're hot shit because they have a badge, a gun, and two weeks of training under their belts. These guys are a whole lot higher up the food chain than that."

"What are they going to do?"

Walter checked his watch. It was past eleven. "Right now they're only taking a looksee, but I don't expect that to last long."

Gillie's usually animated expressions had grown pale and wide-eyed with fear. It was a look Walter had tried to forget from his missions in Nam.

"And what happens when they are done looking?" she asked.

"That's what I'm worried about. Men like them get edgy sitting around. It's not safe here. We've got to beat feet."

Walter scooped up her computer and phone. Gillie followed his instructions and started cramming anything they might need into her backpack.

"Don't forget to put on your shoes," he said on the way to his bookshelf in the living room. There he removed a row of books and pushed open the back panel that revealed a drawer containing cash reserves, a passport, and a war bag. Until he'd decided to get back at Curtis, he never thought he'd need such things again, but his training had made being prepared a habit.

Walter returned to the kitchen wearing his pocketed vest and set his rifle and Colt on the worn laminate countertop.

Over at the table Gillie was stuffing a pile of things into her backpack. Walter enjoyed her big smile when he handed Gillie's laptop and phone back to her. For him it was a token of trust and by the looks of it, she understood.

"Remember, stay away from the windows," he said.

Until now Walter had been acting on instinct and his training, but the weight of his loaded-up vest and his war bag brought home the stark reality of their situation. This was damn serious.

Now he was even more determined to make Curtis pay for what he'd done and to get this girl safely back to her mother. The shoot-first-and-don't-ask-questions types outside were fully capable of dropping them right there on the front lawn without a second thought.

Walter rubbed his back. The searing pain from a sniper's bullet came back almost as vividly as if it had happened just last week. Back then his companions were well-trained, well-armed, and returned fire. This time was different. He was in the company of an innocent kid and didn't dare mess up. Overconfidence had once cost him. He wasn't planning on making that mistake again.

He stuffed extra ammo into his pockets and picked up the kitchen phone. "Good morning, Mrs. Jacober."

"Walter, how nice to hear from – "

He interrupted. "I'll bet you've noticed those men in the blue car?"

"Of course. Do you know who they are?" She sounded so excited, but then again she was intrigued every time a Fedex truck rolled down the street.

"They are here to monitor the neighborhood. I heard they are considering putting in speed bumps to keep those hot rods from tearing up and down when kids get off the bus."

Walter stared at Gillie. She had her hand over her mouth trying to stifle a laugh. Walter wasn't so giddy. He'd assessed the risks. They were low for Mrs. Jacober. Professionals wouldn't bother with a violent response to someone like her. There was no gain in it, but that didn't mean the risks were zero.

"I got a notice just the other day that they would be on the lookout," he said.

"Oh, my. Such nice boys. I bet they are hungry. They look hungry, don't they?"

"I bet a cookie or two would probably taste pretty good to them right about now." Walter glanced at Gillie and rolled his eyes as he hung up.

They grabbed their gear. Walter hustled Gillie down the hall and out the side door. He watched from around the corner, while keeping her safely behind him. In less than a minute Pookie was on the front lawn circling into position and Mrs. J was approaching the blue car with a plate of cookies.

"Now," said Walter the moment her wide-bodied frame blocked the view.

Walter charged toward the van, keeping his own body between Gillie and the men in the blue sports car who were staring at Mrs. J as if she had just grown tentacles. "They'll see us any second. Get in quick."

Gillie jumped in and plopped her backpack in the back. He kept the Colt in his lap. As soon as the van backed onto the road Walter looked in the side mirror and realized that the men in the car had just spotted him.

"Put on your seatbelt," said Walter. The van rocketed forward. He was almost at the end of the street when the men in the blue car peeled away, leaving Mrs. J standing in the middle of the road littered with spilled cookies. When their tires dug in, she hunched her shoulders and tried to hide her face behind the empty plate as a maelstrom of grit and stones spewed in her direction.

Walter saw them coming and made a quick right turn. Then another. He slipped down a narrow grassy path between the houses that was only used by a few of the homeowners. Following the tire-worn trail, he looked for that old shed that was set back off the path, leaving just enough room to accommodate a vehicle. Walter slowed down and turned into the space. There he waited. A large bush next to a tall maple tree helped conceal them from the street.

Gillie was about to say something, but Walter put his finger to his lips. A second later he could just barely see the blue car pulling up from his side mirror. It stopped at the entrance to the path. After a few moments, the car pulled away.

Gillie threw her head back and let out a sigh.

"We aren't out of the woods yet." Walter checked to make sure she had her seatbelt on.

He surged back onto the street, but this time they were traveling in a different direction. Cutting back and forth, he took side roads and avoided culs-de-sac. Like an obsession, he monitored his mirrors, searching for that blue car.

As he was squinting at his left-side mirror they went over a speed bump a little too fast. The van lurched up and down. Tools rained from the shelves in a clatter. Gillie was giggling with her hands in the air as if she were on a roller coaster ride at Six Flags until – *POP-WHAAM-CHINK* – a shot took off the mirror on her side of the van.

♦

AT A LITTLE AFTER ELEVEN O'CLOCK, Lyn threaded her way through city traffic to meet with her divorce attorney. As she navigated the ever busy Main Street in downtown Concord, her mind couldn't help thinking about the detective who earnestly seemed to be trying to help.

She had wanted to tell Determan everything. If only she could. He seemed like just the opposite of Michael. Deter was attractive, but rugged compared to Michael's polished exterior. They both were shrewd and tenacious, but Determan was playing on a completely different field. He was relentlessly after the truth, while her husband was just the opposite – bury the truth, spin the facts, and rewrite history to suit his political ambitions of the moment.

Telling Deter everything would be a mistake. It wasn't that she didn't trust him, rather she feared what Michael was capable of doing. He could end Determan's career with one phone call. And the danger to her and Gillie was far greater. With Gillie living in his house, Michael had Lyn's back to the wall. Any misstep on her part would impact her daughter. It was an unspoken threat she understood all too well. As desperately as she wanted a way out of this mess, talking to Deter might put him in Michael's crosshairs too.

Lyn sat in her parked car staring up at the antiquated office building with its gold-leafed sign that read *James T. Hoffman, Esq.* Right next to it hung a neon sign for a closed water filter business. The whole sight was pathetic. Michael had more than a big wallet and political clout, he had a whole battery of Boston's finest lawyers in his pocket who seemed to own all of New England.

In her mind she was like a tiny mouse in the clutches of an eagle who teetered between tearing her thumping heart to shreds quickly or just playing with her for a while first.

Summoning the best attorney she could afford, which wasn't much on her salary, was probably as helpful as depending on another little mouse for help. Lyn just hoped like hell that they both didn't get eaten.

She trudged up the stairs to the office building that had once been a stately four story engraving business. Now it was just rundown. Even the shrubs looked tired. The door to her attorney's second floor office had the air of something from an old Perry Mason show. The lower half of the door was dark wood and the upper was clear glass with Mr. Hoffman's name carefully etched in professional letters across the pane.

The worn brass doorknob felt cold to the touch as she rested her head briefly on the door frame that smelled like old spar varnish. Lyn took a deep breath to calm her nerves and opened the door.

"Good afternoon, Lyn." said Martha, who had a big friendly smile that welcomed all who entered. The matronly woman was the receptionist, secretary, and an accomplished hand-holder when needed. Lyn thought that in her own way, Martha was a stalwart for the underdog in the fight against injustice.

Lyn nodded, partly to acknowledge Martha's greeting, and partly in gratitude that she'd stopped calling her Mrs. Curtis. "Thanks for fitting me in before lunch, my boss is grateful for that, it's going to be a busy one today. Listen, I wanted to talk with Mr. Hoffman about going back to my maiden name after this is finalized."

"I think he already has that in the works." Martha's mouth was smiling, but her eyes told a different story. "Don't worry," she said.

It was hard not to, especially when Martha had looked away as she said "don't worry" – something was wrong.

The door to Hoffman's office opened. "I thought I heard you out here. Come on in."

Lyn studied Hoffman's back and posture for clues as she followed him to his desk. It was a small office with brown shag carpet that sadly resembled the fur of an old dog with a skin condition. Hoffman's face was drawn despite the forced pleasantries. His shoulders drooped as if crestfallen. But it was the nervous way he fiddled with his Cross pen that raised the hairs on her neck.

"What's wrong?" asked Lyn.

Hoffman looked up at her as if surprised. He settled into position and cleared his throat. "Am I that transparent?"

Her pulse quickened.

"Either that or I've become accustomed to assessing everything as a threat." She shifted uncomfortably. Her legs were sweating and sticking to the Naugahyde seat.

Hoffman pulled his lips tight. "It isn't good news."

Lyn braced herself for the worst. "What does Michael want now? He's got the good car, all the money from our bank accounts, and the house. I've kept up the rent payments and have certified receipts to prove it. He already has *everything,* including my daughter. What else does he want – the damn dog?"

"Apparently he is out for blood. The doctor and one of his employees have filed criminal charges against you. They are claiming that you molested an employee's son while you were babysitting him last year."

Her stomach twisted into a knot. It was as if her brain suddenly became muddled. The words, she'd heard them, but they didn't make sense. Her mind just couldn't comprehend that he'd done something that heinous.

The attorney said something, but she didn't hear it. "I'm sorry. What did you say?"

Hoffman answered patiently. "I said, I know you didn't do these horrible things, but I need to have the details. What did happen?"

Lyn was so stunned she just sat there gripping the arms of the chair. Her breathing came in gasps. *This can't be.*

"Michael, umm… He asked me to watch a little boy, I think his name was Scotty. He was maybe five or six. They were having a meeting and his mother, Terry – I think, needed to attend. I came in and watched him for a little over an hour. He drew in his coloring books and played with a toy car while I stuffed envelopes for them, then I read him a couple of stories. That was it."

"Where did this happen?"

"At Michael's office, in the lunch room."

"I see. So all the witnesses work for Dr. Curtis?"

"Oh, God. They won't cross him. And my job! What am I going to do? I work with children at the library. They were planning on hiring me full-time to lead their literacy program in the spring. If they get wind of this…"

James Hoffman rubbed his hand over his face and sat back in his chair. "I don't know what to say."

Hoffman didn't have to say anymore, she knew he was stymied by something well beyond his control. Now her attorney had a taste of what she'd been through. It wasn't the first time she'd been seared by Michael's unrelenting hatred.

Hoffman tapped his pen against his lips and stared at his desk. "Lyn, there's more. It makes me ill to have to tell you this, but Dr. Curtis has filed a restraining order. – " He tossed his pen onto the blotter. " – I'm so sorry, but even when they find your daughter, you won't be allowed to see her."

Thirteen

Walter's Van, 12:00 noon

Gillie felt Walter's big hand on the back of her shirt, pulling her away from the window just as it exploded. Her scream was almost as loud as the pop of the shattering side mirror. Knobby chunks of glass pelted the side of her face. *Holy crap. What is going on?*

Every time she tried to see what was happening, he'd pushed her head down below the dashboard. "Hey!"

"Keep your head down," he said as he grimaced and turned the van a different direction.

ZING-SMACK. The sound of breaking glass and a bullet whizzing over her head and thwacking into the dash added punch to Walters warning. It felt as if the seriousness of their situation had grabbed her by the throat. "Why are they shooting at us?"

"Like I said, we're a liability."

"Oh, God!" Her pulse was pounding in her ears. "What do we do?"

"Stay down and hold on."

Her knee slammed into the door as Walter skidded around the corner, sending more tools clinking to the floor. The top-heavy van violently rocked as they swerved around pot holes and lurched over speed bumps.

At first Gillie was too scared to be carsick. Looking over at Walter, she realized that he was doing everything in his power to keep her safe as he gyrated around pockets of backwoods homes and occasional gas stations.

Then two more abrupt turns and Walter had his foot to the floorboard. They rocketed down a narrow street at a higher rate of speed than Gillie thought possible. The wind roared through her hair from the shot-out window. She instinctively clung to the center console as if it were a life raft.

Another tight turn and her head started to pound. That thick feeling rose in her throat. Just when she was about to beg for everything to stop, Walter clicked a remote he'd taken from the glove compartment. A garage door rumbled open and the van slowed to a carefully positioned stop. Thank God. Being motionless was good.

It felt as if they'd entered a dark cave. The coolness of the air calmed the queasiness.

"Can I sit up?"

"Are you okay?"

"I guess. Where are we?" Gillie peeked out of the opening that had once been her window. The place had that nasty smell of old grease, but she didn't care. Except for the crinkling noises from the hot engine as it cooled off, all was quiet. Even the stillness helped her pounding head and queasy stomach.

"This is the repair bay of a friend of mine's auto shop. It's closed until he sells it. You can sit up, but stay put." Walter jumped out of the van with his rifle and eased his way toward the open garage door.

Gillie strained to see where he was going. There was something about the way he moved. It was like watching an animal on the hunt. He sure didn't look like an old man now. Everything from the way he backed into the shadows to his alert eyes reminded her of a young guy from one of those super-spy movies, just a few pounds heavier.

Sitting back in her seat, she was stunned that someone would defend her with his own life. Her dad would never do that.

Walter flipped a switch and the van started to rise.

At first, Gillie was startled by the sudden movement of the hydraulic lift and jumped to open the door. She was momentarily confused until a wicked sense of delight overtook her. "Hey, Walter," she said hanging out of the window. "I always wanted to ride up on one of these. This is like totally awesome."

"Shhh. Stay inside and don't move." Walter waved at her to duck and held down a button to close the garage door, but stopped and tucked himself back into the shadows where she could barely see him.

What was he waiting for?

Gillie's leg started to bounce. Her fingers rapped on the door handle until she heard a vehicle approaching and caught a glimpse of the sports car as it crept closer. The sound of the tires pinching the grit on the road echoed in the repair bay.

A beam from a flashlight panned the floors and walls. The bright white circle bounced from a gritty tool bench to large oily drums and then over to a yellow machine with gauges.

The van was perched up high. She just hoped it was high enough to avoid their attention. Walter was out of sight. Trying to calm the jitters dancing in her gut, Gillie held a hand over her mouth and did her best to stay still and prevent the van from moving.

She waited for what seemed like forever. The cuts on her left wrist were starting to itch. As the minutes ticked by her thumb rubbed over the scabs. Only a few days ago she had wanted to die. She'd even planned for it. *How could I have been so stupid? What a dumbshit.*

The crack of gunfire and snap of breaking glass had smacked her into a new awareness and yanked her out of the fog she'd been lost in for the last six months. One thing stuck in her head – more than anything she wanted to live. Gillie slid her bracelets back in place and thought about this man Walter who was doing everything he could to protect her.

The white circle from the flashlight went out. The crunching of gravel and the rumble of the car's engine faded away. Nothing happened. Where was Walter?

CLUNK. Suddenly everything moved. She gulped and grabbed the console. The van inched back down.

What if it wasn't Walter?

◆

DETER HUSTLED THROUGH the police station to his desk and handed his partner Carl a fresh cup of joe and one of those great cinnamon buns from the bakery down the street. "What have you found?" Deter asked around a mouthful of white drizzled frosting. The bite of his hot black cup of coffee cut the sweetness of the pastry perfectly.

"I'm not sure," said Carl. "What I know is that Lovett's wife died of cancer. According to a nurse at the hospital he had one hell of a dispute with YorkCare, their health insurance company, over her treatment. That gives Lovett motive, but we have nothing linking him to the missing girl. There are no ransom notes, no threats, no witnesses, *nada*. We need to see what's left of that file in Curtis's secretary's desk, but we can't do it without a warrant, because I'll bet my last bullet Curtis isn't going to let us touch it."

"What about Lovett's life and his financials?"

"The guy is a saint. Pays his bills on time. Modest investments that fit with his income level. Not even a parking ticket. He has two grown kids – one's a veterinarian and the other is a navy pilot. Neither of them has been in trouble. Oh, and get this: Lovett's a retired Green Beret who served in Vietnam. Not just that – this soldier is decorated. We've got ourselves a Goddamn hero."

Deter wiped his mouth. "This doesn't make sense. If a man with Lovett's skills wanted to get even with Curtis, the high and mighty doctor would just vanish and there would be no trail for anyone to follow. Something isn't adding up here."

The phone rang. Carl answered and held the phone away from his ear. Even from across their desks, Deter could hear the shrieks of a woman sobbing.

"You better take this one," said Carl with his hand over the receiver. "I don't do babies and crying women."

"Next time you're buying the damn doughnuts." Deter picked up the line and didn't say a word. He immediately recognized the voice on the other end. Even though her words were lost in fits of despair, he knew this was Lyn. His first thought was that Gillie had been found dead and his own chest tightened.

"Lyn, take a breath." He heard a gut-wrenching sob and then a sniffle. "I'm here, try to calm down so you can talk to me." After a moment he heard her breathing steady. "What happened?"

"I'm sorry. I can't stand it anymore," she said. "Michael has put me over the edge. You won't believe what that monster has done now."

He put his hand over the receiver and told Carl he was going to be a while. Carl left him a note saying he was going over to Lovett's house to see what he could find.

Deter listened to Lyn recount her tragic meeting with her attorney.

He rocked back in his chair leaving his bun and coffee to grow cold while he listened to the raw emotion in her voice and the questions that he couldn't answer – at least not yet.

"We'll find Gillie. And, Lyn, you are doing better than most in this situation."

"Now do you understand why I told you that Michael is dangerous?"

The intensity in Lyn's voice didn't change, but she seemed to be turning the corner from being shocked and humiliated to just plain pissed. Deter admired her for that.

"The guy is a bully. Don't let him manipulate you. He seems to thrive on that sort of thing. He gave my partner a list of Gillie's old friends. We are tracking them all down, but so far they haven't told us anything new – just that her dad wouldn't let her see them and that Gillie was always complaining about how he treated her. It was a distraction, but I'm damn well certain Dr. Curtis knew that."

"I'm sorry. He got the list from me. Michael asked for it and I thought it might help. One of those kids might have seen or heard something."

Determan was starting to like Lyn despite the warning flares going off in his brain. As much as he wanted to, he couldn't react to the way she drew him in. Lyn was part of his case. That was a line he wouldn't cross no matter how much he liked her. Besides, he had no plans of ever getting into another serious relationship, much less married again. The last two hadn't worked out so well and he told her so.

"I sympathize with you. I've been through two divorces. They were both about as much fun as a root canal without the novocaine. I'm not sure which was worse, the hostility between me and my ex-wives or the attorneys. Looking back, I think the lawyers were the only ones that came out ahead."

Lyn had quieted down and was listening to him. Deter thought it was kind of sweet. In the last twenty-four hours everything she cared about had been ripped away and yet here she was listening to his woes. The woman had such a gentle way about her. She was so damn genuine.

"I don't know why any woman would walk away from an honest guy like you."

Deter chuckled. "Trust me, I'm a lot better at the flirting part than the take out the trash and mow the lawn part."

"Aren't we all?"

"How did you meet Dr. Curtis?"

"It's a little embarrassing, but I met him at a dating service that had just started up online. I thought I had hit the jackpot. At first he was charming with his wavy dark hair and blue eyes. He knew just what to say and I naïvely trusted him. Boy, was that a mistake. It wasn't long after we were married that I found out I was pregnant with Gillie. That's when things changed. For Michael everything is about control. He never could control Gillie and that has made things tough between them. What makes people like that?"

"Often they are determined to get even with someone who hurt them. For others it's an unconscious drive they don't even understand. Many times it goes back to something horrible from their past."

"That fits."

"What do you mean?"

"Michael would never talk about it, but I met his brother a couple of times and he told me a few hints about their childhood. I knew something was strange about his family because they never got together even for holidays and Michael had no pictures. Neil, his little brother, said there had been a "problem" involving their older sister when Michael was young. The family didn't have much – just a single mom who worked all the time. I always thought that was why he was so determined to earn the big salary and live above all that. It was like he had to show the world he was worth more. I'm such a sucker for underdogs. I guess I was taken in. I just kept trying to make things better. I put up with a lot more than I should have."

"Did you ever meet his sister?"

"No. Mike's brother said that one day she just disappeared back when Michael was about fifteen. Apparently, they'd had a fight, but Neil didn't want to talk about it."

"Was she reported missing?"

"She was, but with her drug history and habit of not keeping a steady job, Neil said the authorities didn't put a lot of effort into finding her."

"Do you think Michael knows anything about her disappearance?" Deter was trying to be diplomatic while listening closely to Lyn's reaction. She hesitated like people do when they're trying to make sense of something.

"I asked him about it once. He had his back to me, but I could see his eyes in the closet mirror. They had a dark expression that was like having ice water poured down my back. It was spooky, but by then there was a lot about him that scared me."

"Did he say anything?"

"He told me never to mention her again. Believe me, when Michael tells you to back off – you back off."

Deter wondered if Dr. Curtis's perfectly manicured hands were as clean as they appeared.

Lyn continued to voice her grievances until she suddenly grew quiet. "Oh God. Gillie! You don't think he'd hurt her, do you?

"You know him better then me, but the sooner we find her the better." Determan had been worried from the start about Curtis's troubled relationship with his daughter. "What is Gillie's cellphone number? The one Curtis gave me doesn't work."

Lyn gave Deter Gillie's phone number. "The numbers you have were transposed."

"Why doesn't that surprise me? Do you know what kind of phone she has?"

"He insisted on getting her one of those new touch screen phones. I couldn't afford to activate the internet features on her old phone, obviously he doesn't have that problem."

"Knowing how controlling he is, my guess is that he has been tracking her every move."

"What are you going to do?"

"Find her before he does."

Fourteen

YorkCare Building, 12:30 p.m.

MICHAEL CURTIS'S LUNCH MEETING with his boss had ended early. It had been another frustrating dance with Gerry over their bid to acquire the health insurance contract for all of the veterans in the New England region. It certainly hadn't gone as smoothly as he'd hoped. As usual it was a struggle to keep Gerry on task.

As with most government contracts the deal was lucrative and the competition fierce. The man clearly wasn't a high roller and just didn't get the concept of strategically placed pressure. Nor did he agree with Mike that there were "other options" that needed to be employed to ensure their success. Instead, Gerry just expected Reynolds to roll over and cooperate. Fat chance of that happening anytime soon.

Mike saw Gerry as one of those old-school guys who didn't understand that the VHA's Tim Reynolds wasn't going to be swayed just because the president of YorkCare had turned himself inside out to set up a glittering gala to wine and dine the guy and his board. Cold shrimp, caviar, and cognac only got face time with the man. The food and booze, even if it were from Western France, only filled their bellies. Mike thought they needed some way to be more persuasive.

Reynolds was the last holdout and the key vote for cementing the contract. He had a reputation of being a tough sell. Even worse, the guy took his post at the Veterans Health Administration like it was a calling from God. *Damn boy scout.* That was the last thing Mike needed – some do-gooder stepping in to mess up *his* bonus.

Well, we all have our secrets, don't we? The trick was finding the one thing Reynolds didn't want the rest of the world to know.

Mike was sure something embarrassing could be found. No one was that nice and that committed. He scanned the contacts in his phone and was about to call his "go-to guy" who was good at finding out such sordid details, when it buzzed in his hand. It was Brock, the lead man Mike had deployed just this morning to track down Walter Lovett.

"What do you want?"

"Lovett left the house." Brock sounded tense. "He has the girl with him. What do you want us to do?"

Brock's flustered tone was uncharacteristic of the cold unflinching poise Mike expected of a seasoned assassin. He didn't care what problems Brock was having, the only thing that mattered was taking out Lovett as quickly as possible. "I already know that. I've been following my daughter's cellphone with a GPS app. Didn't you install the tracker on his van?"

"Yeah and it's a damn good thing. You should see the cat and mouse game we've been playing for the last hour. Are you sure you told us everything about this mark? The guy is a lot more talented than we expected."

"You're seriously telling me you can't keep up with an old man – even with real-time GPS?"

Brock's voice became edgy. "I don't think you heard me. This guy isn't your typical old coot. He's skilled – a professional. Some of the tricks he's pulled, I haven't even seen before."

"Bullshit. Move your asses. Get in there and take him out. *Now*."

"I'm telling you he's good. It's going to cost more and take a little more time. We might even need a third man."

"Don't try to scam me, asshole. You're outgunned. Just do what I hired you to do. If you are quick about it and I'm not left with a mess to clean up, we'll talk about further compensation later."

Mike waited. Brock's silence was as cold as a wind off the Bering Straits. Of course, the guy wasn't happy about being cut off, but Mike had to show him who was in charge.

"What about the kid?" Brock asked.

"Scare the crap out of her, bring her back unharmed. I'll take care of her myself." He ended the call without giving Brock a chance to say anything more.

Mike hurled his pen across the room. "We need more time, my fucking ass."

A warm flush crept up his neck. Pacing ruthlessly, Mike twisted the carpet under his heels with each turn. For more years than he cared to count, he'd loathed the anger that triggered deep and dangerous stirrings in him.

How dare they stand in my way. When he handed Brock the go ahead, Mike fully expected a surgical intervention. Slick and clean. After a few hours the job would be done, but it wasn't working out that way. Not even close.

Some professionals. He felt the reins slipping from his hands. More than anything in the whole goddamn fucking world, he hated being out of control.

Mike took a breather.

The private bathroom just off his office offered him a retreat where he could wash his face and collect his thoughts. He held the soap to his nose and took in the fresh fragrance.

After drying off, he stared at himself in the mirror as he combed his hair. Everything about him looked like that of a man who was in charge, but no matter what he wore or how many times he had his hair trimmed, Mike still saw the little boy he'd once been.

If only he could delete the past. Erase it from reality.

He washed his hands, but that too reminded him of how he'd once habitually scrubbed them until they were raw.

After what Mike had seen and smelled, he couldn't tolerate dirt. Even the tiny droplet of water on the mirror broke the illusion of power. He swiped it away before it played with his mind.

As he hung up the towel, the hated memories flooded over his consciousness. Helplessly he remembered the clutter and that stale smell, like that of an old building laden with dust and dead rodents rotting in the crevices. He could see his boyish hands, raw and red and reeking from bleach. Remembering Pop's raspy voice, bulbous red nose, and his ruddy cheeks took him all the way back to Lawrence, Massachusetts. It was 1979 and Mike was just a kid.

◆

MIKE'S FATHER, JEB CURTIS, once owned a comics and collectibles store, back in the day when *Star Trek* was the new big thing. The little shop was sandwiched between a grungy dry cleaners and a vacuum-repair shop in the heart of a working-class neighborhood. It did well for a while until Pops – as Mike called him – started packing it with second-hand knickknacks and shitty periodicals no one wanted. By the time the *Star Trek* movie caused a nationwide resurgence of interest, the little shop was so bedraggled it had already lost nearly all of its customers.

When Mike would lock his ten-speed to the dinged-up green bike rail in front of the shop, he couldn't help over hearing people's comments as they passed by Curtis Collectibles. It was embarrassing.

"A ne'er-do-well runs that junk shop," a man in a tweed vest said.

"That poor child's father is a hoarder," a woman in a pink coat said.

They all called Pops a fool.

Mike called him a no-good bum.

In his opinion his father was too lazy to clean up his own shop. The place fell into disrepair and Mike had been forced to work there when Pops laid off his only employee. Mike was twelve.

He tried to stock the shelves, but since hardly anything was selling, there was no point. Trying to keep it clean with the broken boxes of dusty bric-a-brac piled everywhere was about as useful as a red bow on a pile of horse manure. His dad started drinking and making excuses to Mom about money. Mike saw it all.

The months passed until his dad stumbled onto a solution. As it turned out, the answers to Pop's problems were only the beginning of Mike's. After school one day, he arrived to see his dad shaking hands with a seedy looking guy with greasy black hair. It wasn't the first time Mike had seen him. The guy had been dropping by lately.

"Hank. This is my boy, Mike," Pops said.

Mike felt his dad push him forward to shake the man's hand. While Pops continued to blabber on in the background, Mike stared at the man's extended hand. The fingernail on his little finger was long, curved, and yellowed. Mike withdrew his small hand. Why was this guy here? He never bought anything.

Before leaving, Hank handed his dad a wad cash.

"Son, you go with him. The man has work for you."

That afternoon Hank took Mike to a guarded door just off the alley in the worst part of town. A big guy in a sweat-stained shirt smoking a stogie glared at him as he slipped inside. In the background, a radio with a bent hanger for an antenna played a crackling melancholy tune. Hank hustled Mike upstairs and walked him down a dark hall with battered filthy walls. Each room was occupied by a girl not much older than his teenage sister Becky.

Hank caught Mike's side glances into the rooms and offered a lecherous smile that revealed a red tongue protruding from a gap in his tobacco-stained teeth. "I'm helping these girls by giving them a place to stay. Consider it my community project."

He lied.

Mike went home each night before the arrival of the men he knew were coming and going during the late hours, but the girls never left. At first he was fascinated by the glimpses of female flesh. The real thing was so much better than the old *Playboy* magazines and that one *National Geographic* Pops had hidden under the counter. But then he saw their purple bruises and the raw weeping bite marks. Reality set in hard. So did the smells. After school his job was to clean up the rooms before the real business of the evening started.

Day after day he swept up the used condoms stuck to the floors. The second chore on his list was to strip the beds and wash the sheets. They reeked from sweat and things even worse. Mike learned to love the smell of bleach.

Back at the shop he complained to his father, but he didn't listen. He never did. "Pops, that place is a whorehouse."

"Son, all you have to do is the laundry. It's time you man up and do your part for your mama and the family," he said. "Hank's money spends just as good as anyone else's and his doings are none of your business."

Every day or so, Pops would hold out his hand and Mike would turn over his earnings, but he was pretty sure little of it ever got past the liquor store on the corner. As time went on Mike started holding back a buck or two.

After a while Mike closed his eyes to the horror of it all. Then one day, Hank said he had to leave for some business. He put Mike in charge of the girls.

"Get them off their asses and make them get cleaned up," he said. "There's an extra ten bucks in it for you."

Suddenly, Mike was the man in charge. He looked in the mirror. His scrawny frame and tender age needed something to give him an edge. Mike dug through the office's closets until he found just the ticket. An old baseball bat was propped in the back of a broom closet, covered in cobwebs. That afternoon he walked through the dimly lit halls slamming each door open with the bat.

"Clean up your room and get to the showers," he said as he opened each door.

He hated the girls for the nasty messes they'd left for him to clean up. He hated their stupor, their slurred speech, their watery vacant eyes. He hated the needle marks they tried to hide between their toes and the way they begged for more. And the worst, he hated their vomit. Today they were going to clean up their own puke. He was the top dog now.

The girls learned to fear him, or at least what he'd do with that bat. It was his first taste of power. Hank was impressed and said he had a natural talent for taking command. Mike got his first ten bucks. It felt like a million. After stepping in for Hank again, he got another crisp ten-dollar bill. Each time he kept the money for himself and never told Pops about it.

One day Hank asked him if he wanted to earn even more.

"I've got a lucrative job for you," he said. His breath smelled like something left to rot at the bottom of a trash can.

When Mike realized what he was being asked to do, it was too late to escape. He was cornered. Two of Hank's bodyguards dragged Mike down to a special room where special clients came to play. There his hands were forced to touch things he never wanted to feel. No matter how many times he washed them, they never felt clean again.

For that he hated them all.

That night he left work three hours later than usual. Mike slowly hobbled back home steering his bike along the path next to him. He was too sore to sit down much less ride a bike. His cheeks burned with the bitter sting of humiliation in the cold night air. He'd been betrayed in ways he'd never be able to speak of – not to anyone. Hank's actions didn't surprise him – cuz what can you expect of a pimp? The real betrayal had Pops' face all over it.

Parents are supposed to protect their children.

When he got home he limped up the stairs to the small room he shared with his little brother Neil. The apartment was dark and quiet – everyone was asleep. He pulled the twenty out of his jeans pocket and put it in the tin he kept hidden behind the nightstand.

A long hot shower eased some of the pain.

Afterward, he threw away his bloodied briefs. Curled up in a fetal position on his bunk, his lower lip quivered and his tears soaked the pillow. The windup clock silently ticked away the minutes as he stared out the window and listened to the crickets. Clouds roamed across the heavens like a pack of wolves engulfing the moon. The sky went black.

Many things died that night – his innocence was only one of them. Mike never spoke to his father again.

And it was the last time Michael J. Curtis cried.

Fifteen

The Auto Shop, 12:30 p.m.

GILLIE GRITTED HER TEETH as the hydraulic lift gradually began to lower the van. Inch by inch, it was getting closer to the oil stained cement floor. *Walter, please say something.*

She felt the tires touch first and then heard the creaking sounds of the weight of the van resting on the wheel base. Any second now someone was going to find her. Just as she was ready to bolt, Walter poked his head in the driver's window.

"They're gone, but I expect they'll be back soon. Let's get out of here."

Gillie fell back in her seat and was about to bitch-out Walter for keeping her in suspense until he said, "Shhh."

He took the vehicle out of gear and rolled it backwards off the lift. She jumped out to help even though she didn't really get why he was doing it.

"If we hafta get out of here, why don't you just start the van and let's go?"

"The sound will echo in an enclosed space like this. I want to keep as quiet as we can." Walter looked at Gillie and frowned. "You all right?"

"I'm just freakin' great. My dad hates me, I can't see my mom or my dog or even my friends, and I'm being used for target practice.

Other than that, Mrs. Lincoln, how was the play?" Gillie turned to see Walter's response only to find something about him had changed. "What's wrong? Why are your hands shaking?"

"We need to…" Walter looked around and seemed confused.

Walter looked as if he were pushing a mountain backwards instead of a van on wheels.

"Are you okay?"

"We've got to get out of Hudson," he said as the van cleared the garage.

Gillie was sure his hands weren't trembling because of the two guys that were tailing them. Walter was fearless. She watched the shaking get more violent as he started the engine.

As they drove away she couldn't take her eyes off him. Walter had begun to sweat. *This ain't good.*

Gillie grabbed his wrist and shook it slightly. "What's wrong?"

"Headache." He wiped his eyes and frowned. "And I'm hungry."

Everything felt tilted. It was no longer about her or how much she hated her dad. Something was wrong with Walter. Until a few minutes ago, he'd seemed invincible – well except for his computer skills – but now he was pale. Even though she didn't know how to take a pulse, she could feel his was fast; she guessed too fast. "Come clean. What is this?"

"Get my zipper bag. The green one."

Gillie twisted around and dragged Walter's big bag closer. Inside she found a grooming kit filled with syringes, a few vials of medicine, and a palm-sized machine. "What's this for? Do you need this medicine?" She held up the tiny glass bottle but dropped it.

"I'll get it." Gillie moved her seat trying to get at the vial when she heard the crunch. "Oh, crap. I hope you didn't need that."

"It's all right, just don't pick up the other one."

"But don't you need your medicine?"

"No, I've already had too much of it. I'm diabetic and I haven't eaten enough for the dose of insulin I took earlier. Hand me those glucose pills."

Walter quietly chewed on the tablets and stared out the window.

"Do you want to stop – or I could drive? I have a license."

Walter blinked a few times and started to laugh.

At first she was offended and thought he was making fun of her driving skills, but then she remembered their circumstances and got his humor.

"I get it. *Kidnap victim helps drive getaway car.* Couldn't you just see the two of us on the *Today Show* explaining that one?" His laughter grew and it made her smile, but she was still worried. While packing his vest pockets with his diabetic supplies, his hands were shaking less than they had a few minutes earlier. At least that was a good sign. "Did that stuff make you feel any better?"

"Yes. It did. Thank you." Walter patted her hand as he looked through his side mirror. His eyes went back to looking more focused and alert.

When they stopped at a light, Gillie went to check out her mirror too, but then felt stupid because she'd forgotten it was gone. The light was a long one. She brushed away a few remaining chunks of glass from what had been her window. Her fingers tapped on the door until she realized that the driver of the car next to them was staring open mouthed at the bullet holes and the few remaining fragments of what had been a side mirror. Gillie just grinned. She got a kick out of how bewildered the man looked.

"So, what do we do now?" she asked, hoping she could talk Walter into going through the McDonald's drive-thru. She'd kill for a large fries and a Dr. Pepper.

"Let's get something to eat."

Forty-five minutes later they were on the south side of Manchester watching cars go through a carwash while eating their Big Macs and fries.

She went to look in the glove compartment, but Walter said, "Close it."

Gillie turned on the radio, but he turned it off.

Her foot ran into a big knobby thing on the floor. "What's this?" She picked up the fist sized chunk of metal. "It's ginormous."

"Lug nut."

Gillie blew her bangs out of the way. Walter obviously didn't want to talk.

"I know I can't call my mom, but what about my friend Kip? He could help us."

"Things are already complicated enough."

"Come on. Walter, please." Gillie dabbed a wad of fries in the ketchup and shoved them in her mouth. "Yow'll –" She swallowed and took a couple of gulps of her soda. "Sorry. You'll like him. We've been friends like forever. Besides I trust him."

Just as Gillie was about to plead with him, Walter quickly put down his diet drink and leaned forward to stare out her window. The look on his face told her this was bad news. Gillie's head whirled around, her blonde hair flung into her face. A car was coming at them – *fast*.

"It's them," he said. "Shit. They're blocking the exit. Buckle up!"

Oh, Jeez. She threw the ketchup out the window and dived away from the opening. The sound of gunfire exploded in the air. She flinched and Walter stepped on the gas.

He rocketed toward the only other way out – through the carwash. He laid on the horn and a guy in a Toyota hustled to get out of their way. The blue car accelerated. The man in the passenger seat continued to pop off shots. The sound sent everyone around them running for cover. Walter roared straight into the tunnel.

Without warning he slammed on the brakes, leaned out of the window, and chucked the big lug nut at a panel of switches. Instantly water and soap suds were flying everywhere. Gillie screamed, but she had to admit that her surprise was more delight than fear. A spray of cold water came in through her window and soap bubbles spattered across the windshield. She looked out of the back and saw the car following them into the long row of enormous brushes.

When they got to the end of the tunnel, Walter fired at a gray metal box and the whole system jerked and slowed way down with the blue car trapped inside. Gun shots rang out – *THWAP-THUMP* – the sound was damp and muffled. Gillie saw soapy arms fighting with the long fibrous fingers of the huge brushes and began to cheer. "Walter, you got 'em."

"Damn it," said Walter as he grabbed Gillie and pushed her head down.

Bullets broke out both of the rear windows. Walter fired back. Shots ricocheted off cement blocks and metal. One hit something inside the tunnel. This time the carwash stopped completely and soapy water sprayed in all directions.

Walter sped away, leaving the two soggy men behind to get their seal and shine.

Gillie sat back up in her seat and was about to celebrate another victory over the bad guys until she saw Walter's arm. "You're bleeding!"

"It's just a scratch, Gil."

"That's like uber-gross." It sure as hell didn't look like a scratch to her. She'd be screaming her head off if her shirt was turning all red like that. Her mind and gut twisted at the same time. Walter couldn't be hurt. Not now.

◆

DETER SNATCHED UP the last crumb of his cinnamon roll and wiped his mustache. It hadn't taken long before he'd discovered that Lovett only had a land line. Old school and low-tech wasn't going to help Deter much, but he could track the pings from Gillie's cellphone. On his way out of the station a call came in from Carl.

"Deter. I'm at Lovett's and I think we hit the motherload. Get this – he has a guest room that has brand new plywood on the windows and a new deadbolt lock on the outside of the door. The bed has been slept in and there was makeup and blonde hair on the pillows. I don't know if it was her's, but –"

"It was her. I had a chat with the cellphone company. According to her cell history, that was the last recorded location."

"How in the hell did you get that?"

"Warrant. I told Judge Stromberg what we had. Besides, he owed me the favor of a quick response. Any signs she was hurt?"

"A BandAid wrapper and a bloody paper towel were in the bathroom's trash can. Looks like it was just a minor cut."

"Was there a struggle?"

"Are you kidding? It looks like a damn sleep-over party. He had a quilt for her and a new toothbrush in the bathroom, the wrapper is still on the counter. It looks like he made blueberry pancakes for her. They ate breakfast together – can you believe that?"

"This is one for the record books. Say, Carl, how did you get in?"

"The side door was standing wide open."

"Really? You find anything else?"

"Yeah, it looks like your perp and the vic are both on the run with a couple of goons with guns on their tail. A neighbor, Betty Jacober, came over and told me about two men in a blue sports car who were watching the house. She showed me where they were parked," said Carl.

"Surveillance probably, but who hired them?"

"Don't know. But the neighbor was really miffed – something about cookies. Anyway, I found tire tracks where they had been parked. According to the witness they peeled out after the van.

I found some 9mm casings at the corner, probably from a semi automatic. Looks like they were doing more than just watching. Somebody was serious about doing some real damage. Hold on, Deter, a squad car just pulled up."

Deter continued driving and thought about how kidnappers always cut their losses and run when they think someone is on to them. Typically, they dump the vic and hightail it out of sight. Then again, there was nothing about this case he'd call typical.

After a minute or so, Carl came back on the line. "The Hudson PD saw my car and pulled over to talk. They've gotten several calls of shots fired in the area."

"Any idea where they went?"

"Hell, no. But it was probably as far away from that blue car as possible. Even Jacober said, and I quote, 'Anyone could see that Walter was trying to protect his granddaughter from those bad men.'"

"Like hell that was his granddaughter," said Deter as he played with his mustache. "Say, Carl, since when does a kidnapper risk his own life to protect his vic?"

After ending his call, Deter followed the cell's pings like a bloodhound on the heels of a T-Bone. As he got within range, a blue sports car raced past him. It was a Mustang that appeared to be a few years old. He couldn't help noticing the puffs of soap bubbles blowing off the roof and the trail of water drizzling behind them.

The cell's signal had come from the general area, but appeared to have done an about face. He was about to make a U-turn to follow it until he saw the horizon was lit up like a blow-out sale on Black Friday. Cars and flashing lights were everywhere. Something had just happened. The Manchester PD was arriving in force. Officers with rifles drawn were just starting to secure the perimeter. Other than meth, New Hampshire wasn't exactly the crime capital of the world, which made him curious if this was a coincidence or connected to his case. Being a man who didn't believe in coincidences, he picked up his phone.

"Carl, what the hell just happened at Scrubs Carwash? Half of the Manchester PD is here."

Carl put him on hold for a few seconds and then came back on the line. "There were reports of shots fired. The owner is mad as hell. He says Wash UR Wheels, a rival carwash, is trying to sabotage his business."

Deter pulled up to the scene. "The signal from Gillie's phone was in this area until just a few minutes ago."

"If it was Walter Lovett and the girl, why in the hell would he stop to shoot up a carwash?"

"Let me see what I can find out." Deter put his phone away. He flashed his badge when one of the officers looked up. After a brief conversation Deter got back to Carl.

"There was a shoot out inside the damn carwash. Witnesses say a car followed a white van through the tunnel and was blasting away at them. Everyone ducked so they didn't catch all of it, but one guy said the man in the van wasn't the first to fire."

"Did anyone see the color of the car?"

"Yeah, a blue sports coupe. Someone in that blue car wants Lovett and the girl real bad." Carl sounded perplexed. "How'd they get to Lovett before us? They're not from our office or Feds. So, who in the hell are these guys?"

"Damn good question. I think they passed me on the way here. Put out an APB for a dark blue Mustang driven by two white males. The front fender on the driver's side is whacked. I'll see if I can track it down and get us a license number."

Deter signed off and sped toward coordinates of the latest pings. Who could possibly want Lovett more than him? Did Dr. Curtis hire his own P.I. guys? That didn't make any sense. Private investigators look, they carry, but only use their weapons as a last resort to defend themselves. No P.I. was going to go charging through a carwash with guns blazing. What if Curtis was trying to get to Gillie or possibly Lovett first? Deter already knew there was more to Curtis than met the eye.

Deter called Carl back. "Remember the story Lyn had about that missing sister? It might be worth digging a little deeper into Curtis's background. When you get a chance, why don't you give our friends over at missing persons a buzz?"

Sixteen

Walter's Van, 3:30 p.m.

GILLIE SQUIRMED IN HER SEAT. "I gotta pee."

Walter thought she was unusually pale. "Can you hold it?"

"Not really."

"Are you all right? You don't look so good," he asked.

"Have you looked in a mirror lately?"

Walter found a gas station and pulled up next to the women's restroom. The small building backed up to the woods and there were two ways out of the parking lot. He wanted options in case the Mustang showed up again. While keeping a keen eye on their surroundings, Walter reached over to the glove compartment and pulled out a small dark bottle. "Here, dab a drop of this behind each ear."

"What is it?"

"It's called MotionEaze, it's just an herbal oil, but it's great to get rid of car sickness."

"You are just *now* telling me about this stuff?"

Walter shot her a grin and handed over the bottle. Gillie dabbed a small amount behind each ear. The cab quickly filled with the soothing aroma of fresh mint and eucalyptus.

"Wow. It works. But I still need to pee. Bad."

Gillie went in the women's restroom while Walter checked his wound. Something about all this excitement and the close call at the carwash had gotten the kinks out of his old joints. It felt like old times when he was young and agile. Walter was damn sure he'd lost muscle strength over the years, but his experience more than made up for it. Besides, the most important weapon any man had was his brain. He could feel the shift. His mind had already settled back into a state of alertness that just might keep them alive.

Before he even got his sleeve rolled up, Walter looked up to see Gillie bolting out of the restroom toward the woods.

"Shit." She's running. He opened his door and went after her. If she got away, she was no match for the men in the blue car.

Gillie dropped her pants. Walter hadn't intended to see her thong underwear, but he had.

"Jeez, man. Don't look." Gillie squatted behind a tree.

Walter abruptly turned his back. "What are you doing?"

"The bathroom was like toxic. The woods are cleaner. Sorry. I couldn't wait any longer."

He felt his face flush. It was the first time since he'd asked Helen to marry him that his cheeks had felt like they were on fire. He hadn't realized why Gillie had run into the woods. It all happened so fast. Before he knew it, she'd peeled off her jeans and – well – there it was.

Walter wiped his face on his sleeve and felt relief melt over him. His hand felt for his Colt. It was still right there in his pocket. The sinking sun said it was late afternoon. He stood guard with his pistol like he had so many times before – though it had never been in a situation quite like this. While waiting, he thought about what a stupid mistake he'd made back at the carwash. He knew better than to let himself get cornered. But he'd learned a few things about the guys after them. They weren't looking any longer. Their mission was to take him and possibly Gillie down.

It was time to step up the pace.

Until now, Walter had hoped that he was wrong about being a liability. But after what he'd just seen, it was clear that Dr. Curtis had something hellacious to hide to take the risk of going after him on public streets. As if that weren't enough to twist a guy's shorts into a knot – what kind of monster would go after his own kid?

Walter was annoyed with himself for letting them get close enough to riddle the van with bullets. Beyond the danger, such things triggered all kinds of curiosity especially from cops. That was the last thing he needed.

"Thanks. I feel better," said Gillie as she swaggered around Walter and headed back to the van. He climbed in and stared at a crack spreading across the windshield. It was time to dump the van and find another vehicle, preferably something that wouldn't draw so much attention.

They both just sat there. He tried to say something, but was at a loss for words. After a few awkward moments he said, "Umm, Gil. About the woods. I mean. I didn't…" *Damn it.* He was stumbling over his words and starting to blush again.

"I know you're not a perv, but dude, you've got to get yourself cleaned up."

Walter surveyed his shirt and realized she was right. He'd wiped his face with the bloodied sleeve. He must look like something out of a horror flick.

"Tell me again about your friend, Kip."

"Can I call him? *Please*?" Her eyebrows were up and a smile busted out all over her face.

Walter wanted to give in, but bringing another kid into this was ridiculous. "What do you know about him?"

"Kip's really nice and he's the best friend in the world. He's like so cute. You should see his six-pack – "

Walter just stared at her.

"Okay, never mind."

It was hard to keep a straight face. She reminded him of a little bird with ruffled feathers, especially when she got excited, but he wasn't about to tell her that. He put on his get-to-the-damn-point look hoping it would nudge her to hurry it up.

"He is seventeen, works for his uncle on weekends at the junkyard, and he likes to take old wrecks and make them run again. It's kind of a hobby. Kip is good with anything mechanical. He even fixed my printer so I could use a cheaper brand of ink cartridge."

Borrowing a car from a friend was a much better option than stealing one, which Walter didn't think was right. "Can he get us a car?"

"I think so. Can I call him and find out?"

"Go ahead."

"Oh, shit." Everything about Gillie's expression changed when she pulled out her cellphone. Her thumbs frantically started tapping the screen. The phone went dark. "Umm. I think I know how they found us."

"How?"

"My cellphone was on. Considering that my dad gave it to me, I'd bet anything he has been using the GPS to track us. I'm sorry, I should have thought of that."

"If your dad can track us, the cops can too. They both have to be close."

Gillie slapped the dashboard. "Crap."

Walter rubbed his forehead. It wouldn't surprise him to find a tracker hidden in the van, but he hadn't thought of the phone. He felt like such a fool. How could this get any worse? He was low on meds, his sugars were not well controlled, he needed to attend to his wound before it got infected, the van was shot all to hell, and then there was the matter of the guns who were out to get them.

Gillie's face was in her hands.

"It's not your fault. You weren't supposed to think through all this, that's my job. I'm the one that should be sorry."

"No! My dad is the one that should be sorry. You're wicked amazing. You saved us from them, twice. We can't stop now, because I'm not going back to Dad's house. No way." Gillie picked at a splinter on her palm. "I can keep the phone turned off. That way no one can track us."

"What about calling Kip?"

"I'll turn it on just long enough to call him and I'll make it quick. Then we can be right there to pick him up. Even if they can track the signal, by the time they get there, we'll be gone."

Walter had great reservations about involving another innocent kid in this mess, but what choice did he have? He needed to keep Gillie safe and to do that he needed a car.

Walter moved the van to the pump. After filling it up he sent Gillie inside to pay with cash. He might not know as much about how these newfangled cellphones worked, but he sure as hell knew credit cards could be traced.

After the fill up, he merged back into traffic and headed west. He had to take a route they wouldn't expect. Fortunately, for him New Hampshire towns were strung together by a web of back roads woven through a landscape of small lakes and woods.

Going around the city took time, but it kept them off the grid. Finally they left Manchester, crossed the river, and headed into a rural area near Lake Glen.

"Turn here," Gillie told him.

The van entered a small tract of homes in Goffstown that were nestled within a pine and oak forest. Gillie's friend lived in a typical New England neighborhood where the roads were lined with trees, instead of street lamps. A gray squirrel scampered between two small Cape Cod Colonials and took refuge under a trailered snowmobile.

Walter stopped next to a huge pine tree. Gillie pulled out her phone, while he rolled up his sleeve and slapped a bandage over the inflamed wound.

"Kip, this is Gillie."

"Oh, my God! Are you all right?"

◆

GILLIE CLOSED HER EYES and let herself enjoy the sound of Kip's voice. It was so good just to hear him, even if he was nearly shouting. She held the phone away from her ear. "Shhh. Not so loud, you dope. Someone will hear you." She giggled. "Hey, I need your help."

"What do you want me to do?"

"Come down to the corner by the big tree. I'll be there." Gillie hung up and figured her dad had probably noticed the signal. "Too bad, so sad." She pushed the off button on the top of her phone. *Track this, asshole.*

The sun had turned into a big orange ball hanging low in the sky. Gillie drummed her fingers on the dash until she saw someone coming toward them. The wave of hair sticking out of a ball cap and that sweatshirt with the pocket on the sleeve – she'd recognize them anywhere. The door creaked as Gillie pushed down the handle and started to jump out until Walter's hand slowed her down.

"Are you sure about this guy?"

"*Yes*. Kip has always had my back. That isn't gonna change now."

Walter let go and she bolted out of the door.

Gillie's legs ran so fast she nearly knocked Kip over. His arms wrapped around her and pulled her right off the ground. He seemed taller than she remembered, but he still looked like a surfer with those blond streaks. Even his hands smelled like board wax.

"I can't believe you're here. I saw your picture on the news. That was like crazy. I was so worried."

She wanted to just stop and hang out, but obviously this wasn't the time for that. "Look, I'll explain everything, but we need to get to somewhere safe."

Kip said, "I know where we can go." He still sounded worried, but when his hand wrapped around hers, it felt like she belonged in this world again. She just wasn't sure what he would think of the man in the van. Before she could tell him about Walter, Kip's grip tightened and he stopped. He glared at Walter who stared right back. "Who's that guy?"

"Let's just get in and I'll explain everything."

Gillie jumped into her spot in the passenger seat and Kip slid open the side door and hopped into the back. When Walter turned around to look at Kip, the boy jumped out of the fold-down seat and stumbled over the spilled tools.

"Kip, this is my friend Walter. He kidnapped me, but he is really nice. Honest."

"What? Are you kidding me?" Kip scooted to the back of the van and picked up a hammer.

Walter looked at her with that big scowl of his, only this time the blood smeared all over his face made him seem a lot scarier.

"So, that didn't really come out the way I meant it." Gillie took a deep breath and tried again. "My dad doesn't just hate me, he is the reason Walter's wife died. And Dad's gonna kill a lot more people, including me and Walter, if we don't stop him."

Kip's long legs reminded her of a startled moose caught in the high-beams of an eighteen wheeler.

"Why are you with this old guy? He looks like something out of a paranormal flick."

"I trust him as much as I do you." From the corner of her eye, Gillie caught Walter's sudden blink. It wasn't that he smiled – because he didn't – it was the way his eyes softened that got to her. "The blood is because he got hurt protecting me."

"*Seriously*?" Kip dropped the hammer.

"Just give him a chance. You'll see."

Walter leaned over and whispered in her ear. "I told you this was a bad idea."

"I know he can handle it." Gillie wanted to resolve the standoff, but Walter's jaw was set like a chunk of concrete and Kip was in the back still acting like a trapped animal. *Men.*

"Walter, he surfs. Get it – the ocean here is freakin' cold. Anybody who can stand that is really tough. Besides, he's smart and we need him."

Walter took a deep breath and unfolded his arms. "Kip, Gillie is right. We need help, but I can't ask you to do this. It's too dangerous. Her father has sent gunmen after us. This is no joke."

Kip sat back into the folding seat. "What makes you think you can get away from them?"

"I know a few things that they don't."

Gillie tapped Kips arm. "Walter did Special Ops."

"Oh." Kip still had his fist in a ball as if he were ready for a fight and didn't take his eyes off Walter.

"God, you guys. Please. I need you both. So, could we like work together and just get going?" Gillie reached out and held Kip's hand, forcing it to relax.

"Okay. What do you want me to do?"

"We need a place to rest and a car," she told him.

Kip finally calmed down, but Walter's hands were shaking again.

Seventeen

Deter's Subaru, 4:00 p.m.

DETER WAS NEARLY upon the location of the signal when it disappeared. He'd lost them again. He was probably too far from a cell tower. It was a common problem in a state so sparsely populated. Dead zones were a routine annoyance, but it was a small price to pay for lush forests, clean water, and fresh air.

He checked his watch and waited. Being a detective was a collage of extremes, not to mention tough on the waistline. Until recently, when he'd cut down and switched to drinking coffee, he'd filled the long hours of waiting with eating doughnuts and junk. He knew it wasn't good but most of his colleagues had the same problem. They'd sit around waiting for hours, then suddenly something would pop and they'd be sprinting into a fight for their lives.

Deter did some work on his laptop. How come they never have to do paperwork on those damn cop shows? Just as he felt his eyelids getting heavy, he popped a peppermint Lifesaver into his mouth and sat up. His laptop registered an alert. Gillie's signal was pinging off a cell tower on the other side of Manchester. Apparently she was heading west. How the hell did they get way over there?

Deter turned his car around and did his best to make a beeline to their location. Just as he neared Goffstown, the signal went dead.

"Damn it!" He pulled off the road and slapped the steering wheel. Playing with his mustache, he scanned the parking lot next to him. Deter couldn't believe his luck. Up ahead on the other end of the strip of shops was the blue Mustang.

Deter called in his location to Carl and gave him a heads-up. "I'm going to tail these guys."

"Roger. You want backup?"

"Nope. I don't want to tip my hand just yet. I'm going to hang back and see what they're up to."

Deter followed behind the car with the two men inside. One thing was for sure. If they were here, Gillie had to be close. They'd been on her and Lovett all afternoon.

It was tough getting close enough to read the license plate, but a few miles later a stop sign gave him the opportunity he needed. As soon as the numbers were visible, Deter had Carl on the phone.

"Run a twenty-eight on this for me. Call me when you have the results."

Deter expected that it would take at least fifteen minutes before he heard back, but in less than two Carl was already back at him. "It's a plate from a red Ford Ranger that was reported stolen six months ago."

"That's just bitchen."

"Deter. I've got a feeling about this Mike Curtis. I talked to some ex-employees. You know how they are always eager to dish dirt, but not these guys. Not one of them would say a word – even the one he fired a week before Christmas. She can't be happy with him after losing her health insurance just four weeks before her baby was due. Everyone of his former employees acted like they were scared."

"Maybe they have reason to be. What if Curtis is the one that hired the guys in the Mustang?"

"And what if Walter Lovett and this girl have a lot to say – maybe too much?"

"I've been thinking the same thing."

"What about her phone? You're following the pings, right?"

Deter sighed. "The signal's sporadic. She must be turning it off. I have an idea. Get out that list of her friends. See if any of them have an active cell number operating near these coordinates."

◆

WALTER LOOSENED HIS SEATBELT and glanced over at Gillie with Kip's cellphone up to his ear. While he waited on hold, she shifted in her seat and put her feet up on the dash. *She must be sick and tired of sitting in the van, I know I am.*

"Charlie, this is Walter Lovett. Say, could you please refill my prescriptions?"

With the phone between his shoulder and ear, Walter handed Gillie a pen. She filled the time by drawing stars on a pad of paper she'd found in the door pocket. He'd noticed how she'd drawn similar ones on the flap of her backpack.

"Sure. When do you want to pick them up? We'll be open until ten."

The last thing Walter wanted to do was to run the gauntlet again and go back into Manchester, but he needed enough of his medicine to see him through this. "I'm on my way over now. But listen, could you get a vacation extension for me? I'm going to Florida for a few months to check out some vacation property."

Gillie tapped his arm and mouthed "*Florida?*"

Walter just rolled his eyes.

Finally, she caught on and nodded that she understood the ruse. At least she was quiet about it.

"It might take longer down there than I expect. You know how banks are these days."

Meanwhile, he couldn't help keeping a watch on Kip. The kid hadn't taken his eyes off Gillie. Obviously he cared about her.

Gillie turned to talk to him, but before she could make a sound, Walter reached out and touched her arm.

"Would a two month supply do ya?" said the pharmacist.

"Make it three."

"No problem."

Walter tossed the phone back to Kip. "Thanks."

On the way to the pharmacy, Walter listened as Gillie filled Kip in on everything that had happened and what she'd figured out about her dad. At first Walter just concentrated on the road and kept a look out for the blue car. He wondered how they had been able to track them so easily, it had to be more than her phone. Before he had time to ponder the idea, Kip laughed at something Gillie had drawn. The boy was easy enough to read. He listened before talking and his calloused hands were a good sign that he didn't shy away from real work, but Walter wasn't ready to warm up to him just yet.

He couldn't blame the poor kid for his reaction. *I wouldn't trust a stranger with blood all over him either.* Kip seemed like a good kid who had a calm confidence Walter appreciated. His steadiness was probably one of the things that drew Gillie to him. Poor girl, her life has been anything but steady of late.

"Trust me. You are not half as surprised as I am," Gillie told Kip. "My dad sent guys after us that were shooting at us with real bullets. Can you believe that? I knew he was a jerk, but I didn't know he was *that* bad."

Hearing the story in Gillie's own words made Walter feel like a complete ass. He couldn't help reconsidering what he was doing. Was this really the right thing? Putting himself at risk was a choice he'd made, but these were just kids. Part of him wanted to drop them off somewhere safe and leave.

Walter interrupted. "I shouldn't have brought either of you into this. Of course, I expected Curtis to come after me, I just never thought he'd put his own daughter at risk. Just for the record, I would never hurt either of you."

"Sir, I'm not surprised at all. Gillie's mom is really nice, but her dad is a total whackjob. He treated me like a piece of shit – sorry, sir – but it's the truth. And he was even worse to Gillie. I'd love to help you get that dick. He deserves it."

"I'm not sure if it is worth risking your lives. At your age, you have the whole world in front of you." Walter was about to go find Gillie's mother and leave the kids with her when that defiant expression over took Gillie's face.

"Walter. With or without you, I'm gonna finish this."

"Me too," said Kip.

Gillie bounced the pen on her leg. "If we stop now, you'll get arrested and I'll be forced to go back to my dad. I'd never see my mom or my friends again. And that's the least of it. If he thinks I'm a threat, then there's nowhere safe for me – especially with him. It's too late to go back."

Cornered by a sixteen year old, Walter didn't know what to say.

Gillie stared at him insistently. "So are you going to help us or not?"

He wrapped his fingers around Gillie's hand and squeezed gently. He loved her spunk, but God he hated himself for having drawn her into this. Unfortunately, she was right. If he left now, she didn't stand a chance and neither would all the others that Curtis would cast aside as unjustified expenditures.

He sighed heavily and shook his head. "Young lady, I think you redefine the word stubborn. Okay. I'm in. However, if we are going to do this I need to get my medicine and grab some rest – *and* – you both need to listen to what I tell you to do from here on out."

"Agreed," they said, nearly in unison.

For the next several miles, Gillie and Kip were busy grinning at each other and talking quietly while Walter considered what they would need for resources for the next few days.

Lights were just beginning to come on around the city. The days were definitely getting shorter. As buildings flashed by, he stretched his left leg and wished the van had cruise control. It wasn't all bad though, they made better time getting through Manchester than he'd expected.

As soon as they pulled into the side parking lot of the Rite Aid, Gillie immediately began to bargain for a Coke and a bag of gummy bears. Walter drove to the back of the building by the delivery dock to find a place to stash the van. With all the damage it wasn't possible to park out front. A few turns of the steering wheel and it fit neatly behind a couple tall stacks of crates and a large bin of boxes that hadn't been broken down yet. Hopefully, they wouldn't be gone long enough for an employee to notice it and get curious about all the bullet holes.

Walter was about to open his door when Gillie grabbed his arm.

"You can't go in there like that," she said.

He checked the mirror. "Mother of God. I look worse than I thought. Sorry Kip, no wonder you were taken aback."

Walter flipped off his vest and dirty shirt. After putting a new bandage on his arm, he threw on a clean shirt and the rest of his gear. His vest had frayed edges that were soft to the touch. The old thing had been with him for so long it was part of his system for traveling fast and light. While he stuffed more ammo into the ample pockets, Gillie helped wipe his face.

Now that he was presentable, the three entered the brightly lit pharmacy with its polished floors and neat rows of brightly packaged products.

"Go get drinks and things to eat that don't need refrigeration." Walter enjoyed watching her face light up.

She grabbed Kip's hand and dragged him off to the aisles where candy and soda were in abundance. Walter met up with them a few minutes later with a basket that carried a small assortment of bandaging materials, antibiotic ointment, and Motrin.

Walter handed Gillie the basket and stepped up to the prescription counter. Charlie, the pharmacist, was buried in his work, but he took the time to wave anyway. Walter waved back as usual. It was a ritual between them, only this time he paid for his insulin with cash.

With the white bag of medicine in hand, they all went to the main register up front to pay for their supplies. While he and Kip waited in line, Gillie was off trying on sunglasses and chattering away. The whole scene felt strangely normal until Walter looked through the glass entrance and saw the two men from the blue sports car dash by.

Eighteen

Deter's Subaru, 5:00 p.m.

Deter had been cautiously tailing the Mustang when it pulled into the Rite Aid parking lot and stopped within clear view of the entrance. He slipped his SUV into a space next door at the liquor store, turned off the engine, and waited. Why in the hell were they at a pharmacy?

Deter answered an incoming call from Carl. "What have you got?"

"That depends. Where are you?"

"I'm in Manchester at the Rite Aid parking lot just off route three, not far from the Intervale Country Club. Why?" he said as he picked up his coffee.

"You won't believe this, but according to his CID number, a friend of Gillie's is somewhere in the area or at least his phone is," said Carl. "The kid's name is Kip Jordan."

"After all the screwy things in this case, why am I not surprised?" Deter toyed with his mustache. "Let me look into this. I'll call you back."

Deter had just taken another sip of his lukewarm coffee and grimaced when the doors of the sports car flew open. His pulse quickened. Two men emerged as he put down his cup. A gust of wind blew open one guy's coat to reveal a rifle. The other one in a

Mountain Dew T-shirt grabbed a shopping cart and together they headed toward the building. Watching these two gun-packing yokels trying to look like shoppers was just plain amusing. The hurried walk of the distracted men with a poorly concealed rifle barrel gave them a Darth Vadar does Walmart sort of look. It was just all kinds of wrong.

Expecting them to enter the store, Deter had already picked up his phone and was about to call for backup when he looked up to find the cart rolling toward the entrance without a driver. He snapped his head around and saw the tail of a trench coat disappear around the side of the building.

Hound that he was, Deter went after them. He turned up his collar to give his quick gait the appearance of a regular guy anxious to get out of the wind, until he peeked around the corner.

A few more steps and he took cover behind a large box compactor. From there he spotted the white van. *Holy crap*. It had taken some serious fire. It looked like a junker that had been used for target practice.

The license plate confirmed it was Walter Lovett's. The hardened face of the taller man in a Mountain Dew T-shirt caught Deter's attention as the guy strolled around the vehicle, looking through the blown out windows. Meanwhile, the shorter one in the trench coat ducked down on the other side and did the dirty work of examining something on the undercarriage. Deter suspected they were monkeying around with a tracker.

Lovett couldn't be far. Deter cut to the chase and snapped up the opportunity to look for the girl while the gunmen were still preoccupied with the van.

When he got to the front of the building, the store's bright interior glowed through the glass walls of the entrance. Customers past him like bugs drawn in by the light. He peered inside and right there, trying on sunglasses of all things, was Gillian Curtis.

She looked just like Deter had pictured her, but it pained him to see her acting like nothing was wrong. It amazed him how victims, especially kids, will cooperate and even identify with their abductors. On the other hand, Deter had to admit that her father was such a jackass, why wouldn't she be glad to be away from him?

Walter Lovett came into view. He hurried Gillie along, but in a protective, almost fatherly way. Deter's eyebrows went up when Lovett bought the sunglasses for her and then, as if that wasn't enough, she hugged him.

A teenage boy, probably the one Carl had told him about, stood next to her with a cellphone in hand. Deter couldn't believe his eyes. She was laughing and seemed genuinely happy until Lovett's head whirled around and he stared out the front door.

Thinking that Lovett had spotted him, Deter pretended to be looking at the newspaper stand. The exterior lights came on as the sky transformed into blazing streaks of orange and purple. His mind was scrambling for his next move. He slipped his hand under his coat and flipped off the safety strap of his shoulder holster. Now it was a matter of waiting for the right moment to pounce.

His fingers tingled like they always did prior to jumping into action, but before he could intercept the trio, he realized the two men from the blue Mustang had just sprinted around the side of the building in a dead run for their car. Oh, Jesus, the last thing he needed was to have two innocent kids caught between Lovett and what were surely Curtis's hired guns. He had to protect those kids.

Just as he was about to enter the store to contain the situation, Walter Lovett picked up a bag and headed toward the front door with the two kids snug behind him. The door was bottle-necked by a gaggle of older women who were cheerfully greeting each other. Lovett was still inside.

Deter abruptly moved to face a movie-rental machine. Standing in front of the big Redbox, he did his best to look like a regular guy scoping out the latest releases.

As soon as those women got out of his way, he was going in. If Lovett stayed in the store just a little bit longer, he'd be able to separate them and button this whole mess down. On the other hand, if Lovett got outside, all bets were off. He didn't relish the idea of doing scene control with so many civilians milling about. Just keeping up with Lovett and those kids was more than enough.

Deter stepped beside the Redbox and peered back inside the store. Sure he'd seen Lovett's DMV photo, but it was fascinating to see the retired Green Beret in the flesh. It was interesting what time had done to a man with that kind of history.

At first glance, Lovett appeared to be an ordinary older guy, but in a lot better shape than most. He had a good head of graying hair, but it was the man's stance and especially the striking sharpness in his eyes that made Deter suspect that Lovett hadn't forgotten a lick from his days in the Army.

Lovett nodded to the ladies and strolled out the door with both kids right behind him. Deter watched him eyeing the parking lot. Most criminals were edgy or arrogant, but not this guy. Lovett's head was high and his big shoulders relaxed as he walked toward him. The kicker was the way he scanned the scene and protected those two kids. By the book all the way.

The guy was clearly used to operating on his own and looked even more determined than the gunmen. They wore the swagger of thugs hungry for power, but Lovett looked more like a man who had grown comfortable with the formidable set of skills he had under his belt.

Deter found himself wanting to just sit back and watch. *This guy knows what the hell he is doing.*

The only problem was Deter stood between Lovett and his route to the van parked in back. He was briskly herding his charges toward Deter when tires squealed and the blue car raced toward them.

THUMP-POP-POP-THWACK. The sounds of gunfire sent people screaming and diving for shelter. Two moms picked up their toddlers and raced back into the store. An older man with white hair blowing in the wind clung to his walker and tried to shuffle away until two bystanders hauled him to safety inside the liquor store.

Before Deter could unholster his weapon, Lovett knocked him to the ground and pinned him against the concrete. "Keep your head down," Lovett said in Deter's ear. "And your mouth shut until they're gone."

He was stunned that Lovett was barking orders at him. Deter turned his head to see as Lovett pushed away and used the bulk of the big red machine to cover the kids.

As the car sped away Lovett moved closer to the van. He nestled the kids behind a masonry planter. Next to them was a display of trash cans and bags of composted manure. Deter hesitated. They were only twenty feet from him with a clear route to the van. *What the hell do I do now – recover the girl or help fend off the gunmen?* He pulled his weapon from his shoulder holster and was about to force Lovett to release the girl when the sports car skidded around to take another run at it.

The car hadn't gotten more than fifteen feet before Lovett spotted their approach. Tires screamed and the engine roared. He pushed the kids back down behind the masonry blocks and pulled Gillie's backpack up over their heads.

Just as the car pulled up on the other side of their cover, Lovett leveled his big shoulders full-force into the stacks of trash cans and fertilizer bags. A gun barrel slid out of the car's passenger window.

Deter heard one round and saw a burst of yellow petals as the slug ricocheted off the planter and took out one of the mums. Deter drew his gun as Lovett spun around and shot out the sports car's windshield with a Baby Glock.

The display came tumbling down on top of the vehicle. Lovett fired again and blew one bag of fertilizer wide open as it plopped through the broken windshield. The odors of gun smoke and cow manure inundated the air.

While the driver of the car peeled away with a guy in the passenger seat screaming his head off, Lovett hustled the kids out of there. With the gunmen gone and no bystanders in immediate danger, Deter's mission to recover Gillie left him with little choice but to hurry after Lovett, who was making a dead run for the van.

The guy was almost to the vehicle when he skidded to a stop and signaled the kids to hold back. He dropped to one knee to look at the undercarriage. Apparently he saw something that spooked him. He jumped up and sprinted away from the van with all his might.

Arms pumping, he was wide eyed, stiff necked, and charging right at Deter like some crazed, red-faced bull in a full tilt stampede. "Run!" Lovett screamed at the kids. He kept pushing Gillie and her friend out in front of him. At first Deter thought Lovett was using the kids as a shield, but then he was waving his arms at Deter to get down.

Like hell I will. He raised his arms and locked them straight out with his weapon drawn and ready. "Police! Hold it right there."

As the last word left his mouth a flash of light and an ear-splitting explosion blasted him off his feet. His ears were ringing like a drunk at Sunday morning services. At the same time a wave of nausea hit him like a freight train. Deter threw his arms around his head, trying to protect himself from the barrage of hand tools and hardware that were zinging through the air like strange do-it-yourself shrapnel. A crow bar skidded across the ground and thwacked into his thigh.

The blast set off an odd chorus of car alarms. As his stomach and the whirling scenery settled, Deter lifted his head. Smoldering debris and knobby chunks of safety glass were everywhere, including in his hair. He touched his face. The skin felt gritty and sore.

Deter propped himself up on his elbows. He hadn't a clue where his gun had landed. Black smoke choked the air and a confetti storm of shredded cardboard rained down around him.

He couldn't believe the sight in front of him. Pieces of the burning van decorated the macerated foliage of a nearby wooded lot. The smaller bushes were flattened completely. Tools had taken out the signage on the side of the building. One fender was in a tree and the bumper had scattered the neatly stacked pallets like they were a deck of cards. *If I'd been only five feet closer.* Deter decided not to think about that one.

He slowly turned to look behind him only to discover he was eye to eye with Walter Lovett.

Apparently he'd also been knocked down. As Lovett quickly shifted to search for Gillie, the whites of his eyes blazing through the grime and grit that blackened his face reminded Deter of seeing the faces of those rescued miners as they were pulled from the earth. Lovett turned his gaze back to Deter. Both men's eyes locked for a second, each sizing up the other.

"I told you to keep your head down."

Deter chuckled. "Well, Sergeant, how about you give me the girl and we'll talk about cutting you a break?"

Lovett didn't even flinch. Instead he used his cuff to wipe his face. "It's Master Sergeant, detective. *De Oppresso Liber.*"

"So, you're *liberating the oppressed*? Is that what we call kidnapping now?"

"Detective, if you're half as good as I think you are, you already know there's a skunk behind this mess, but you ain't lookin' at him."

Deter's eyes narrowed. "Was I that obvious?"

"You weren't really looking at those movies."

"How the hell do you know?"

Lovett harrumphed and wiped some more grit from his ears. "You didn't have your wallet out. You looked in only one spot. It was obvious you weren't scanning movie titles. And besides, when I pushed you down to keep you from taking a bullet, your pant leg rode up. Your ankle holster gave you away."

Deter grabbed at his ankle. Sure enough, the holster was empty. But there was no use in complaining about it now. His legs were still so wobbly that taking on anyone in his current condition – especially Walter Lovett – just wasn't going to happen. "I'm curious. What were you most highly skilled at?"

Lovett rose to one knee and responded as if Nam had happened just yesterday. "We were all cross-trained to do manhunts and recon, but my *MOS* specialty was *CSARs*."

"Combat search and rescues?"

"Yes, sir."

Deter was punchy, sore as hell, and giggling like a teenager. He just couldn't help himself. *Holy crap, Curtis is in deep shit.* What he would do in those designer trousers, if Lovett ever got a hold of him. Still chuckling, Deter held his aching sides and rolled over onto his back. "I've gotta take the girl back with me."

Lovett stood. "You're shell-shocked. Go see a doctor."

Sitting up slowly, Deter was still astounded at the surreal destruction. It looked as if he been frisked by a tornado. Everything from his pockets littered a ten-foot fan around him. Even his shoes were gone.

Naturally, Lovett didn't have that problem. His boots were tightly-laced military fashion and right next to his right foot was the small notebook with stars drawn on the cover. Deter felt his pocket. *Crap.* It was the one from Gillie's bedroom. Lovett picked up the damn thing and took it with him.

Out of the corner of his eye, Deter caught sight of his service pistol. The Glock 22 was lying on the asphalt up against the building and was way beyond his reach. He helplessly watched as Lovett picked up the gun and started walking toward him.

Deter's mouth went dry.

If only he wasn't shoeless. If only he could take cover, but there he sat like a bull's-eye stuck to the pavement.

After glancing over to check on Gillie and her friend, Lovett skillfully removed the clip and flung the weapon into the bushes.

Deter relaxed his shoulders. "You wouldn't happen to know where my Baby Glock got to, would you?"

"You mean this one?" Lovett pulled it out of his pocket. "It's not bad." He looked down at the pistol in his hand and turned it over a few times. "A light twenty ounces with ten rounds of serious fire power. Accurate. Not too much kick. Nice." He released the clip and tossed the gun into the bush. Deter craned his neck to see where it went. Lovett dropped both clips at Deter's feet and nodded toward the woods. "Don't leave them there for some foolish kid to find."

"No shit. Do I look like a fucking rookie?"

"Just makin' sure. I've learned not to assume anything," he said, as he went about picking up things from the ground.

Deter held his aching head in both hands. Much to his surprise Lovett took the time to toss his battered cellphone and badge into his lap. After removing the electronic key fob, Lovett pitched his keys over to him. "Don't use those until the ringing in your ears stops and you feel steady enough to drive. And see a doctor," he said before walking away.

Lovett returned to Gillie. They quickly picked up their scattered bags and disappeared from view.

Deter sat there for a few minutes and kicked himself for not calling for backup. The chunks of debris on the pavement poked at his tender feet as he struggled to stand. At least he still had his socks on. His head was spinning and his legs were pretty shaky. After regaining his bearings, he searched the bushes until he found his weapons. "This damn case is one for the books," he grumbled to himself.

Deter shook off the kink in his knee and passed by the front of the pharmacy on his way to his car. As he neared the liquor store, he stared at the empty parking space.

"Goddamn it." His car was gone.

Deter panned the parking lot. At the exit on the far end, his car had just left and was merging into traffic. It drove right past the emergency vehicles that were arriving en masse.

Deter hit the speed dial. "Carl, get over here. I've got a problem."

Nineteen

Deter's Subaru, 5:45 p.m.

GILLIE TOSSED THE BROKEN SUNGLASSES aside and blankly stared through the windshield as they left the parking lot. She barely noticed the passing sirens. Every moment of the explosion played in her mind like a movie stuck in replay. It was as if her brain was still back at the pharmacy trying to make sense of what had just happened.

◆

FOR GILLIE THE FLASH CAME before she heard or felt the blast.

The pressure hit, making it hard to breathe. Her ears hurt. She found herself pressed against the ground with Kip on top of her and his shoulder shielding her face.

A vague sense of him wrapping his arms around her stuck in her head, but she wasn't at all sure if he'd pushed her down or if they'd been blown off their feet. Now the weight of his body felt comforting – even though he made it harder to see what was going on.

"Are you hurt?" Kip asked. The worry in his eyes was hard to miss with him being that close.

"My God, what was that?" Gillie pushed Kip out of the way so she could see what was happening. Walter was picking up things from the asphalt and talking to a man who was on the ground. Just a few minutes ago she'd seen the same guy at the Redbox. Apparently he'd been blown off his feet too.

"The van exploded," said Kip.

He rolled off her and she sat up. Poor Walter. The van was tacoed. His tools were blown everywhere. Gillie stared in amazement at his favorite screwdriver buried in the wall with only the red handle sticking out.

"Walter made a living with that van and those tools. This sucks."

Kip held up what was left of the steering wheel. "We definitely need a new ride now."

He was so close to her, she could smell his wintergreen gum. That was awkward. For the first time ever she felt shy around him.

Car alarms hollered somewhere in the background like a strange squad of cheerleaders. Sure she and Kip had hugged and been close a bunch of times like when he'd tackled her to get his shirt back after she'd played keep away, but it never felt like this. They'd had staring wars, but he'd never looked at her like this, either.

Kip pressed against her. "I'm glad you're all right. Sorry about your new sunglasses, they're demolished." He put what was left of them on the ground next to her. As he pulled his hand away, he stroked her arm with the back of his fingers.

The thumping of Gillie's heart made it seem as if every cell were vibrating like a subwoofer on overload. Of course, she loved him. Kip was her best friend in the entire world. It was just that she'd never thought about him in *that way* – at least not until now. But there he was, so close and so sweet. And despite all the craziness, he'd trusted her and stayed to help even though he'd been skeptical of Walter. Now he had protected her with his own body.

Kip bent closer – close enough to kiss her. She held her breath and was just about to close her eyes, when she heard steps running toward them.

"Are you kids all right?" She could hear Walter's voice, but he sounded a million miles away thanks to the dreamy moment that almost became her first kiss from Kip.

Kip flinched as if awakened from a trance. Jumping to his feet, he helped her up without saying a word, but the heat of his touch was electrifying. A flush instantly warmed more than her face. She marveled at the sensation. Curiosity, excitement, and a bit of embarrassment all mixed together and made her gasp in a breath. While Walter checked her briefly, she couldn't help thinking the whole world could see every tingle and wondered if he had noticed. Fearing that he would, she didn't dare look directly into those brown eyes that usually saw everything. Thankfully, he was in a hurry and didn't notice – maybe.

"Come on." Walter picked up his little bag of medicine. "We gotta get out of here. Now."

"But how?" Gillie was really confused. She wanted the world to stop and give her time to make sense of it all. "Walter, we don't have a car."

"I think I can borrow one." He pressed an electronic key fob and listened to the beeping. She and Kip gathered up their spilled bags and followed without daring to look at each other.

Sure enough the beeping took them to an old black Subaru Forester. Gillie had no idea where Walter had found the fob. Once inside he reached under the dash and demanded that she not watch. "This is a skill you don't need to know."

The car rumbled to life.

As they sped out of the parking lot Gillie felt Kip's hand slip between the door and the seat. He'd just touched her fingertips when Walter shot him a look in the rearview mirror that could have taken down a rhino.

Within seconds something weird caught Gillie's attention. "Umm. Walter. This is bad – like real bad."

She gawked at the computer, handcuffs, and rifle sitting there in the car they'd just jacked from the parking lot. This stuff definitely did not come standard on any regular old Subaru.

"Don't worry. I'm going to return it. Besides, he has backup willing to come get him. It's better than taking the car of some poor mom who needs to go pick up her kid."

"But this is a cop's– "

"Yes, this is the detective's car."

"Seriously – that guy was a detective? Are you crazy? He'll catch us."

"I can get you another car," said Kip, sounding as if he were trying to be helpful.

"Good, because I'm not planning on keeping this one any longer than necessary."

◆

WHILE KIP GAVE WALTER DIRECTIONS to the junkyard, Gillie watched the traffic go by. She had spent many summer days at the yard hanging out with Kip. She loved the place because it was a thrill ride for her imagination. It was just creepy enough to be fun.

By the time they arrived, the sun had dropped below the horizon. The world around them turned purple and an eerie mist rose around the pole lamps.

Long sinister shadows reached out from the piles of wrecked cars and twisted metal. Gillie shook her head and thought about how she'd once tried to talk Kip into making it into a haunted junkyard for Halloween, but his uncle said the risk of injury was too great with all the sharp metal around.

It was weird how one day could change everything. The junkyard didn't seem nearly as scary as it used to. Not after today. Not after seeing real monsters – up close and personal. The scariest part was that they didn't look like the evil-eyed villains portrayed in movies. The two men in the blue car just looked like ordinary people. Even the one who had stuck his gun out of the window was sort of cute. *That's just not fair.*

Then there was her very own father who was the worst one of all. Gillie stared at the shadows almost in shock. It was clear that he didn't care about a lot of things. He was too cheap to spring for a pair of running shoes for track, but he had no problem spending big bucks to send gunmen after her. Unbelievable. *I could have been killed!*

If she hadn't heard the bullets or seen Walter's van explode, she wouldn't have thought any of this possible. Gillie rubbed her tired eyes and tried to relax.

They parked near a chain-link fence. Kip went ahead to unlock the gate, but instead he just stood there motionless. Gillie waved at him to hurry up. Then she saw the large German shepherd inch closer. Brown-black fur glistened in the security lights as the dog cautiously came up to the gate with her nose sniffing the air. Kip relaxed and whispered something to the dog, who began to wag her tail so furiously it swung her butt back and forth with each swish.

"Shadow," said Gillie. She jumped from the car and went over to reach through the fence and bury both hands in the silky fur around the shepherd's neck.

Kip pulled open the gate and motioned for them to come in, but Walter hung back.

"Where's your uncle?" he asked.

"He's in Virginia for some kind of auction."

Walter nodded. "Is there somewhere I can put this car out of sight. Just for a few hours? I'm not hot on the idea of leaving a stolen car on your uncle's property, but I need a break."

Gillie untangled a sticker-bur from Shadow's coat and watched as Kip opened a shed and drove out an old Crown Victoria. He'd been telling her about it for months. Finally, she got to see it. The burgundy paint looked really messed up, but the engine purred as if it were fresh off the dealer's lot. The way Kip commandingly guided Walter as he backed the detective's SUV into the shed made her proud of him. He was so good at stuff like that. On the other hand, Gillie was just glad she'd learned to parallel park.

When Shadow rolled over for a belly rub, a wave of homesickness washed over her. What she'd give to go home and sit on the front porch with Cody. How she missed talking to her mom and her cooking, especially the baked apples. It felt as if she'd been through a time warp and was in the wrong place – almost like Dorothy in *The Wizard of Oz*, only this time the man behind the curtain was her own dad. That was a freakin' scary thought.

While they waited for Kip to lock up the shed, Gillie brushed some dirt off Walter's sleeve. "I'm worried about my mom. What if Dad thinks she is a liability too?"

Walter's face bunched into one of his I'm-thinking frowns. "Why would he do that? She doesn't know about what he's doing at work. Does she?"

"If she did, I would have heard about it. Mom would go apeshit over stuff like that. I don't think she knows about the spreadsheet, but she knows some. Before he left, they really got into it. She said that they were practicing medicine without a license by forcing people into treatment plans made up by his insurance company – not the doctors. She said it was a conflict of interest because insurance companies were all about making money, instead of doing what was right for the patient."

"She's right. What did your dad say to that?"

"He got all pissed off and left. He expected her to be all happy about his big bonus, but instead she was upset that the money people had paid for insurance was going into VIP pockets instead of paying their doctors' bills. She said it was crap like that which made health insurance unaffordable for regular folks. What she said really made him mad."

"Gil, I think I like her already. She sounds a lot like you – spunky and smart. I think she'll be fine. But first I need to check my sugars. How about we work this out after I get some rest?"

Shadow excitedly ran big circles around Kip as he led the way.

Gillie kept pace through the enormous stacks of flattened old cars and rusted-out trucks. She jumped when a mouse ran from a giant pile of worn out tires. It was a strange place when she thought about it. There was something just odd about junk sorted into neat orderly piles. It didn't matter, the important thing was that they were safely on the inside surrounded by a tall fence topped with razor wire and the bad guys were on the other side.

Kip's phone rang. "Mom, hi," he said. "Sorry. I forgot to call. I'm at the yard. Uncle Phil won't be back until Monday and I promised him I'd take care of Shadow. Remember?" There was a long pause. "I'll call you."

Gillie was still watching Kip after he'd hung up. "I didn't lie. I really was supposed to watch the place, I just hadn't planned on having company. We have four days until my uncle gets home. While he's gone we can hang out in the trailer home in the back."

Shadow showed them the way. The trailer was old, dirty white, and pretty shabby looking. A painted deck with steps to the entrance was peeling and the metal front door was all dinged up with rust creeping out of the seams. It was a sad little place, but tonight Gillie thought it looked like a piece of heaven.

"It ain't much, but we should be safe here," said Kip. "Especially with Shadow around. She's very protective."

Even if it wasn't as cheerful as Walter's sunny yellow bedroom, Gillie was so tired of being in a car that the cozy quarters were a welcome sight. At least it had the basics: a couch, an old recliner

Kip had put there himself, and Shadow who liked to stretch out in the middle of the room on a braided throw rug. There was a tiny kitchen and a hallway that led to a bathroom, a small bedroom, and a backdoor at the end of the hall.

She could tell Kip had spent time here recently. Surfing magazines were piled up on one of the end tables, gummy-bear wrappers were on the countertop, and his work boots were by the door.

Gillie dug through the bags of groceries and put an assortment of beef jerky, canned peaches, a couple of apples, and pretzels out on the coffee table for everyone to share.

When she went for a jar of peanut butter she saw the pizza box in the trash. She'd kill for a pizza about now, but they were all exhausted and Walter had on that look he got when he was busy thinking and didn't want to be interrupted. Gillie could see that he was tired, but at least his hands had stopped shaking.

Twenty

Pharmacy, 6:05 p.m.

Deter was already unimpressed by a local beat cop who was doing his damnedest to get nominated for cop of the year. With a voice an octave too high for a grown man, he kept taking notes and eyeing Deter as if he were a suspect. This was taking forever.

Officer Erickson squinted at Deter. "Where did you get that badge and gun?" It was the second time he'd asked the same stupid question.

Deter had to hand it to him. The guy had just enough sense to have plenty of backup on hand. Deter eyed the two crewcut bruisers in uniform that flanked him on both sides.

"I told you. I'm a detective."

Erickson looked Deter up and down and made more notes. "Sorry, sir. I've just never seen a detective on scene without shoes."

"I just survived a bomb blast, for Christ's sakes."

"Bomb blast, uh-huh." Erickson continued to scribble away in his little notepad.

If Deter weren't so hot to get back on Lovett's trail, he'd toy with this doofus who sounded like a twelve year old. Come on. His badge number was just too easy to check. The guy must be a rookie. He had that too-eager look about him and the real give away – he had too much crap hanging from his belt and stuffed into his pockets.

Deter threw his hands in the air. "My shoes were blown off. I told you." He was about to lose his temper when a welcome sound came up from behind.

"Officer, I can vouch for this character," said Carl, looking pleased with himself. "He might be a pain in the ass, but he is my partner, just like he says." Carl flashed his badge and holstered Glock just to prove the point.

Officer Erickson nodded and went off to pester other traumatized witnesses.

"Thanks for the vote of confidence, partner," said Deter.

"Hell, you can hardly blame the poor guy. Look at yourself."

Deter checked his reflection in one of the few intact panes of glass on the front of the store. The ribbon of blood on the side of his head reminded him that his scalp was stinging. Deter brushed a layer of dust off his pant legs and realized that his shoeless feet did look kind of stupid. His toes were sticking out of holes in his black socks and were cut all to hell. They didn't look much better than his head.

Carl chuckled. "Can't wait to hear how you got your badge and gun, but lost your shoes."

"If you think this is so goddamn funny you can be the one to explain to the captain how I lost the car."

"No way. Buddy, that honor is all yours."

Deter told his tale of woe all over again to Carl while a paramedic attended to Deter's scalp wound.

"Sir, do you feel dizzy?"

"No."

"Are you seeing double?"

"No."

The paramedic leaned in to check Deter's ears. "Do you hear ringing or any high-pitched or irritating sounds?"

Officer Erickson came back carrying a pair of shoes. "These yours?" the officer said in that voice.

Deter leveled a look at Carl and the famous Deter giggle started to bubble up.

"Don't go there," said Carl.

Deter turned his head away. He had to, otherwise he was going to bust out laughing, then Carl would join in and there would be no stopping either of them. "Nope, I'm just swell," he said, biting his lip.

Carl turned to the paramedic. "He's fine. He always gets punchy after he gets his bell rung."

Deter and Carl watched Erickson wander off with his back up crew. It was such a huge scene, the processing teams were using the lights from fire trucks in addition to their own. Between that and the big staging lights, the place was lit up like high noon.

By the time Deter followed Carl to his car every inch of Deter's body felt like he'd been beaten with a baseball bat.

After standing around and fielding questions for over two hours, he finally was able to sit down. Easing into the passenger seat, Deter felt the relief of being off his throbbing feet and threw the shoes on the floor. Putting them back on seemed like too much effort.

The ringing in his ears had become annoying. Lovett had warned him not to drive for a while. *Why the hell would he care?*

Usually he and his partner fought over who would take the wheel, but not tonight.

Deter was happy to let Carl take him away. In the side mirror, silhouetted figures floated through the devastation like ghostly cranes pecking at the debris. Never again would he wander into that store without remembering the strange slow-motion impact of the blast and what it was like to stare up at Walter Lovett. The hair on his arms stood at attention and he started to shiver.

"Carl, turn the damn air off."

"Seriously, Deter. What's up with you?"

"This case makes no sense. Lovett just saved my ass – twice. He pushed me to the ground and told me to keep my head down. Then he deliberately stepped in front of me and took more of the blast than I did. That old bugger is as tough as they come. He walked away with little more than a layer of dust. I've never seen anyone move like that. And he had every opportunity to shoot me – even with my own pistols – but he didn't. He just took out the clips and gave them back to me. I don't get it."

"What about Gillian Curtis?"

"Are you kidding? Lovett would give up his own life before he'd let anyone hurt that girl. You should see how he dotes on her. Hell, she's safer with him than anyone else right now."

They had just pulled into the department's parking lot when Carl slammed on the brakes. "Deter? Isn't that your car?"

There was his SUV neatly parked in the front lot.

Deter jumped out of the vehicle, shoeless feet and all. "I'll be damned. How in the blazing hell did that get here?"

By now Carl was standing next to him. "You gotta be shittin' me. Looks like Lovett just saved you an ass chewing too."

"Let's go look at the cam feed."

Everyone turned and looked at the pair as they entered the building.

Deter knew he must be quite the sight. Captain Morrison walked by looking all squared away, as usual. He took one glance at Determan and said, "I don't want to know. Just fix it." A wave of chuckles and clapping rose like popcorn around the room. Carl and Deter largely ignored them as they headed over to their desks.

A couple of calls and a few minutes later a courier came downstairs with an envelope. Deter was busy putting on his shoes and grumbling when Carl returned with a glass of water and the Advil. Deter down a healthy dose and tried to gather up his scattered thoughts.

He and Carl went into the AV room to watch the recording. According to the time stamp, while they were cajoling Officer Erickson, Deter's car was being returned to the station and carefully parked right where he would see it. There were two people inside and a third one drove an old Crown Victoria. As the doors opened it became obvious who they were.

"Do you see that?" said Carl. "There's that Jordan kid. Lovett and Gillian Curtis were right here in our own parking lot."

Deter studied the screen and watched Lovett locking up his car. He wasn't a thug and he sure as hell wasn't a thief. "Damn considerate perp if you ask me."

Carl was squinting at the screen. "What are we missing here – besides the girl?"

◆

MIKE LOVED HIS HOUSE and especially this room. He swirled three tiny cocktail onions in his dry martini, then bent over to pull them off the sterling silver pick with his teeth – one savory orb at a time. He closed his eyes and took in the tangy crunch mingled with the icy burn of gin. Not just any gin. This was Tanqueray Ten with just a whisper of vermouth. Perfection. He stretched back in his custom black leather lounge chair and let the buzz wash over him.

The rich smell of Italian leather and glitz of a fully equipped media room and bar surrounded him in his personal cocoon of comfort. Right from his chair he could dim the lights, start a movie, or watch any televised game. He was warm from the buzz of the booze and at ease and looking forward to a good night's sleep.

All was well until he clicked the remote to catch a few minutes of the news. Pandemonium displayed across his enormous LED screen as reports came in about what had happened at the Rite Aid store in Manchester.

The voices of people screaming and the howl of sirens clamored in the background. A camera focused on a bumper in a tree and then panned the scene.

Mike sat forward and caught a glimpse of detective Determan getting into a car with a man he knew was the cop's partner. The camera went back to what was left of a smoldering white van.

"Jesus fucking Christ." Mike held his forehead in disbelief and called a number in his favorites list.

"Tell me this wasn't you."

Brock was silent.

"Didn't you draw enough attention at the carwash? You couldn't corner him in a remote area where the damn deer don't give a shit? No. You had to blow up a fucking Rite Aid with – what? – fifty witnesses or more observing the spectacle?" Mike was hot.

"I can explain –"

"No, you can't. I thought you were a professional – the best."

"We were planning on cornering him until the cop showed up. The bomb was for backup and he still got away. He's not so easy to corner."

"Apparently that's the understatement of the day."

"Don't put this on me. I told you from the beginning that he has serious skills. Lovett shot my partner and took out the windshield of the car. I'm picking up a new one and bringing in two more guys and the price just doubled."

"What you are going to do is follow orders. Lay low." Mike's mind was racing. "I want you to disappear for a little while until you hear from me. I have another job for you."

Mike clicked off the television and slugged back the rest of his martini.

He bent forward in his chair to think about this fiasco. If there was one thing he was good at, it was getting the upper hand. It was a bit of a specialty he'd learned a long time ago.

Back after that horrible night at Hank's when he was just a kid, Mike had decided right then and there he would never again be anyone's victim. Tonight would be no exception.

He wiped his hands after putting his martini glass in the bar sink. Before his eyes were bottles of premium liquors glinting in the soft light. The Bushmills 1608 sat on the shelf, mocking him. For reasons he couldn't explain he opened it. Even though he paid over a hundred bucks for this bottle it still smelled like whiskey.

His memory opened up like a vault that refused to stay shut. First it was a flood of pictures, but it was the smoky fragrance that took him all the way back to the weeks after leaving Hank's flophouse.

◆

A SHORT TIME AFTER that night in the special room, Mike sat in the weed-filled grass of his front yard. He smiled as he read an article in the newspaper about an anonymous tip that had led to the closing of the flophouse. The papers said investigators had found drugs and that a number of the girls were minors. Oliver Hanks, also known as "Hank," had been arrested and was expected to do twenty to life for a long list of charges.

Two days after the article in the paper, Pops fell asleep after making friends with another bottle of Jim Beam. The comic store burned down, with him in it. The fire chief said it was a tinderbox just waiting to go off. They concluded it was an accident – what with all that old paper and the bottle of spilled alcohol and his lit cigar that had fallen to the floor and missed the ashtray.

Mike was happy to let it be. What the cops didn't know wouldn't hurt anybody. Besides, Pops was a fuckup.

Parents are supposed to protect their children.

He went back to school. Every morning, Mike would make himself a peanut butter sandwich and stand at the corner bus stop. On the ride to school, he'd brace himself, even tried sitting with one leg under him as a cushion, but when they went over speed bumps the bite of his still painful injuries only made him more determined. He bit the inside of his cheeks to keep his emotions in check.

Sometimes he remembered the sounds of Pops screaming and the roar of the fire, but even that helped drowned out the tomfoolery of the other kids on the bus. While blocking spit-wads, he decided that from then on he was going to take his slice of the pie and it was going to be a big one.

Mom couldn't stop him. She was too busy working at the grocery store by day and at that stupid convenience store by night. Neil was too little to understand. It was his sister who was the pain in his ass. She'd watched his every move, including catching him snatching money from Mom's wallet.

He'd deal with her just like he had with all the milky-eyed, slack-jawed girls at the flophouse.

Mike told himself that someday he was going to be a big man with clean sheets that were laundered by somebody else. Someday he was going to eat thick juicy steaks instead of dry sandwiches on cheap stale bread. And at all costs, he was never again going to allow anyone to hurt him.

◆

MIKE ABRUPTLY EMERGED from his thoughts and realized he was standing at the bar with the whiskey bottle still in hand. He carefully slipped it back on the shelf in front of the mirrored wall. The bar light flickered and he caught a glimpse of his own reflection.

What would Pops think of him now?

A few years back, after another promotion, Mike had his driver cruise through his old neighborhood in a slick black limo. He'd settled triumphantly into the backseat, expecting to declare victory over his past by flying his flag of success for all to see. The sad truth was no one cared – in fact, no one from his past was even still there. So what did any of it matter now? Maybe it only mattered to him and that was all that counted.

This night was growing short and it was time to get down to business. He went to his study and turned his attention to his computer and that damn detective. The internet was such a handy tool. Hours went by until he found an old headline that read: *RAMPAGING COP SUSPENDED*.

The article in the *Union Leader* showed a young detective Andrew Determan who had gotten himself in hot water by being too aggressive with the interrogation of a suspect. There were allegations of police abuse and tampering with evidence related to a drug bust. Speculation abound that he was driven by an unsolved crime – the kidnapping of his own five-year-old son, Ryan. Detective Andrew Determan was on paid administrative leave until the matter could be fully investigated.

Leaning back in his chair, Mike stretched out his long legs. Life was nothing more than gamesmanship. You won only if you knew how to play your cards.

A ray of light filtering through a small crystal globe on the corner of his desk caught his attention. He snapped it up and twirled it before his eyes. The tiny continents etched into the surface played before him. His long fingers closed around the cold sphere, enveloping it in the middle of his fist. Gillian threatened his world. He had to get the detective to back off so he could get to her and Lovett first. He tossed the orb into his other hand and then back and forth until an idea came to him.

Mike smiled. Determan would never see this one coming. With the phone up to his ear he cracked open a cold one and said, "Brock. About that job."

Twenty-One

The Yard, 9:00 p.m.

Back at the trailer, Gillie rolled a tennis ball across the floor and watched Shadow eagerly scamper after it. It felt good to do something ordinary after the freaky adventure to return the detective's car. The shepherd quickly returned the ball and dropped it next to Gillie's hand. Dogs were so ready for fun and so trusting. She'd been kind of like that – at least until today. She couldn't help smiling at Shadow's alert ears and bright eyes that were totally focused on the ball in Gillie's palm. Kip and Walter were in the living room too, but they were quiet. Too quiet. Gillie felt like she was gonna bust wide open. *Didn't anyone else need to talk about all that had happened?*

"I was like terrified that a bunch of cops were gonna come blasting out of the station and arrest us," said Gillie. She couldn't believe Walter had driven the detective's car right into the station's parking lot.

"I wish I could do stuff like that," said Kip, hunching over to rest his elbows on his knees.

"Come on now, you have no business being involved with such things," said Walter. "Besides, it wasn't that big of a deal. It was dark."

"Weren't you nervous or scared or something?"

"Back when I was a clueless recruit, I used to think the whole world was watching my every move. Then I realized no one gave a hoot about me. People are so focused on themselves, they don't take notice. As soon as I got right with that, the nerves went away. Today it's even easier, with so many people obsessed with their phones – they make themselves easy marks."

Kip picked a sticker off a green apple before biting into it. "I don't know, dude, what you did took serious *cojones*."

"It's not about nerve or muscle. It's about patience and thinking ahead. In any fight the most important weapon you have is being smarter than the other guy. Think about it. If you were a cop, where would be the last place you'd look for someone who had stolen your car?"

"I get it. You're too much," said Kip. Gillie watched him adding a glob of peanut butter to his apple and taking another huge bite. Of course, she'd noticed how he'd barely taken his eyes off her since the blast.

Gillie turned to Walter. "Why did you become a Green Beret?"

"I was drafted. Back when I got out of high school, if you weren't in college you had two choices: go to Canada or go to Nam. I had no idea what kind of a career I wanted – so off I went into the army."

"But why Special Ops?" asked Kip.

Gillie had wanted to ask him that one since she first heard about his training.

Walter smiled. "I wasn't cut out for their two-step-rah-rah boot camp where they spent most of their time marching around trying to sound tough. I was more comfortable operating on my own. When I was a kid, my dad used to call me 'Wild-Man Willy' because I spent so much time in the woods behind our house." He chuckled. "I used to take my duds off in the laundry room.

My mother insisted I do my own wash after a frog jumped out of the hamper followed by a bunch of spiders spreading out over the floor."

Gillie shivered. "I hate spiders."

"Stuff like that never bothered me. Anyway, it didn't take long for the Army to figure out I knew how to shoot. Once they saw I was pretty good at it, it was a done deal. I guess I thought it would be something I could do, but even more importantly, I wanted to make a difference. I wanted to come home knowing I'd done something right."

It wasn't hard to see Walter running through the woods and hiding in the bush. Even now he looked the part with his hiking pants that could be made into shorts by zipping off the legs. For an old guy, Walter was very cool. "With all those medals on your uniform, you must have been some kind of hero."

Walter's smile faded. "It wasn't like that. It was a no-win situation. Our mission was to engage the Viet Cong with the same guerrilla tactics they were using on us. We caught holy hell from all sides: conflicting orders, protestors back home who thought we were all potheads or warmongers, and we even caught flack from the people we were trying to help. I'll never forget the old, toothless-Vietnamese woman who threw chicken shit at me after we saved her village from being burnt down.

"We were usually so deep in hostile territory that while we were hot and heavy with the enemy we also had to contend with being strafed by friendly fire and sprayed with Agent Orange. Lots of good men died. Johnson. McCloskey. Joey was only nineteen. And that guy from New Jersey, what was his name?" Walter sighed. "There were so many of them. If you lived long enough to come home, you were welcomed back with jeers and pelted with tomatoes." Walter shook his head. "There were no heroes. Just sacrifices and a war that seemed like it would never end."

Apparently it was a lot different back then. No one would dare do that now. Gillie had seen people at the airport spontaneously applauding men and women returning home in uniform. "Weren't there any good times?" she asked, trying to cheer him up.

It was a relief to see his face brighten up a little bit.

"Sure. A couple of buddies and I used to raise hell. Firestorms were business as usual, but we managed to look beyond it and find something to smile about. We saw each other through a lot of shit."

Gillie listened intently to the conversation. Walter's stories came alive when he opened up. They were so real. When he talked about what he believed in, there was an honesty to his words that she found amazing. Her dad never did that. Walter was smiling again and teasing Kip. It seemed like they enjoyed each other's company.

After the exploding van and dodging bullets, there they were huddled around the beat-to-hell coffee table sharing their secrets and snacks as if this were some strange summer camp. It felt like a campfire where people talked about stuff that mattered. Somehow there was comfort in the three of them being together. Even Shadow was relaxed and breathed a heavy sigh every time someone stroked her belly.

"I feel really bad about your van and all those tools," Gillie said. She worried about what Walter would do when this was all over.

"The van was old. Things like that can be replaced."

"What about your rifle?"

"Oh, hell, it was a good companion, but nothing like the M24s that they use today. Now that's a weapon."

"But, Walter, what about all your stuff?"

"Gil, I don't wear this vest to make a fashion statement. I keep the important stuff on me. It's an old habit." Walter opened a few of his pockets and showed her an assortment of cash, a small flashlight, diabetic supplies, ammo, a small pair of binoculars, matches, a roll of wire, and a key he held up with a grin.

"What's that for?"

"Plan B. I have a safe deposit box, just in case this goes on longer than I expected."

"Jeez, dude. Hanging around you is like being a guest star on *NCIS*."

"You really are stuck on that show. Anyway, I told you I had planned ahead. There were just a few things I didn't expect."

"Like me?"

Walter raised his eyebrows and ran the back of his fingers over the stubble on his chin. "You were a surprise, but a nice one. Oh, I almost forgot." Walter pulled a small notebook out of his pocket and tossed it to Gillie.

"Oh my God. Where did you get this?"

"It was blown out of the detective's pocket."

"How the heck did he…?" Gillie knew right then that the cop must have been at her mom's house. "Thank you. The password to my dad's computer is in here."

"You sure that spreadsheet will prove what your dad has been up to?" Walter asked as he opened a pocket.

Gillie tried not to watch when he used a lancet to prick the back of his forearm. A small bubble of red rose on the skin and was sucked up by a narrow white strip he fed into his meter.

"Not just that – I can get at his notes and the formula he uses to sort incoming claims. I've been thinking about it." She watched Walter pull out a syringe. "I'm sure the claims from the people Dad flagged as 'reds' went to what he called his 'special claims review committee.' I doubt they even bothered reading them. MacAbee and Hollister and some others were on the committee too. There was even a pediatrician on his team – can you believe that? How could you let a little kid…" Gillie shook her head. It was too much to think about.

She grimaced as Walter loaded the syringe. He tapped the barrel and squirted a bubble out through the sharp needle. She turned her head just as he opened a zipper on his thigh to inject himself. She didn't watch, but she couldn't help smelling the alcohol wipe. *I'd never be able to give myself a shot.*

Kip drummed his fingers on the table and said, "How could he do stuff like that? That's so bogus. Why hasn't YorkCare just fired him?"

"Money," said Walter. "My guess is that they were too happy with their bottom line to care. These big insurance companies have rockstar egos. They see themselves as so powerful, they can get away with anything as long as it's couched in politically correct terms. It's amazing how many ways they can spin the words 'care' and 'managed.' "

"But they are supposed to help pay people's doctor bills. These jerks aren't doing what they promised," said Kip. "It's just not right."

"Oh, it gets worse," said Gillie. "Dad showed me the processing department. If claims are backing up too fast, the processors just delete them – gazillions of them – and the system automatically sends back a report that says there was missing information. It's a lie, but Dad said it saves them tons of money. They even know what percentage won't bother to refile. They use all kinds of tricks like that."

Walter was chomping on a stick of gum. The way the muscles of his jaw pumped told her that he was mad. "Everyone should have affordable health insurance, but the way the system is now, it's just too open to abuse. And those trying to regulate it don't see what's happening."

"This is so huge. What the hell can we do?" said Kip. "They probably have people in Congress covering their butts. The police can't do anything."

Gillie suddenly realized how great it was to be around people who cared. After spending six months with her dad, never again would she take friends for granted. "I think we can stop him," she said. "Maybe if we made this public, everyone would get so hacked off they would force a change. But first, we have to go to his office and get the proof."

Leaning on his elbows, Walter hunched over and stared at the floor. "I can't go any farther right now. I still need that nap."

Gillie wanted to keep talking and hanging out, but Walter had already stretched out on the couch and closed his eyes. Within seconds his foot was twitching and he was snoring.

Kip nodded toward the bedroom. Gillie slipped after him as quietly as possible considering how much the stupid floors creaked. Once they were in the room Kip asked, "Gillie, are you sure we can get those documents? Isn't this like crazy dangerous?"

"If we do nothing it's dangerous. He isn't going to let us go. The only way to stop this is to stop him. If we don't we're all dead."

Kip flopped on the bed and rolled over on his stomach. Shadow had followed and was pawing at him for attention.

"Aw, *crap*. Kip, I forgot about the alarm code."

"I thought everything was in your notebook."

"No. That only has the computer passwords. There's a different one for the door to his division. It's in my old phone."

"And where's that?"

"At my mom's house."

Kip looked relieved. "I thought you were going to say it was at your dad's house and I don't think going back there is a brilliant idea."

"Yeah, but I still need to run over to Mom's."

"When Walter wakes up we can go."

"No way. By the time he wakes up she will be home from work and it will be too late. I have to do this now. I'll be back before he knows I'm gone. I promise."

"Seriously. By yourself?"

"No one will even know I'm there. I'll keep my phone off. They can't track me. The only one there will be Cody and he'll protect me. Do you have a car I can use?"

Kip rolled off the bed and onto his feet. "The truck and the Crown Vic are the only ones with registration and licenses."

Gillie stared up at him through her bangs and cocked her head. "Please?"

"I'll come with you."

"Good God, Kip, it's just to Mom's house. I'm not twelve and I'm not a freakin' damsel in distress. Besides, Walter's hands have been kinda shaky. I know this is hard on him. What if he needs his glucose pills again and no one is here to help him?"

"I don't want you to go by yourself."

"I won't be alone. Cody will protect me. Come on, *please* – we're wasting time."

Kip caved, but didn't look too happy about it. He dug into the pocket of his jeans. "Here's the truck key. You better get back here soon."

Gillie snatched up the keys with a grin and tiptoed into the kitchen. She grabbed her phone from the charger. Walter shifted. She held her breath and froze. After he went back to snoring, she relaxed and returned to the hallway.

Kip looked so sweet when he was all worried about her, she couldn't help giving him a hug. Before slipping quietly out the back door she turned to look back at him.

"It's all good, dude. I'll be right back. I promise."

Twenty-Two

Deter's Car, 9:00 p.m.

DETER POPPED INTO the driver's seat. Everything felt off. His feet couldn't reach the pedals. He hated it when other people drove his car. It was an invasion of a man's privacy, like borrowing a guy's swim trunks and returning them with the lining all stretched out. Deter yanked at the crank between his legs and scooted the seat forward. He went too far. His bad knee collided with the dash. Deter closed his eyes and swore at himself.

With the seat finally in place, he carefully checked the mirrors. The Forester was the oldest one in the fleet, but he was used to it and it was a great car to drive. Finally, after all his adjustments, it felt like his again. He repositioned his computer and made sure everything was in its place.

Deter scanned the interior. Nothing was missing. Even his rifle was still stowed right where he'd left it. Clearly Lovett wasn't trying to rob him. Hell, he'd even left the key fob in the cupholder.

The car immediately came to life when he turned the ignition. He went to flip the sun visor out of his way and found a note sticking out right in front of his eyes. On the back of one of his business cards the handprinted words read *KEEP YOUR HEAD DOWN – CURTIS ISN'T WHO HE SEEMS.*

"No, Shit." That was hardly a surprise. The real question was, what did Lovett have on Curtis that he didn't? On one hand, his mission was clear. Walter Lovett had the girl and it was his job to get her back; on the other, the facts were telling him that damn note was right.

Deter had been suspicious last night when he had watched Curtis's act in front of the camera, but this morning he'd been certain of it when the doctor strolled into his office like a guy who didn't have a care in the world. Curtis was the man they should be investigating, not Walter Lovett.

The weirdest part of this whole mess was the dawning discovery that Lovett and he were on the same side. They both wanted Gillie safe. Truth certainly was stranger than fiction.

Deter shook his head and quickly remembered it was still pounding after the blast. It was hard to think. His arms felt as if he were trying to run a marathon while carrying buckets of cement, and he didn't even want to know how long it had been since he'd slept. That old familiar sense of exhaustion seeped deep into his bones. He yawned, leaned back against the headrest, and closed his eyes. As much as he wanted to give in right there, he needed to get home.

Rallying what few reserves he had left, Andrew Determan sat up, took the wheel, and pulled out of the parking lot. The black Subaru headed back to his apartment. Enough was enough.

Once there he sat on the edge of his bed, knowing he needed three things: a nap, a change of clothes, and a desperately needed shower – just not in that order. His brain was long past organized thought.

He could deal with just about anything after some shuteye. Maybe his head would quit hurting by then too. Deter lay back onto his bed and wiped his tired eyes with his thumb and forefinger. While a heaviness settled into his limbs he thought about what he should be doing next. *Maybe in a few minutes I'll be able to get my shit together and do something productive.* Images of Lovett, the barrel of that rifle sticking out of the car window, the exploding mum, and his son Ryan's face all rained down in his mind like the cardboard confetti at the blast site. *I'll get up in just a minute and...*

◆

GILLIE RUMBLED ALONG in the pickup truck. It felt good to be alone for a little while. Not that she wanted to go back to how it had been at her dad's house. The quiet drive was a nice break that gave her time to think.

The truck was fun because she sat up so high. The night air rushing through the open window felt fresh and inviting until shivers ran up her arms. She wasn't sure if it was the sight of her old neighborhood or the chill of the dropping nighttime temperatures. Either way, her Aéropostale sweatshirt wasn't warm enough. Gillie made a mental note to get a warmer one out of her closet.

Comfortable in her surroundings, she turned onto her old street and approached the house. The windows were dark. Mom was obviously at work. She always took the closing shift on Thursdays. Gillie had kind of hoped that she would be home and that they could talk – at least for a little while. Mom would have given her a big hug and told her that everything would work out. Gillie loved her so much for being like that. No matter what, there were always welcoming arms that waited for her. Gillie parked the truck in the driveway and went to the back door.

WOOF-WOOF-EEROO. Gillie started to laugh at Cody's howling. Clearly he knew she was home. She could hear him pawing at the door and his tail thumping against the wall.

Gillie fumbled with her keys and opened the back door as fast as possible. As soon as she was inside she dived into the furry greeting of her pooch.

"Hey, boy. How have you been?" Gillie broke into giggles as she got her face washed. As Cody shook, his dog tags flopped back and forth from the D-ring on his collar. "I see your bling is still slapping you around." The retriever just sat there wagging his tail.

"Come on, Cody." Gillie clapped her leg for him to come and skirted through the parlor, around the little table, and down the hall toward her room. The dog dutifully followed. She took in the smell of home. Pictures of her life hung all around her, just like the moments from Walter's life hung on his walls. Her footsteps slowed. It seemed as if the smiles were trying to tell her something.

Gillie's hand touched a spot on one wall where they had planned to hang this year's photos. It was empty. Her story was unfinished. She thought her life was like that bare wall, all the happy times had stopped the day she'd moved.

By her mom's room were dozens of pictures: there were ones of Gillie blowing out trick birthday candles, her toes in the sand at Hampton beach, and her first bike tied with a big red bow. Over on the other wall was her high school's marching band picture and next to it the awkward picture of Gillie with her front tooth missing. She looked closer at all the happy times when she and her mom had laughed until they cried or had gotten soaked at Six Flags.

Gillie studied the one of her mother singing. What would she do if her mom was lost like Helen?

The freaky part was that this wasn't much different from Walter's house: they both had pictures of smiling faces, birthdays, and moments of backyard fun. Gillie remembered Walter's uniform, the picture of the kids asleep on his shoulders, and Helen's wig on that faceless stand and the pink slippers that would never be worn again.

Gillie held her sides and sank to the floor. Everyone is someone's mom or friend or brother or wife. How many others were gone? How many people had her dad let die? How many would never sing or share ice cream or read stories to their kids again just because of him? Her lip quivered. *This sucks so bad.*

She could still see that stupid sponge he'd pointed at her. Wrapping her arms around her knees, her father's hateful voice echoed in her brain. Only now she knew he really meant every cold word. He didn't know her at all and never had. Even worse, he didn't want to.

Cody pawed at her arm and licked at the damp streaks trickling down the sides of her face. She rubbed his head. "You silly dog. I love you so much. God, I've missed you." Her voice became a hoarse whisper. Her nose started to run. She no longer cared and gave into the sobs.

After a while her eyes felt scratchy and sore, but the tears were gone. Gillie jumped when the cuckoo clock in the living room chimed, declaring it ten-thirty. Wiping her eyes, she realized it was time to get busy and back to the yard before Walter woke up. She pulled herself up and sat with her back against the door frame of the bathroom. A yawn over took her face and she tried to refocus.

Across the hall from her was the bedroom her mother had made into an office. The door was open and the desk was cluttered with piles of paper and files. But it was the pencil cup and a stapler on the floor that hung her up. Mom never left stuff on the floor.

Gillie rose to her feet and entered the room. Empty cans of Coke and a half full mug of coffee were left next to the computer. Things were pulled from the drawers and closet and piled so high she could barely walk through the room.

Boxes, bubble wrap, and packing tape were all over the place. What was she doing? At first Gillie was drawn to the open cartons. Her mother had been going through Gillie's baby things. A small toy giraffe with the nose chewed off and pair of pink booties were on the floor next to official looking papers and an empty wine glass. Mom never did that either.

The first paper had a docket number on the top. They were divorce papers. That wasn't exactly a news flash. "If only I could divorce him too."

It was the second paper that took her breath away. The words "court order" were printed across the top. It was a restraining order. The words were there, but she just couldn't believe what they said even though she read the words out loud. "Lynsey Ann Curtis is prohibited from any and all contact with a Miss Gillian Marie Curtis."

She sank to her knees and then sat on her feet to read the next paper. It was a criminal complaint filed by a Michael James Curtis, M.D. on behalf of one of his employees, for child molestation. A notice was attached to appear for a hearing next week to enter a plea.

"Are you freakin' kidding me! That asshole." Gillie picked up a stapler and hurled it against the wall. Cody bolted out of the room only to return and sit at the doorway. "Cody, there's no safe place for any of us. Not until we stop him."

Twenty-Three

Deter's Apartment, 10:45 p.m.

DETER'S OWN SNORING woke him up. A foul pasty feeling had taken over his tongue and his throat felt like he'd swallowed a chinchilla.

Looking around he quickly realized he'd fallen asleep on his back, fully clothed, with his feet still on the floor. Even his gun was still in the shoulder holster. He sat up with a start and checked the time – he'd been asleep for nearly two hours.

After the showerhead pounded his back with a jet spray of hot water and some fresh clothes that didn't smell like spent explosives, he was back on the road with a steaming cup of coffee, thanks to the saving graces of Dunkin Donuts. In the rearview mirror, a pair of head lights were following him.

He took a few turns – they boldly stuck to his bumper like a horny poodle – even as he entered the highway. Only when he slammed on his brakes and almost got rear ended did they back off, but only a few feet.

BAM – POP. At first he thought they were shooting at him until his car lurched to one side. *Shit – a blowout.*

His hands fought to hang on to the vibrating steering wheel. He let off the gas. The car slowed. Adrenaline put every nerve in his body on high alert while his white knuckles struggled to keep the car in the lane. Finally he was able to get the vehicle off onto the shoulder and stopped just as a semi roared by. Deter sat for a second to catch his breath. He didn't see anyone in the rearview mirror, but he wasn't taking any chances and pulled out his gun.

Deter got out of his car and slammed the door. His eyes rapidly scanned the traffic, the shoulder in both directions, and the clump of trees along the road. A blast of air blew open his coat and pelted him with a flattened Pepsi can as a rusty panel truck zoomed by. The residual stench of an engine about to crap out was all that was left as it rumbled on down the highway. *Where the hell did the guys tailing me get to?*

At the front of the Subaru he holstered his weapon. The beam from his flashlight confirmed that the right tire was shredded. "Goddamn it." Deter knelt to get a closer look. The wheel well was marred by a small explosive device that had left behind a starburst of black, torn metal, and the outline of a box about the size of a pack of cigarettes. The tire was ruptured from an exterior source. Deter pricked his finger when he felt around the tire rim and found a sharp piece of metal still embedded in the rubber. *No wonder there was a double pop. The assholes sabotaged my car.*

He went to stand when something hit him hard from behind. "What the hell?"

Hands were all over him. He couldn't see their faces. Deter grabbed for his shoulder holster. Two hands wrenched his arm away. They pinned the other arm behind his back. His bum knee hit the ground, sending a sharp pain up his leg. He twisted and turned. The last thing he remembered was a fist in his face.

◆

STILL FURIOUS AT HER FATHER, Gillie marched down the hall to her bedroom. Inside, the smell of a vanilla candle surrounded her. It had been so long since she'd been there. Her big hippo still sat on the bed. The room felt strange and familiar all at the same time. Things were where she'd left them – except for the junk someone had pulled out from under her bed. That was embarrassing. The detective had been here for sure.

Her closet was filled with tops and pants she'd forgotten about. Hanger by hanger she searched until she found her heavy purple hoody with the furry lining. Her hand dug deep into the pockets and grabbed her old phone. Pockets made such great hiding places.

Snuggling into the warm jacket, she sat on the floor and plugged the phone into its charger. Under "Bucko" in the contacts she found the code and quickly transferred it into her new phone, which slipped nicely back into her waistband. Then she dropped the old one back into her pocket.

Her dog laid on the floor next to her. His soft fur curled around her fingers. She missed him and her room. She missed her friends and her mom. She missed all of it. "I'm gonna come home, Cody. I promise."

Back in the kitchen, she took a slurp of a Coke she'd found in the fridge. It made her shiver. The house felt chilly. The old phone bent back her fingernail when her hands dived into the pockets to warm up. Gillie bit at her throbbing finger and tossed the old phone on the kitchen table.

Torn between desperately wanting to stay home and returning to the yard, the temptation to call her mom or at least text her grew. But how would she explain everything? What if Mom called the police? They could stop her from getting the spreadsheet and Dad would walk, which meant that stupid restraining order would stick. She took another gulp of her soda and put one of Mom's sticky notes on the fridge. With a Sharpie she wrote, "I'll be home soon. I love you, Gillie."

She sat at the table and listened to the sounds of Cody sniffing around the floor. On nights like this when her mom had been working, she used to watch TV or text her friends and draw. It was crazy how much had changed. The dog pawed at her leg.

"Hey, your dishes are empty." Gillie took another sip of her soda. As she filled up his kibble and water bowls she wondered when Mom would be back. It would probably be at least midnight. She put the dishes on the floor and listened to the dog chomping kibble and lapping up gulps of water until something caught his attention. The knob on the back door moved just slightly.

The fur on Cody's back rose into a fierce mohawk. His eyes intensely focused on the back door and a deep snarl rumbled in his throat. Gillie froze.

◆

LYN WAS ALMOST HOME. Her shoulders, her back, and her heart ached. The last few days had been the worst ones of her entire life and that was saying something.

She had been scheduled to work at the coffee shop, but was so upset by the charges Michael had filed against her that she had decided to take the day off. Instead, she spent the time gathering the things she needed most and moving them into her brother's garage for safe keeping. It had been his idea. Steve was good with things like that. In fact, he'd been protecting her for as long as she could remember.

She had no memory of their father. Steve said he'd drifted away when she was only two. Their mother, on the other hand, had been a thoughtful woman, a great mom, and a social worker until they were in their late teens. Then Mom got sick. Unfortunately, she never got any better even after the tumor in her head was removed. Ever since then her mother had been at the nursing home.

Lyn used to take Gillie to visit and admired how she would cheerfully talk with Grandma for hours. That girl had such patience. She was never put off by her grandmother's slow speech and twisted sense of reality, rather she seemed to get a kick out of it. For Lyn things weren't so simple. The worst part was that her mother no longer recognized her, which made the visits painful.

Steve had helped hold Lyn's life together back when they were kids. Even now, he paid for anything that Mom needed. Lyn tried to help with what she could scrape together from her coffee shop wages. It infuriated her that she was married to a doctor and couldn't do more. No matter how big Michael's paychecks had been, he was never willing to help, and now Lyn was in no position to do much. The last six months and especially the last few days were even worse than when her mother had gotten sick.

The future seemed so uncertain. She had already lost her mother and her marriage. Living without her little girl was too hard to imagine.

Once again, Steve held her together. He'd helped her get a fireproof safe to stash away some extra cash and her important records. If Michael was going to gut her life, she was going to do all she could to protect herself. Tomorrow, she'd finish up. For now she was taking her exhausted body home.

As she drove she wondered how she was going to sort through her keepsakes. Gillie's handprint from when she was three, the vase she made in second grade, and all the pictures. She couldn't bear the thought of leaving them behind. Those were the best of times and she wanted it all back.

Lyn couldn't help thinking that things had to get better. They sure as hell couldn't get much worse.

Just as she turned the corner she saw the strange pickup truck in her driveway and the dark green SUV parked in front. Lyn pulled over to the side of the road. Michael had forced her into survival mode and she was taking no chances. She hadn't planned on guests and wondered who'd parked their vehicles at her house.

On her limited budget, she'd developed the habit of turning off the lights before leaving and was certain she'd done so this morning.

Now all of her lights were on.

Lyn rolled down the window. Cody's barking could be heard down the block. It was more than his usual grumbling at a cat in the yard. Gillie had always said they had an "organic doorbell," but tonight's woofing didn't sound like that either. He sounded frantic.

She thought of calling Steve, but instead Lyn dialed Deter's number. It rang and rang and finally went to voice mail. "This is detective Determan, leave me a message."

"Deter. Where are you? Someone is in my house. Call me as soon as you get this."

Cody's yelping intensified. What was going on? Lyn got out of her car and snuck around the far side of the porch, away from the driveway. The lights were on in Gillie's room too. Lyn peered through her window. The closet door was open. She hoped like hell it was Gillie and not a robber.

Lyn continued listening for any sounds from inside. At the back of the house she stopped to peek around the corner. There on the back stoop was a strange man who had his hand on the doorknob.

Twenty-Four

The Yard, 11:00 p.m.

WALTER FELT SOMETHING nudge him. He kept his eyes closed and stayed still until he was more awake and had a few seconds to listen to his surroundings. Slowly he opened one eye to see two golden-brown eyes looking back at him. Shadow licked her lips and was resting her chin on his chest.

"What do you want?"

Her tail wagged.

Walter sat up. Kip was sound asleep in the recliner. Walter could see why Gillie liked him. In a way, he reminded Walter of Benny, his army buddy. They both had that same quiet resolve.

Walter hadn't heard from Benny in years. He had been sent home to recover after a roadside bomb had rolled his Jeep. Walter missed him. It would be real handy to have him by his side about now. Back in Nam they had kept each other going. What one didn't think of, the other did. It was the best of times and infernal torture – all jumbled together. But he could always count on Benny to crack a smile or a joke to keep things in perspective.

Walter put down a bowl of water for the dog and patted her head. As he straightened up, he realized that it was too quiet. He looked around the living room and hurried into the bedroom. It was empty. The bathroom door was open. Inside was dark. He went back to the kitchen. Nothing. A knot twisted in his gut.

Where was Gillie?

Back in the living room he slapped the recliner upright, catapulting Kip to the floor. The startled kid was staring up at him. Walter could feel cold sweat popping out on his upper lip and the tightness in his throat even before he opened his mouth.

"Where in the hell is Gillie?"

"She'll be right back." The kid glanced around the room like he was looking for a place to hide.

Walter bolted to the front window. He checked outside and then shoved his Colt into a pocket. With one hand he grabbed a wad of Kip's shirt and yanked him to his feet. "You have some explaining to do. Let's go. Move it."

Walter ran, pulling a stumbling Kip behind him into the cold night air. The car's engine roared to life. Shadow whined and paced back and forth and turned in circles as they left the yard.

"I'm sorry. She insisted. Gillie said she would be right back." The sound in the kid's voice was pitiful.

"Where'd she go?"

"Her mom's."

"Good God. After seeing them blow up my van, you let her run off alone?" Walter sucked the night air in through flared nostrils and forcibly kept his emotions under control. "What were you thinking?"

"I guess I wasn't, sir."

"Damn right. Can you call her?"

Kip pressed some numbers on his phone. "Hey, Gillie, we're in the car. Where are – "

The kid went wide-eyed and handed the phone to Walter. He heard a dog barking and the sound of heavy breathing. "Gil. You okay?"

"Oh God," she said.

The sound of panic in her voice soured his stomach.

"Someone is here. He's at the back door." Her last three words nearly tore his heart out. "Walter, I need you."

"Keep your phone on and hide it. I will find you."

The last sound he heard was her scream.

◆

AS SOON AS SHE LET OUT A SHRIEK, Gillie knew it was a mistake. A tall man in a gray Mountain Dew T-shirt flung open the back door and blocked the exit. Her eyes went wide when she recognized him as the guy who'd been driving the blue car.

There in her mom's kitchen they were eye to eye. He had a gun. She had a dog. Gillie tugged at Cody trying to pull him back. "Come on, boy."

Hoping Cody would follow, Gillie charged toward the living room.

The man leapt at her and missed. His sudden movement sent Cody on the attack. The dog snapped at his arm and he kicked back – hard. Cody yelped and limped to Gillie, shaking and twitching his hind leg.

She wanted to ditch Dew man and split with Cody out the front, but that wasn't happening. The guy was already too near. The closest thing to a weapon she could see were a busted umbrella or the fireplace tools. Gillie snatched up the poker. The pressure of being so pissed off at her dad cut loose.

Where does this jerk get off coming into my house?

She'd had enough of men trying to push her around. Gillie's get-the-hell-outta-my-face attitude took over. "Dew man..." Her voice exploded in the small room. She smacked his hand away with the poker. "Don't you ever touch my dog again."

Cody went bonkers. The man backed up, but only a little.

"You are coming with me. Tie up your dog or I'll shoot him."

Gillie stepped in front of Cody without taking her eyes off the intruder. The dog squirmed, whined, and tried everything he could to get around her. Finally he broke free and went for Dew man's neck.

The man raised his gun.

Gillie screamed "*STOP!*" and ran at him with the poker. The barrel of his gun was pointed right at Cody's chest when a kitchen chair came down over the back of the man's head.

He crumpled to the floor like one of those balloon people who had lost its air.

"Mom?" Gillie was so stunned to see her mother standing there with the chair still in hand, she dropped the poker.

Her mom yelled, "Look out."

The gunman grabbed at Gillie's ankle and knocked her off balance. Mom kicked his hand away. Cody jumped into the fray. His teeth were pulling so hard on the man's shirt that it ripped. Arms and elbows flashed in a furious whirlwind. Gillie saw Cody fearlessly sink his teeth into any parts he could get at.

The gunman stumbled to his feet. From there on it seemed that everything whirled out of balance in slow motion like some sick carousel. He slammed Gillie's mom against the wall hard enough to knock the clock off the nail.

"NO!" Gillie shrieked at the man.

Her mother looked dazed. One hand slid down the wall while the other hung limply at her side. Gillie tried to grab Dew man, but it was too late. The butt of his gun smashed into the side of her mother's head. He pushed her at the dog just as her knees buckled.

"Oh, God. Mom!"

Gillie belted the man with everything she had, but he got a hold of her anyway. She tried to pull away to get to her mother, but his hand grabbed a hunk of her hair and yanked her toward the back door.

"Mom? Please get up."

Cody frantically nudged and pawed at her mother.

On the way out of the house the intruder pocketed her old phone from the kitchen table and slammed the door behind them.

As he dragged her further and further from the house Gillie felt as if everything she'd ever loved was up for grabs.

This was worse than when she'd thought about killing herself. Seeing her mother assaulted right in front of her turned her whole world upside down. Panic made it hard to think straight. Was Mom okay? Or worse, what if she wasn't?

Her scalp sizzled with sharp stabs of pain as he tugged her toward the front lawn with his fist still clenched in her hair. Gillie fought to get away, but the more she struggled the tighter he gripped and the harder he pulled.

She could hear Cody barking and see him frantically running from one window to the next looking for her. Like a furry-blond soccer ball he bounced up to see over the sills. It was impossible to get the image of her mother's face out of her head – especially the awful part when the butt of the gun smashed into her skull. The whole thing made Gillie want to hurl. She just prayed that it looked worse than it really was.

Gillie's fears grew as Dew man continued to overpower her. Nothing she did seemed to stop him. He just kept dragging her toward a green SUV parked out front.

Awful sobs started to come until she remembered something Walter had told her. He had said smarts were more important in a fight than physical strength. Gillie's throat relaxed. She didn't have a weapon, but she did have a voice and knew how to use it. The only thing she could think of was how adults always got so hacked off when teenagers used swears.

As the gunman shoved Gillie into the backseat of the car she could hear Cody continuing to howl for help. She saw her shot and took it. She flipped over and landed a kick solidly in the middle of the man's face. He staggered backwards holding his nose. A cut opened up across the bridge between his eyes. A thin line of red trickled from his nose and his eyes watered.

"You bitch. You fucking broke my nose."

"HOLD IT, Bucko," she said. "You broke into my house, tried to kill my dog, bashed my mom's head against the wall and abducted me at gunpoint and you're pissed at *me*? Really? Are you stupid or something? You're the bad guy here – own it, asshole."

The man cuffed her in the mouth, splitting her lip. Gillie spat the blood at him.

"Oh, now what? You feel better because you beat up an unarmed girl that's half your size. Wow. You're really a badass now. Jerkoff."

"The name's Brock, not jerkoff. And if it were up to me I'd shoot you right here. Right now."

Gillie quickly got the idea that he was hired to bring her back, which meant if she were seriously injured, Dew man here wouldn't get paid. "That only proves my point, fuckface. You're nothin' but a hired douche."

"Shut your goddamn mouth." When Brock jumped in the driver's seat, his ears were burning bright red and she knew there wasn't a damn thing he could do about it.

Gillie felt better already. She eyed the bite on his arm and his torn shirt. "What you gonna do now, get a new T-shirt that says 'I beat up girls and old dogs'? Bet your pals will be really impressed with that one – *NOT*."

Brock's jaw set and the veins in his forehead pulsed. He grabbed his gun, leaned out his window, and fired three rapid shots into a tree.

"That's swell, hotshot," said Gillie. "Now you can add squirrels to the list."

Brock stomped on the gas and sped away.

Gillie felt her lip. "Great. I've been abducted twice in two days. I feel like the freaking Boardwalk card in a screwed-up game of Monopoly."

Twenty-Five

Deter's Car, 11:45 p.m.

DARKNESS SURROUNDED DETER. It seemed as if he had fallen into a well. His disoriented brain tried to make sense of the dampness.

The passenger seat felt soaking wet and some of his seat was moist. He checked his crotch – at least he hadn't embarrassed himself.

One whiff and the stench of hooch assaulted his nostrils. From what he could see, everything around him tilted at the wrong angle.

Something dug into his neck. Deter fought against the restraints compressing his chest and soon realized the stupid seatbelt had locked. He fumbled around and pushed the release button. At least now he could breathe.

His eyes viewed his surroundings through lenses fogged by thoughts that only came in fragments and bizarre ones at that. Of all the stupid times to remember the cat from his childhood.

I'm so fucked up.

Something started tickling him. His damn cellphone buzzed in his pocket. He answered it.

"What?" Deter felt his tender cheek bone.

"This is Walter Lovett."

"We have to stop meeting like this," said Deter as a chuckle surged to the surface. "Shit, my head hurts. This damn case just gets weirder by the minute."

"What's wrong with you?"

"How the hell did you get my number?"

"You really are having a tough day. I borrowed your car remember? You keep your business cards in the pocket on the sun visor."

"Oh, yeah." Deter suddenly realized why he was sitting at such an odd tilt. "Holy crap, my car."

"I need your help. Where are you?"

Deter tried to make sense of his surroundings. "By the looks of it, I'm in a ditch and I don't have a bleeping clue how I got here."

"I'll bet my last round it wasn't black ice. Can you see anything?"

"I'm about five hundred yards from a McDonald's and I can see a sign for route three. Last I remember, I was looking at a blown tire and a fist coming at my face."

"Sit tight. I'll be right there. Gillie is in trouble and I need your help."

Deter's head was spinning. This was a first. Since when did a perp call a cop to ask for help?

♦

GILLIE PEERED THROUGH THE DARK. Where in the heck was this Brock guy taking her? A sign up ahead gave it away – "Manchester Family Care Center." The names Daniel B. MacAbee, D.O. and John Edward Hollister, M.D. were listed, along with somebody who was a P.A.

Lights mounted up high on the building lit up two cars in the parking lot. Thank God none of them were her dad's. She half expected he would be there. Her old man was the last person on the planet she wanted to see right now or maybe ever.

Brock forced her through the waiting room and into the back toward some voices and he wasn't gentle about it either. His grip made a stinging band around her arm, but she wasn't going to admit it hurt – especially in front of these jerks.

That's gonna leave a bruise.

Gillie squinted at the bright fluorescent lights and pulled her arm away. "Let go of me, asswipe."

"MacAbee, this one is all yours," said Brock.

A hand was in the middle of her back shoving her toward the doctor. Gillie lunged forward with her right foot to keep from falling. Pivoting around, she shot Brock one of her looks, and then sized up the doc. He didn't seem nearly as imposing as she had pictured him.

His buzzcut, round face, and glasses that made a straight indention just above his ears reminded her of one of the geeks at her old school.

Two guys she hadn't seen before were gawking at Brock's bloodied arm, swollen nose, and torn shirt. Gillie joined in. "Mr. Hot Shit just kicked ass: he hurt an old dog, beat up a girl, and scared the crap out of a couple of squirrels. You got yourself a real tough guy here," said Gillie, dramatically rolling her eyes.

The men started to snicker. Gillie enjoyed dissing Brock until he stuck a gun in her face and reminded her that this wasn't a joke.

With Walter she'd sensed he didn't want to hurt her from the beginning, but this guy was different. Even so, she wasn't about to look weak and play the victim bit. They were going to shoot her or not – either way, she wasn't gonna give them the satisfaction of being all weepy and scared.

"What, genius? You're gonna shoot an unarmed kid?" said Gillie holding up her hands. "Get over yourself."

"Brock! Put it down," said MacAbee. "You know the rules. We deliver her unharmed."

"Oh, right. Whatever you do, don't piss off the high and mighty Dr. Curtis."

Gillie wished it had been her dad standing there all torn up. He'd deserve it.

Brock lowered his gun, but didn't take his dark eyes off her.

She crossed her arms. "Don't give me the hairy eyeball, asshole. You're the moron that started this."

"Enough. Put her in exam room five," said MacAbee, waving his arms in the air like he was some big-time band director.

Brock forcefully escorted her into a small room that smelled like rubbing alcohol and Pine-Sol. It was a typical doctor's exam room with a small sink, a counter, and an exam table in the middle of the floor. She caught sight of the foot stirrups and grimaced. With both arms pushed out in front of her, she made a cross using her index fingers.

Above the exam table a poster of a tropical island was stapled to the ceiling. A few feet away was some kind of fancy smoke-detection system.

Outside the door MacAbee sounded like a cruise director ordering Brock and the others around.

Gillie opened up the cabinets. They were loaded with more than enough supplies to wreak havoc on her captors and piss off Brock one more time. She thought about all those MythBusters programs and the cool stuff she could remember from Mrs. Nobel's Chemistry class. Most of her lectures had been boring, but today having stayed awake for at least some of them was going to pay off.

First Gillie checked the window to make sure it was big enough for her to fit through. It was – just barely – but it wasn't the kind that could be opened. Gillie stared at a small crack in the corner of the window and bit her bottom lip.

I know what would work.

She put the fire extinguisher from under the sink on a chair near the window along with a thick pile of patient gowns. Then she squirted the liquid hand soap over the floor by the door.

In the first cabinet was a stack of pink kidney-bean-shaped bowls like the ones she'd used last fall when she had gotten food poisoning. She put one of them on the exam table and filled it with alcohol and a wad of paper towels. No matches were to be found, but a big round exam light with a magnification lens on an arm hung from the ceiling.

Oh, jeez, this is great. Gillie flipped on the switch. A bright white circle lit up the exam table like a searchlight from a UFO. Gillie adjusted the lamp and positioned the magnifying lens, focusing the beam into a searing pinpoint in the middle of the dish of rubbing alcohol. "Oh, no! Captain, we're being invaded."

Next she was about to break one of the biggest rules she could remember from Chem class: never – *EVER* – mix ammonia and cleanser. She put another bowl on the counter just inside the door and filled it with ammonia. Next to it she put the can of Comet Cleanser.

Over at the exam table, a thin ribbon of smoke was already heading for the ceiling. Any minute the smoke detector was gonna start wailing like Susan Nelson's spoiled little brother.

Gillie gulped in a deep breath. *Time to roll.*

Covering her mouth and nose with a thick wad of paper towels, she shook the Comet powder into the basin of ammonia and stirred it with a tongue depressor. "Let's see how you guys like chlorine gas."

"Holy crap." Gillie jumped back, stunned by how fast the smoke and fumes filled the room. The smoke detector let out an ear-piercing shriek. Holding her breath, she smashed the window with the fire extinguisher and padded the jagged opening with the gowns before shimmying outside.

Voices shouted. The exam room door flew open. Gillie glanced back inside just in time to see a man slipping on the hand soap and going down hard. Her legs charged through the dark parking lot toward the woods with all her might. Halfway there she smirked at the sound of the cussing and coughing behind her.

She was almost to the woods when a man, running flat out, tackled her from the side. The weight of his body surprised her as they skidded over the blacktop. The pavement dug right through her jacket's sleeve and into her elbow. With the air knocked out of her lungs, she was stunned by the pain in her chest. She couldn't talk, much less run. Finally big arms pulled her to her feet and hauled her back toward the building. Gasping for air and trying to ignore the stabbing pain in her elbow, she fought back. "Let go of me, jerk."

The man just kept shoving her forward. "Shut up," he said.

Inside the brightly lit office, a red-faced Dr. MacAbee was on the phone. "Sorry. It's a false alarm, the cleaning crew had a rookie who set off the system by accident."

Gillie hated how his voice sounded so sympathetic while his buggy little eyes told a very different story.

Again he reminded her of that kid at school, George Ashton. Geeks were cool unless they were like George. He pretended to be all sweet and innocent on the outside, but he was always scheming behind people's backs, taking credit for others' work, and trying to be all that. No one trusted George. MacAbee seemed just like him, only old. He had to be at least thirty.

"Where do you want her?" said the jerk holding her. Every time she moved he'd yank the arm behind her back up until her shoulder screamed for mercy. Gillie locked her jaws and refused to make a sound.

MacAbee pointed to his office and dismissed them with a wave of his hand. Gillie was frogmarched into a modest office nowhere near as fancy as her dad's. "Early Target. Impressive," she said. If only Walter were here. He would kick this guy's butt.

"Brock. Where is her phone?" asked MacAbee.

Gillie almost laughed out loud when Brock pulled her old phone out of his pocket and tossed it to MacAbee. *Dumbshits.*

The doctor turned to look at her over the top of his glasses. "Miss Curtis, you will sit quietly in my office and not touch anything. If I have any more trouble with you, I will let Brock here go back to your house and do whatever he wants with your mother and dog. Do I make myself clear?"

Twenty-Six

Crown Victoria, 12:00 midnight

WALTER KNEW there was no point in going to Gillie's house – Kip's phone gizmo showed she was already gone anyway. It didn't surprise him. He knew whoever took her wasn't going to spend much time at the house, it wasn't an easy position to control. Nope. These men needed somewhere secure. Somewhere beyond neighbors with prying eyes and fingers all too willing to call the cops.

The question was where? One thing was for certain – Walter could be walking into a trap and he needed more backup than a teenage boy. Walter scanned the side of the road looking impatiently for Determan. He had already wasted too much time trying to hone in on his location.

Kip pointed to a spot just ahead. "Look up there."

Walter saw a flash of light where he was pointing. Finally. Off the road on the right, flashing tail lights protruded from a ditch. He parked and double-timed it over to get a firsthand look at this mess. Kip was right on his heels. The grass was flattened, but not torn up. Obviously, the brakes hadn't been applied when it rolled over the edge. If they had, there would have been skid marks. Most likely it had been pushed.

The detective was sitting at the bottom in the driver's seat – alive, but disheveled. The door was wide open and he looked lost.

Walter called down to Determan. "You okay?"

"I'm just bitchen. I dumped my car in a ditch just so I could sit here and watch the goddamn stars come out. Whaddaya think?"

Kip chuckled.

"You stay here." Walter hustled down to the bottom of the gully and reached into the cab to turn off the ignition. The car was in neutral. Someone had rolled it into the ditch, all right.

It also stunk – not from the overturned cup of coffee, but from a nearly empty bottle of Jim Beam on the floor.

"You been tying one on?"

"Are you out of your fucking mind? Thanks to you, I don't have time to get in trouble. Besides, I hate whiskey."

The detective's breath smelled of coffee, not booze, but the passenger seat was soaked in it. It didn't take long for Walter to figure out what had happened. They put the car in neutral, tossed in the open bottle of whiskey, and pushed the car over the edge. It wasn't a real crash. The damage was minimal and the air bags hadn't even deployed.

Determan had to have been in the drivers seat, so why hadn't he slammed on the brakes or fought back? Hell, his weapon was still right there in his shoulder harness.

Walter looked around. Something else was missing. "Detective. Where in the hell are your shoes?"

Determan stared at his feet. "Damn. That's the second time today. I can't keep a pair of shoes on my feet to save my ass."

Walter knelt down and grabbed his bare foot.

"Hey. What the hell are you doing?"

"Button it and hand me the damn flashlight, will ya?"

Determan tossed Walter the flashlight. He focused the beam on a space between the detective's toes and pointed out the needle mark. "Pal, you've been drugged. You know anyone who would do this?"

"Hello? I'm a detective. I arrest people for a living."

Walter glared at him and crossed his arms.

Determan threw a hand in the air. "There are lots of people who'd love to see me six feet under, but most of them are behind bars enjoying three hots and a cot for the next twenty to life." The detective toyed with his mustache. "There's only one guy that I can think of who has an itch to get me out of his way. He's been doing his damnedest to derail this investigation from the very beginning."

"Curtis, right?" Walter said.

Determan nodded and then stopped and held his head as if the movement hurt.

"How do you feel?"

"Like a rodeo clown after a bad day at work."

Walter quickly assessed Determan's condition. He felt sorry for the guy. The man was up to his neck in something he didn't understand and Walter didn't have time to explain it all now.

It seemed that Curtis knew no bounds.

Going after a cop like this? What was he thinking? That was the kind of thing drug cartels did, not white collars. Not in America.

It made Walter pissed as hell that he and so many of his buddies had sacrificed so much to have some idiot back home allowed to operate like this. There were moments when Walter wished he and Benny could go in and do a little clean-up work – not maim anyone – just get them behind bars where they belonged. They'd be quick about it too. No one could clear a building like he and Benny could.

Walter was about to help the detective up when he caught a glimpse of something in the backseat. "Looks like you've been more than drugged. My guess is that powder and those pills aren't supposed to be in a cop's car."

Determan's head whirled around. "What the hell?" A pained look overtook his face. "I'm in deep shit."

As the wide-eyed detective stared up at Walter sirens began to wail in the distance.

◆

WHAT WAS IT ABOUT SIRENS that always got Deter's adrenaline going? Tonight it cleared his head enough to give the backseat a more critical look.

Small bags of a white powder and pills littered the seat and floor behind him. The packets likely contained meth and Oxycodone, the current drugs du jour.

"Let me guess. Those have your fingerprints all over them," said Walter Lovett.

"Probably."

"Sounds like the shit is about to hit the windshield."

"Roger that."

Lovett just stood there looking at him. "Well? You gonna sit on your ass or do something about it?"

Deter looked up at Lovett in disbelief. "What the hell do you expect me to do? The captain is going to fry my ass for wrecking another car."

"I need your help. I'm sorry about your car and your boss, but I don't have time for this crap," Lovett said.

"I can't just walk away."

"You have to. If you don't it will be too late for Gillie."

Lovett pulled him from the car with one hand. Damn that man was strong. Next he lurched into the backseat and scooped up the packets. "I'll be right back."

Deter watched as Lovett charged up the embankment toward the woods. After examining a few trees he deposited the stash into a deep natural hollow and topped it off with a handful of rocks, and pine needles.

He returned just moments later. "You can deal with that mess later. Let's go."

Working his way out of the ditch, Deter realized that the pounding in his head was in sync with the sirens that were noticeably louder. *Good God.* He moved a little faster.

They were heading up to what looked like the same beat-up Crown Victoria he'd seen on the station's video feed. And standing next to it was a tall slender silhouette. As he got closer, he could see the boy and the car more clearly. The Crown Vic was old, but Deter would bet it still had balls. He'd driven one back in the day when he was a city cop. It was one his personal favorites for keeping up with gangbangers and their juiced up rides.

The slope was steep and slippery. Deter tried his darnedest to keep his balance in the dark. In front of him Lovett charged to the top like a bull. Deter wasn't about to be outdone by an old fart, even if they guy did have skills and shoes.

He wanted to complain when cold mud – or at least what he hoped was mud – squished through his toes, but he didn't. That's just bitchen. Rocks and twigs and God knows what were poking at his tender feet as he tiptoed a crooked path up to the car. On the last stretch, the boy offered a helping hand.

At least Deter made it over the ridge and into the car without looking like a total fool. His throbbing feet weren't the only thing having a rough night. Thanks to the drug's aftereffects, his brain was processing about as fast as the old computer he'd taken to the dump last week. The kid sat in the front seat and glanced over his shoulder. Deter figured him to be Gillie's friend. "Thanks for the hand. Jordan, right?"

"My name is Kip and you're welcome."

"You can call me Deter, everyone else does."

Lovett smiled at the kid, turned on his lights, and pulled out into traffic. After making a U-turn he traveled on as naturally as if he'd done this every night of his life. Three cruisers and a fire engine roared past them going the other direction and Lovett didn't even blink.

Deter wondered what concoction they'd given him. He'd always been a clean cop and wasn't used to this feeling. Even though this wasn't his fault, he was damn sure he wouldn't pass a drug screening and that bothered him. At least they hadn't given him a larger dose. That could have been a disaster. Then it registered. They could have killed him. This wasn't a hit. It was a message to back off.

He also thought about the dope in that tree and how he was going to retrieve it and enter it into evidence without having to explain too much. Then he realized Lovett was watching him in the rearview mirror.

"Don't worry, I'm not about to leave that crap there. I'll make sure it gets taken care of."

Lovett nodded.

Jesus, it was like the man could read his thoughts.

"I've got to call Carl and tell him what happened. The captain is going to kick my ass from here to Texas."

Lovett looked up at him through the mirror. "You know Curtis is behind more than setting you up. He's what this whole mess is about."

"I figured. His guys have been on you like a pair of tights. My guess is that they put a tracker in your van way back at your house."

Walter Lovett shrugged and continued to look worried. "I understand why they would be after me, but why you?"

"I should have seen it coming. Curtis had to know I was getting close. All he had to do was flip on the news to see that. Reporters and cameras were all over the Rite Aid scene."

"But why the setup and the drugs?"

"My guess is that he wanted me thrown off the case. Curtis must have been desperate to get to you and Gillie before I did."

Lovett's face had that intensity that first tipped him off that this guy was no idiot. "But no one would believe you'd taken drugs and crashed your car, would they?"

Deter rubbed his neck. "They'd believe it all right. Nine years ago my son was kidnapped and I didn't deal with it very graciously."

Lovett eyed him closely in the rearview.

"I was like most parents. Desperate. My wife blamed me. After all, I was the detective. I was the one who was supposed to be able to find him. We were divorced the next year. I was angry. I got a little too loud. Pushed a little too hard. I never was a bad cop, I just wasn't a very nice one. I lost a lot of friends. Eventually I was accused of police brutality and allegedly planting drugs on this gangbanger. The guy was a real prick going for his fifteen minutes. The press tried me on the front pages without benefit of a judge, a jury, or the law. I was on admin leave. After the investigation all charges were dropped, but some of my colleagues never trusted me again. I never got my boy back either or the asshole who took him."

"How old was your son?"

"Five."

"I'm sorry. That shouldn't have happened," said Lovett. "So they set you up thinking it would look like you went over the deep end again because you were on another kidnapping case?"

"Something like that."

"Well, I guess that makes us a team. You're now on Curtis's shit list along with the rest of us," said Lovett.

"Gillie's mother warned me about him. The only problem is, I think he's a lot worse than anything she ever imagined."

Twenty-Seven

Crown Victoria, 12:30 a.m.

WALTER CHECKED HIS WATCH. It was after midnight or "O-dark thirty" as his buddies used to call it. They were driving through an area of Manchester that started to look familiar, even in the dim light of the occasional street lamp. The screen on Kip's phone was lit up like a candle in front of his nose. A small blue dot on the GPS was moving over a tiny map in sync with their car. "How in the hell are you doing that?"

Deter opened his mouth first, but Kip beat him to the punch. "Gillie and I both have this app. I can see where her phone is and she can see mine."

Kip was like a lot of people Walter had observed of late. They always had their heads down and were constantly absorbed by their phones. Even in restaurants, some people would play with their phones rather than talk to each other. He didn't get it. In Walter's opinion it was a stupid distraction. The damn thing was a phone, not a dance partner.

The boy still had his nose up to the tiny screen. He seemed pretty pleased with himself until Walter reminded him of his screwup. "I'm still pissed at you for letting her go."

"I'm sorry. It was just supposed to be to her mom's house and right back. Besides, have you ever tried to tell that girl 'no'?"

Walter chuckled. "I've gotta give that one to ya, son."

Kip shot him a grin and continued to give directions.

Walter's head swiveled to the left at the intersection. "What the hell? I know this place. We're close to MacAbee's office. My wife used to go there."

"MacAbee's in on this," said Deter. "I'll bet that's where they took Gillie."

"Then I guess we better go take a looksee. Kip, put that damn thing away. I know where I am." Walter had to work to keep his imagination from playing the thousand ways to kill, maim, and torture an asshole game. He hated MacAbee almost as much as Curtis. Helen should have been seeing an oncologist, not a bumbling family doc, but MacAbee wouldn't give them a referral and the specialist wouldn't see them without one.

Just past the Dunkin Donuts, Walter pulled into a strip mall. Each shop was closed and dark. A wooded lot separated them from the doctor's office. The three scooted from the car and into the cover of the tall evergreens and oaks. Deter's light tan coat was like a warning flag waving in the darkness. "Detective, move slowly and stay down or your coat is going to give us up."

At least Kip had on dark clothes.

Deter slowly sank back into the shadows while Walter crept in for a closer look. On his belly and covered by branches, he pulled out his binoculars and searched the area around the office. At night the interior lights shining through the windows made it ridiculously easy to see anyone inside.

As soon as he got back to the detective, Kip was chattering away and eager to help. "Gillie has to be in there. We could grab her and run. Maybe we should disable their cars first, but how? That thing about putting sugar or salt in the gas tank doesn't work. I tried it myself on junkers but it didn't do anything."

Walter didn't have time for chitchat. "You should have put it in the engine oil."

He wasn't sure which was more amusing – the bunched-up frown on Deter's face as he thought through the implications or how the kid was so easy to impress.

Walter led the detective and the boy to the edge of the woods. Their target was a New England-style house with blue siding and white shutters that had been turned into a medical office. It looked like a big old blueberry muffin plopped in the middle of a parking lot.

Steps and a handicap ramp were in the front, along with a black BMW that glistened in the headlights of passing cars. Walter had made too many trips up and down those steps. The last time he'd had to hold onto the rails with both hands when his knees nearly buckled. Seeing the place again brought back a sickening knot in his belly. Walter closed his eyes for a few seconds. He pulled down an exterior calm like a ski mask and forced himself to refocus.

In addition to the BMW, two SUVs were parked close to the building but facing the street. By his count there were at least three people inside – plus Gillie, if he was lucky. At first everything looked well cared for and orderly. There was the smell of new cedar mulch and the glow of new iridescent parking stripes. Then he caught sight of a window on the side of the building that looked as if it had just been busted out. That was out of place. Walter reminded himself of the old adage that "Anything that looks off, usually is."

"Kip, you stay with Deter. I'm going to move in and check this out."

Creeping in closer to the building, Walter made sure to stay out of sight. He looked back at the woods just in time to see the detective push Kip's head back into the shadows.

Walter snugged up to the side of the building. Damn. It sure looked like they'd had some action. It was obvious that the window had been blown out from the inside. Cloth patient gowns layered the bottom and sides of the window. Several had fallen out onto the asphalt. It had all the markings of an escape, except that Gil would have called if she'd gotten away.

He cautiously peeked through the broken window. A thin ribbon of yellow-green fumes seeped through the opening and hung in a thin layer at the ceiling. His nose told him it was chlorine gas. Deadly stuff. That got his attention.

He grabbed another glance inside, looking for the source of the fumes. He caught sight of the can of cleanser and bowl by the door. The corners of his mouth quirked into a subtle grin.

Walter covered his face with his handkerchief. Every few seconds he'd wipe his burning eyes. He heard the voices of several men talking, one of whom he recognized. Dr. MacAbee was barking orders and complaining loudly.

"Just look at my exam room. I can't believe she did this. How the hell am I going to explain all this to my staff tomorrow morning?" MacAbee sounded as if he was about to tear someone's head off.

Walter's smile grew bigger. There was only one person who could get a man that pissed. Gillie had to be here.

He scooted around the back where he knew MacAbee's office had a window. There he peered through the vertical blinds. Walter steadied himself by pressing his palms over the cold pane of glass and let his eyes adjust. Someone was sitting at the doctor's desk. It was Gillie.

He hotfooted it back to the woods and told Deter and Kip about the destroyed exam room and how MacAbee's voice was breaking he was so mad.

"That crazy girl," said Kip. "We gotta get her outta there before she gets hurt."

Deter shifted to stand on a pile of softer leaves. "He's right. Maybe there is a back door we can bust through."

Walter took stock of his two comrades. He had a kid as green as fresh mowed grass and a barefoot cop with a drug hangover. Swell.

"I have a better idea. Let's get them outside in the open. Deter, you provide cover and do your cop thing when they come out. Kip and I are going to go raise some hell."

The detective ducked back behind a snarl of wild berry vines.

Kip stayed behind Walter as they worked their way over to the front of the building and hunkered down in the dark behind the BMW he assumed was MacAbee's.

The kid was all wide-eyed and breathing fast. "What are you gonna do?"

Walter leaned over so Kip could hear him. "I'm going to create a diversion to get them outside."

"We should disable their cars."

"How?"

"We could pull the distributor wire."

Walter shook his head *no*.

"Or we could pop off the valve stems on the tires."

Walter stood up and glanced at the two SUVs and then back at the BMW. "This one has a car alarm. I've got a better idea. Help me lift this thing."

Walter scuffled over to a heavy clay pot filled with wet sand and cigarette butts. They grunted and lifted it high in the air and then hurled it into the windshield with all their strength. The car's alarm immediately started to squeal as the grit and spent butts littered the shiny hood.

Kip held his ears and ran for cover while Walter brushed off his hands before joining him.

The kid flipped his hair out of his way. "Why did you do that?"

"It was faster than breaking into the car to pop the hood to get at the distributor wire. And easier than yanking off valve stems. Noisier too."

"But they could still come after us. We should've disabled them."

"I still can – anytime I want. I have a special device for that."

Walter pulled out his Colt and smiled.

Kip just rolled his eyes.

As they hustled around the corner to the back of the building, Walter heard the clambering and shouting behind them. At MacAbee's office window, Walter tapped on the glass. Gillie jumped out of the chair. The instant she recognized them, that goofy grin lit up her face. She ran over and put one hand on the glass where Kip was pressed against the window and the other where Walter was standing. He pointed to the crank and hoped she would get the idea.

Thankfully, she understood. As soon as the window was open wide enough, Walter cut open the screen and helped pull her out. Just as she cleared the frame, the door to the office burst open. Walter ducked to the side, pulling both of the kids safely to the other side of him.

Gillie grabbed his arm. "That's Brock, he's a real ass – "

PHOOW – the windows next to them exploded. Razor-sharp shards *CHINKLED* to the pavement. Walter pushed the kids further back and slid up closer to the opening.

MacAbee's voice echoed in the hallway. "Are you out of your fucking mind? I have to open for business tomorrow. Get out. All of you – out, out, out!" His voice faded back toward the front of the building. The doctor was muttering something about "never again."

Walter patiently waited for the guy who'd fired the shots.

Sure enough, the man Gillie called Brock stuck the barrel of his Beretta out of the window. This fool wasn't trained for urban maneuvers. Slowly his head emerged – nose first.

Without hesitation Walter did a big ol' roundhouse on Brock's face. Blood sprayed the twisted window frame. Walter wiped off his hand and rubbed his knuckles while taking a quick look to make sure the guy was down. Brock had been knocked out cold.

That's gonna hurt tomorrow.

Walter raced for the woods, keeping himself between the kids and the office. Someone in the front parking lot was shouting and pointing at them. One man lifted a rifle, but before he got a shot off a crisp *POP-POP* zipped out of the bush where he'd last seen Deter. The man's limp body fell to the pavement.

Walter just made it to the edge of the pines with the kids when more rounds rocketed past them.

The shots were coming from where Walter heard footsteps of another guy running for the woods. They were safe but the bullets chewed the hell out of a tree trunk. Deter yelled at them to get down.

THUMP-THUMP-CRACK. More slugs zinged over their heads and Deter fired back.

Gillie and Kip huddled together. Walter listened to the volley of bullets which had stopped suddenly. "Someone will have heard the shots and reported it. We gotta get out of here."

Kip bolted ahead into the dark brush toward the car.

Gillie lurched ahead to follow until Walter grabbed her arm. "You're staying with me. I'm not losing you again." She smiled that grin and held his arm as they moved forward.

The man from the parking lot stepped out from behind a huge tree. "Hold it right there."

He had Kip by the neck with his Ruger 9mm pistol pointed at the kid's temple.

Deter reacted. In a flash his Glock 22 was leveled at the gunman. "You don't want to do this. You don't need him. It's not worth it."

"Turn over the girl or I'll make a squirrel feeder out of his head."

Kip's chest started to heave as he turned red and started breathing from his mouth.

"Okay. I hear you," said Deter.

"Shut your trap and hand over the girl."

Mother of God. He was trying to talk the guy down.

Deter continued in a calm voice. "Listen, these are just kids. How about – "

In a snap Walter drew his Colt and took off the man's ear. Half of his head went with it.

"I can't hear." Kip held his ears and whimpered as he curled up on the ground. Blood covered the side of his head.

Gillie got to him first. Down on her knees, she tried to talk to him. Off to the right, Deter gingerly picked his way through the underbrush barefoot. Walter handed Gillie a flashlight and clasped the boy's head between his hands. Thank God, the blood was just splatter. Then he checked his eyes. Walter took a deep breath and sat back. The poor kid was shaking like a new recruit. He had every right to be scared.

"How many fingers am I holding up?"

"Two."

"What's your name?"

"Dumbshit."

Walter laughed and hugged him. "The ringing will stop. You did good." He hoisted the kid up and slapped him on the back.

"That was a gutsy shot," Deter said. "And damn nice aim too."

On the way back to the car Walter gave the detective a ration. "I wasn't going to sit around and chew the fat with the guy. Besides anyone who would point a loaded gun at a kid is too stupid to live."

Gillie shot him one of her looks as she got into the car.

"I said *loaded*."

Twenty-Eight

Crown Victoria, 1:30 a.m.

Deter sat in the backseat next to Kip, trying to keep a spring in the lumpy seat from skewering his ass when his own words – *these are just kids* – came back to haunt him. They were so young. They had never witnessed the horrors he knew Lovett had seen over in Nam nor even what he'd experienced on the force.

He couldn't help thinking about his son as he watched Gillie staring out the windshield in silence.

"Gil, are you all right?" Lovett's voice took on a gentleness that surprised Deter.

"You killed that man," she said, pulling on a lock of her hair. More than her voice was trembling.

Lovett's head pivoted between watching the road and looking at her. He reached over and held her hand.

"Sweetie, I had to. I didn't have a choice." Lovett's tone was not that of a proud marksman who'd just reduced another target, rather it carried genuine sadness. It was the sound of someone who had learned the value of life.

"I know," she said.

After a few more miles in silence, Lovett asked what had happened at the house.

Gillie told him about Brock. "This whackjob in a Mountain Dew T-shirt just busted into the kitchen and every thing went nuts. Cody was barking his head off trying to protect us and that jerk kicked him."

"Us?" asked Lovett.

"Yeah. My mom showed up and tried to protect me. The guy went nuclear. After he kicked Cody, he hit my mom so hard she passed out. We hafta go make sure she's okay. Please. Besides, MacAbee said if I gave him anymore trouble he was gonna let Brock do anything he wants to them."

Deter was relieved when Lovett said, "Call her, now." He turned the car around as Gillie directed him toward her neighborhood. She pulled out her phone and dialed her mother, but the call went directly to voice mail.

Lovett kept moving at a good clip, but in Deter's opinion light speed wouldn't have been fast enough. Each second seemed like hours.

While Lovett asked her why she'd gone home in the first place, Deter kept an eye on Kip who hadn't said a word. The kid began rubbing his ear, but stopped. He seemed grossed out by the blood. After wiping his hands on his jeans, he just vacantly stared out the window. It looked like his mind was on a different planet. It was time to pull him back. "Where'd you get this car?"

Kip's eyes slowly turned back toward Deter. "What?"

"Where'd you get the ride?"

"Oh. I fixed it up myself from leftovers at my uncle's junkyard and he let me keep it. He's cool like that."

"So you're good with cars?"

"I do all right," said Kip. His expression relaxed some.

"Sounds to me like you did a great job, I should have you work on my car."

Kip smiled.

There was nothing like talking about wheels to brighten the spirits of a teenage boy.

Deter looked up at the strip of cloth hanging from the overhead. Lovett took a tight turn. Deter's weight shifted and the spring bit him hard. Obviously the upholstery wasn't part of the fix-up plan.

He took off his coat, folded it up, and sat on it for relief.

The boy's eyes were locked on Deter's shoulder holster when he felt his butt buzzing. His phone was vibrating. His hands fumbled with his coat pocket and the spring took another nip out of his buttocks before he was able to answer. The call was from Lyn, but he was too late. Not only that, it wasn't the first one he'd missed from her that evening.

She'd called him while he was stuck in the ditch. Damn it.

He quickly called her back. "Lyn, this is Deter. How are you?"

Gillie twisted around, her eyes were riveted on him. "I'm sorry I missed your –"

Lyn interrupted. "Gillie was here. Oh, God. They took her."

By now Gillie was begging to talk with her mother. Deter held up his finger to hold her off for one more second.

"Who was there?"

"I don't know. A big guy in a Mountain Dew T-shirt. Oh!" Lyn's voice went silent. Something crashed to the floor in the background. A dog barked.

"Lyn?"

"Mom!"

The knuckles on Gillie's hand blanched waxy white. It looked like her fingers where about to tear a chunk out of the worn maroon seat back. Kip put one hand on her shoulder and stared at Deter.

Lyn was back on the phone. "Did I hear Gillie. Where is she?"

Deter took a deep breath. "Are you sure you're okay?"

"I tripped. I'm a bit dizzy, but all right. Do you know where Gillie is?"

"Listen to me. Lock the doors and stay where you are. We'll be right there. And there's someone here who wants to talk with you." He handed the phone over to Gillie.

◆

THE MOMENT THEY STOPPED behind the truck in Lyn's driveway, Gillie jumped out and bolted toward the house. Even before Deter could extricate himself from the man-eating backseat, mother and daughter were hugging, crying, and filling the air with shrieks of pure elation.

Gillie gently pulled her mother's hair back to look at the marks on her face. As they hugged again Cody jumped up to get into the middle of it all. Their laughter was so contagious Deter couldn't help feeling an enormous sense of relief. As they went inside Kip eagerly jogged toward the kitchen to join them.

Deter was about to follow when he realized that Lovett was still in the car, staring at the dashboard, and looking like a displaced person.

"Come on. You might as well get this over with."

Lovett shook his head. "I shouldn't be here."

"Are you nuts? If it weren't for you, that reunion would never have taken place."

After raking his fingers through his hair, Lovett slowly emerged from the car looking like a man who thought this was a really bad idea. Deter nodded toward the house. Lovett reluctantly followed him into the kitchen.

Inside, Gillie's mother was about to give Kip a hug until she saw the blood on his face. "My God. What happened to you?"

"It's been a tough night, but he's okay," said Deter. "He's a brave kid. I'm proud of him."

She handed Kip some paper towels and pointed to the sink before returning to kiss her daughter on the forehead. Something about the way Gillie and Lyn grinned from ear to ear and chattered away left Deter captivated. There were no words for seeing a mother and her daughter reunited. These were the moments that made sense of his life.

Lyn's bright eyes overshadowed the horrible swelling and bruises that were spreading over her face. Even the late hour didn't dampen her welcome. It was the first time Deter had seen her look truly happy. He couldn't help wondering what she'd do when she realized who the man was that had walked into the kitchen right behind him.

Lyn turned toward Deter with that smile that took his breath away. "Deter, how can I thank you? You said you'd get her back and you did."

"As much as I'd like to take the credit, I can't." Deter stepped aside so she could see Lovett, who stood there awkwardly straightening his shirt and looking at the floor.

"Mom, this is Walter. He's the one who saved me," said Gillie.

Lyn looked puzzled.

"Well, that was after he kidnapped me."

The room went silent. All color drained from Lyn's face as she reached for the support of a chair back. Deter caught her arm and said, "There's something you need to know –"

Lovett put up his hand. "Ma'am, Gillie's right." Lovett raised his head and looked directly at Lyn. "I owe you a huge apology. I don't expect you to forgive me." Lovett's face softened when Cody came to him, tail wagging, and sat on his foot.

"I don't understand." Lyn's fair skin flushed, but she continued to hear him out. "Why on Earth did you do this?"

"My wife died because of your husband." Lovett put a hand over his mouth as if saying the words out loud had burnt his tongue. Then he dropped his hand and said, "What Curtis did to us was unthinkable. I know this was foolish – a stupid mistake on my part

– but I just wanted him to feel the same loss I had for at least a few hours. Helen was sweet and gentle, like you." Lovett's eyes turned red as he cleared his throat. "Gillie talks about you."

Lyn nodded, but didn't take her eyes off him.

"I promise you, I would have given up my own life before I would have allowed anyone to harm her."

Something in Lyn's expression shifted.

Gillie grabbed her arm. "Walter even made me blueberry pancakes and you should taste his grilled cheese sandwiches. They're like amazing."

Lyn stared at Gillie.

"Mom. He's my friend and I'd trust him with my life."

"Me too," said Deter, enjoying the look of surprise that passed over Lovett's face. "He's saved my sorry hide more than once. Unfortunately, we all now understand your warning about Dr. Curtis. He sent hired guns after us. If it weren't for Lovett, none of us would be standing here now."

Lovett shrugged. "It doesn't matter. I should never have taken her. I am sorry. I never intended to cause you pain." He held out one shaking hand. Lyn grabbed it with both of hers.

"You're right – " She pointed a finger at him. " – you shouldn't have, but Michael had already taken her away." Lyn's voice soften. "You are the one that brought her home. For that I will always be grateful."

Lovett relaxed his grip on her hands. "Gillie is a great kid. I can see where she gets it." He patted Lyn's hand.

She smiled until she saw Deter's bare feet. "Aren't you freezing?"

"It's been a long night," said Deter. In truth the warmth of her kitchen was helping defrost his cold toes.

"Come on. Sit down," said Lyn.

With Gillie's help Lyn offered them all a hot cup of coffee, some fresh bread from a bakery called When Pigs Fly and soup she heated up in the microwave. The rich smells made Deter's stomach grumble. He couldn't even remember the last time he'd eaten something that didn't come from a drive-thru window.

With sore spots on his keister, he sat down carefully at the kitchen table. After what he'd been through, this simple meal seemed like a king's feast. While stuffing his face and slathering butter on a warm, thick, chewy slice of Oat and Honey bread, Deter told Lyn all about what had happened at MacAbee's.

Kip had cleaned himself up and seemed to be feeling better as he watched Gillie telling how she'd caused mayhem in the exam room. Lovett laughed out loud and patted Gillie's hand. "Nice job. Quick thinking."

Lyn listened contentedly with a bag of frozen peas sandwiched between her head and one hand.

"That bruise must smart." Deter said.

She shrugged.

Lovett leaned over. "Mind if I take a look?"

Deter toyed with his mustache and watched in amazement at the gentleness of Lovett's touch. He felt her skull, examined the bones around her eye, and the angry swelling on the side of her face. Her eyes followed his finger back and forth and she squeezed his hands.

"That had to hurt." Lovett's voice was as soft as his touch. "Ice it for the next twenty-four hours. Take ibuprofen for the pain and call the doc if you notice any changes at all."

Kip returned from the bathroom and plopped a box of Band-Aids in the center of the table. Observant kid. A nick on the side of Deter's foot had left dots of red on the floor. The Band-Aids were passed around like salt and pepper. Deter took a few and tossed the box to Lovett who pulled up his shirt sleeve and put a couple of them on a wound that looked like a bullet graze.

What really caught Deter's attention was when Gillie started showing Lovett all her cuts and bruises. He dutifully checked each one, cleaned up her elbow, and replaced a small Bandage on her finger. It was sweet the way they talked – his gentleness and her warmth said it all. If Deter hadn't known better, he'd swear this was a girl spending time with a beloved grandfather.

It struck him that this man that he'd been tracking as a perp had exhibited nothing but concern for the wellbeing of others – well, except for the guys shooting at them. It was obvious that he cared about each person sitting at that table.

Deter wasn't concerned about the dead men, that had been self-defense. It was the outstanding warrant for kidnapping that worried him. He hoped like hell that he wouldn't find himself in a position where he'd have no choice but to arrest this good man. That would make him sick.

While Deter wondered how in the hell he was going to explain all this to the captain, he listened to the sounds of everyone talking and laughing even though they were all so tired and beat up. If you didn't listen to the content of their conversation, this could have been a normal gathering of friends – but, of course, it wasn't.

Deter took an accounting – the flesh wound on Lovett's arm, the gunman that had scared the shit outta Kip and left him splattered in blood, Gillie's collection of cuts and bruises after being abducted twice, and then there was the side of Lyn's lovely face, all puffy and purple. Even the dog had a slight limp.

This was just a taste of what would come if Curtis had his way. The truth sat before him – stark, brutal, and inescapable. Each one of them was smack in the middle of something that could get them all killed.

He and Lovett knew just how much danger lay ahead. Deter wrestled with his conscience and his desire to stay employed and avoid being arrested. He'd lived every day on these streets trying to keep the innocent out of harm's way. Now a teenage girl was at the heart of one of the most twisted-up, confounding cases he'd ever been assigned. To take down Curtis, they needed irrefutable proof. Unfortunately, it was all too clear that Gillie was the only one who could get at the documentation that would do just that.

Shit. Sometimes Deter hated his job.

He wanted to call captain Morrison and put an end to this, but if he did Curtis was untouchable. Lovett would end up in jail. And Gillie would be sent back to her father. Even worse, when Curtis finished with Gillie, he would hunt each one of them down until no one was left to tell the real story.

"Folks." Deter clanked his spoon on his coffee mug. "We need to have a serious discussion." He looked over at Lovett, who was nodding. "I think we need to take a look at our situation and Lovett should be the one to spell it out."

"Hold it. Don't you think it's high time you call me Walter?"

Deter snorted. "*Walter*, please brief us on our options."

Walter folded his big hands on the table before him. "It's pretty obvious to all of us that we are loose ends that Curtis can't afford to leave hanging. We know too much about what he is up to and he apparently will spare nothing to shut us up – permanently if necessary. His hired assassins aren't going to leave us alone. And it's only going to get worse, unless we stop him."

Walter's warm expression had turned steely cold. His set jaw made it clear he was all business.

"Obviously, Michael is after me too," said Lyn. She held Gillie's hand and started to tell her about the restraining order.

"I know, Mom, you're not even suppose to see me. Forget about it. No way is he gonna keep us apart. And I know about those bogus charges too."

Deter stared at the ceiling fan wondering what Morrison would think of him not enforcing that court order. *This is gonna be ugly.*

Lyn cupped her hands around her coffee mug. "The library left a message on my phone. I lost my job – I'm suspended, pending the outcome of the charges. They shouldn't have found out so fast, but knowing Michael, it doesn't surprise me. He must have called them. The worst part is that I can't talk to them to explain my side until this is over."

Walter rolled up his sleeves. "He is a lot worse than you know."

"Mom, he is preventing people from getting the care they need and letting them die just so he can get his big bonuses. And he is trying to get the veterans contract. He'll do to them what he did to Helen."

"Part of me wants to grab Gillie and run, the other wants to slap that man silly. I just don't know what to do."

"I do," said Walter. "We need to go get his emails, documents, and anything else that will incriminate him, so Deter can arrest him. Without solid proof, no one is going to touch a guy with his connections."

Gillie picked at her peeling nail polish. "It's all in his office."

"But you said you couldn't get to your dad's emails," said Kip.

She raised her eyebrows. "I couldn't from *his* computer, but MacAbee's was wide open. Remember how Dr. Dumbshit put me in his office? His password was the date he graduated from medical school. The stupid certificate was hanging on the wall right next to his computer. Anyway, you have a very interesting email waiting for you, detective. I forwarded everything they talked about."

Deter felt his jaw drop. "How the hell did you know my email address?"

"Remember when we jacked your car?"

Lyn sat up and stared – first at Gillie and then at Deter.

"Oh, right. How can I forget? It's been one hell of a day and my ears are still ringing."

Lyn frowned. "Why are your ears ringing?"

"Dad's gunmen blew up Walter's van right next to the Rite Aid store. It slammed us all to the ground. Deter was in front and didn't get down when Walter told him to."

Lyn threw her hands up in the air.

Gillie put an arm around her mother. "Anyway, I got your email address from the business cards you keep in your car. Now all I need is ten minutes in my dad's office. Fifteen max."

Lyn dropped her head into her hands.

"What about the computer passwords?" asked Walter.

"I have them in my notebook."

"So that's what those numbers were," said Deter. Now it made sense. Smart kid.

"I needed only one more code. That's what I came home to get. It was in my old phone. There is just one more little thing." Gillie looked over at Walter. "We need to get past the building's alarm system."

"I can do that," said Walter.

"My career is flashing before my eyes. I'm going to be in jail right next to all the badasses I put there. Shit." Deter could just see Morrison's face as he tried to justify this one. This had handcuffs written all over it.

Walter leaned in closer. "I know how you feel. You're a good cop. You do your job. And this is way out of your field of play, but here's the deal, one of two things is going to happen here – Curtis is going to stop us or we are going to stop him. Your choice."

Deter's phone buzzed. It was Carl.

"I've been worried sick." Carl was yelling so loudly everyone at the table could hear him. "Where the hell have you been?"

"It's a long story."

"How the hell did your car get in a ditch? The captain is ripshit. What am I supposed to tell him?"

Deter sat back in his chair and looked at Walter. "Tell him the truth," he said. "Go into my emails – the password is under my pencil tray – and look for something that was forwarded in the last few hours. Attached are some very important documents I want you to show Morrison. Make copies and guard them with your life."

"Sounds like Curtis is even dirtier than we thought. What's our next move?"

"I'm going to catch him. And Carl, you were right about Walter Lovett. The guy is a hero. If it weren't for him I'd be dead right now and so would the girl."

"Where is she?"

"Sitting across the table from me drinking a Coke."

Cody's head suddenly rose off Walter's foot and a deep rumble rolled in his throat. Gillie's eyes went wide.

"Carl, I've gotta go."

Twenty-Nine

The Curtis House, 2:30 a.m.

SLEEP HAD ELUDED MIKE. He had too much yet to do. His eyes were fixed on his computer screen. His fingers flew over the keyboard in a moment of less than noble inspiration, but what the hell, it was effective. He couldn't help being pleased with himself as he typed out his phony "press release."

>VHA GOLDEN BOY'S CAREER BUILT ON LIES
>
>The Veterans Health Administration is red faced after the discovery that their golden boy, Timothy Reynolds isn't who he seemed. After his own son was killed by land mines, Reynolds had been revered for his tireless lobbying on behalf of veterans until a recent investigation revealed that Reynolds' past has a darker side.
>
>The stalwart of the VHA wasn't always so loyal nor so reliable. More than two decades ago, Tim Reynolds was courting Washington's elite, vying for power, and carrying on an illicit liaison with a cocktail waitress. The affair ended with the birth of a son no one knew existed – including Reynolds' wife.
>
>Tens of thousands of dollars were allegedly paid to keep his name off the birth certificate. Over the years, Reynolds' illegitimate son, Matthew Silverman, had a reputation for getting into fights and blogging against the military. Several reports show he was a frequent patient in two psychiatric hospitals. Three years ago Mr. Silverman was arrested for firing a rifle at the White House.

Checkmate. Thanks to Mike's network he'd discovered the real story, but this juiced-up version and the threat of what the consequences would be for Reynolds if this story were leaked to the press would be a far more useful tool than the boring truth.

In reality, Reynolds had spent an evening indulging in too many Mai Tai cocktails and had a one-night encounter that could hardly be called an affair.

Matthew Silverman was the son of the waitress, but the paternity issues surrounding him had never actually been determined. The boy's real troubles stemmed from occasional depression, a common condition that was nothing more than a chemical imbalance for which he'd sought treatment.

His blog was a forum of passion about the plight of those he'd seen during his own venture into searching for care. The report said he went to Washington to call attention to the fact that many people with perfectly treatable symptoms went without care because of the prohibitive cost of health insurance and hospitals that routinely charged 600 to 1200 percent more than established pricing in the area. His survey showed that hospitals charged over five-hundred dollars for a test that only cost them three dollars.

The shot at the White House was actually a blank fired into the air, apparently in the hopes of gaining a few minutes of press time, which was why he was currently on probation and not in jail.

To Mike the facts were irrelevant and he had no intention of highlighting healthcare's dirty little secrets.

He knew that reporters hungry for a juicy story would snatch his hyped-up exposé in a heartbeat. By the time the story hit the airwaves and was bantered about by the morning shows, no one would care about the truth. The important thing was that by then the damage would be done. Reynolds would be finished – unless he had a change of heart and agreed to cooperate. In which case,

Mike would be all too happy to bury the story. Naturally, he'd keep a copy filed away for safekeeping.

Mike was patting himself on the back and about to make the call to rein in Reynolds when he got a call from an irate Dr. Daniel MacAbee.

"What gives? You said your guys were professionals. My office is shot all to hell. I can't even open for business tomorrow."

"What are you ranting about at this hour? Go to bed."

MacAbee sputtered on. "Brock brought Gillian here. Now I have one exam room that's in shambles. Windows all over my office are busted out. There's blood all over the parking lot. The cops will be at my doorstep any minute. What the hell am I supposed to say to them? Having two dead bodies in the parking lot isn't exactly good for business."

"Do you still have Gillian?"

"No. She's gone. Lovett and some others came for her."

"Where'd they go?" Mike asked.

"How the hell should I know? What about my office?"

"Daniel, shut up. Get out of there now. Call your office manager from home. Tell her there was a break-in. Give your staff two paid days off and keep your mouth shut. If the cops ask, you speculate that it must have been druggies looking for pain meds. After tomorrow night it won't matter. You can retire to someplace tropical and spend the rest of your days drinking rum out of coconuts."

Mike had already taught Daniel MacAbee better than to argue. His ass was on the line too. The last thing Mike needed right now was for MacAbee or anyone else on his committee to fall apart. Stakes far higher than his petty little practice were hanging in the balance.

The poor bastard didn't even realize that in a few years his practice would be gone anyway. YorkCare wasn't the only insurance company gradually forcing all primary care docs into working for hospitals by lowering their payments until it was impossible to cover the overhead of a private practice. At the same time, insurance companies were quietly buying up hospitals and insolvent practices, one by one. Eventually, all doctors would be salaried staff in facilities run by insurance companies. The trick was making sure YorkCare had a healthy chunk of that market.

Tomorrow's healthcare industry was indeed going to be a brave new world. This new lucrative industry was where physicians would be nothing more than hired help, care would be rationed, and fortunes would be made – including Mike's, which he expected to make Donald Trump's assets look like pocket change.

"Where's Brock?" asked Mike.

"After I taped up his face, he went after Lovett and your daughter. He was so hacked off his blood pressure was off the charts."

"How much did Gillian see?"

"She certainly saw me and she saw your cowboys shooting up everything in a two-mile radius of the office. She sure as hell knows you're involved."

"How do you know that?"

"She got Brock so riled up he put his pistol to her head and I had to yell at him to cool his jets. When I ordered him to follow the rules, she taunted him by saying he shouldn't piss off the high and mighty Dr. Curtis."

"Damn it. I wanted this taken care of before she knew about the Lovett case. Whatever she knows or thinks she knows – it's too much." Mike paused. "Put Brock's anger to use. Take him off leash. He needs to finish this – now. Call him and tell him I said to take them both out, but make damn sure it looks like Lovett did it."

◆

GILLIE JUMPED UP from the table and was stunned by how her dog's happy-go-lucky tail wagging could so quickly turn into bared teeth and snarls. His ears were back and the fur over his shoulders looked like it had been gelled to a razor-sharp edge.

Until now, she had enjoyed hanging out with everyone at the kitchen. Deter had just put away his phone when a figure flashed by one of their windows. The conversation died instantly.

"I can't do this again," said Mom in a voice that sounded more desperate than anything Gillie had ever heard.

"Get down!" said Walter. Before anyone could move, he was out of his seat with his gun drawn. Cody was right next to him, following his moves.

Gillie peeked around the corner at the living room. Outside a figure flashed past the window over the love seat toward the front door. *Oh, crap*. Brock was back. The guy was like the freakin' Terminator.

Both the front and back doors blew open at nearly the same time. Everyone hit the floor, except Walter, who refused to back down. The intruder aimed his rifle at the table and didn't even see Walter on one knee next to the wall. Two *POPS* later, Walter had him by the collar and was dragging the screaming man toward the laundry room. The guy was twisting and grabbing at the red splotch on his thigh.

"Quit your whining. You'll live, if you shut your trap." Walter yanked him past the table and into the laundry room.

Deter was on the other side of Gillie. With their backs against the adjoining wall to the living room, she wedged herself into the corner and listened as Deter drew his weapon. They both heard the footsteps in the front room.

Brock was inside. That stunk.

Gillie looked at Kip and her mom huddled under the table. Everyone she loved was in that house. Only this time she was sure Brock hadn't come to abduct anyone. Any other day she would have been frozen with fear, but now it just pissed her off.

Her house was old and quirky. It had to have something she could use to slow him down.

After a few seconds, she scurried past Walter, who was busy tying and gagging the injured man with Cody still at his side. She slipped out of the laundry room and into the parlor with the sagging floor. Hiding behind the bookshelf with her back pressed against the wall, Gillie ever so carefully slid one of the shims out from under the front with her foot.

The shelf was quiet for the moment, but very unstable. She ducked her head back against the wall while her heart pounded out a beat in her ears. Through the arched opening, she saw Brock crouched down behind the couch, inching toward the kitchen. If he had looked to his right he would have seen her.

She pressed harder against the wall. With one eye she peered back around the bookshelf. Brock brought up his pistol and pointed it in the direction of the table where Kip and her mom were hiding. His face was so gnarly she barely recognized him. His nose looked like a disgusting growth that was held on with strips of white tape. One eye was swollen nearly shut. *Serves you right, asshole.*

Gillie quietly moved toward the laundry room. When she felt the door frame she let her voice rip across the room. "Hey, Jerkoff!"

Brock's head whirled around and he launched himself toward her at full throttle. The barrel of his gun swung around to take aim when the bookshelf quivered. The sound momentarily distracted him.

He looked back at Gillie and charged across the floor right in front of the big bookshelf, slapping the little table to the side. The loose floor boards shifted under Brock's weight. He cursed and awkwardly crumbled to the floor. In a split second, he was up on one elbow and raising his gun just as Walter's big arms pulled Gillie from the room. A bullet soared through the air and splintered the door frame just as the bookshelf came crashing down right on top of Brock.

The sound of hardbacks slapping together and the rumble of tumbling books filled the small room. Brock was screaming and fighting to get out from under the weight on top of him.

"Gil, go with your mom," said Walter as he ran back toward the parlor.

She followed him and peered around the corner. *I gotta see this.*

Across from Walter, Deter had moved to the archway between the two rooms. Both men had their pistols aimed at the gunman.

Brock inched backwards trying to pull himself out from under the crushing pile. His butt and legs came out first. What he didn't know was that her dog was watching his every move. Gillie was sure that Cody remembered the smell of the guy who had kicked him because his jowls rose into what she called his nasty-dog face.

The retriever silently moved in closer. His white fangs were just inches from Brock's butt pocket. The dog was waiting for the next movement. Then it happened. Brock jerked backward and Cody sank his teeth in hard and deep.

Brock shrieked, twitched, and blindly swung his gun around. Before he could get a shot off, Deter kicked the pistol out of his hand and said, "Don't move, asshole."

The rest of what happened was a blur. Gillie felt Walter picking her up and whisking her back into the laundry room. Then he hustled all of them, including the dog, out of the house and into the car. Deter was the last one to hop in the Crown Vic.

As they left the driveway Deter said, "I cuffed Brock to the handle on the fridge. It'll slow him down, but I don't expect it to hold him until Carl gets here. We need to beat it."

Gillie looked out the back window. Just as they turned the corner she caught a glimpse of Brock limping to his SUV with the white handle from the refrigerator dangling from his wrist.

She was in the front seat with Walter who was going maddeningly slow.

"Stomp on it! He's gonna catch us."

Walter's eyes shifted between his rearview mirror and the cars around him. "That is exactly why I'm *not* speeding. I don't want to draw attention to us. When you're being pursued, you don't want to go fast."

"But you did last time."

"That was because I had no choice. Instead you need to put yourself out of their line of sight – like behind a sign or going in the opposite direction – or like this."

Walter pulled into a used car lot and parked in the second row between two other vehicles of similar color. After waiting less than a minute, they saw Brock driving right by. He never saw them.

"You want to blend into your environment. See? It works every time, even when you're on foot. You want to be hidden where they don't expect to find you."

Gillie looked into the backseat at her mom who had Cody in her lap. "Mom, see what I mean? Walter is like having your very own Gibbs."

NOON – DAY THREE
Friday, October 12

Thirty

The Yard, 12:00 Noon

THE NEXT DAY GILLIE WOKE with a start. The brightness of the sunlight blaring into the bedroom declared that it must be lunchtime. She rolled over to find her mother lying next to her. Mom was sound asleep and breathing softly. It was a relief to be back in the junkyard trailer and surrounded by the high fences topped with coils of razor wire.

Even with the security of her mother next to her, and the buffer of sleep, the events of last night were still too near. Brock shoving that gun in her face would haunt her thoughts for a long time.

What had she done to cause all of this? What horrible mistake had she made to make her own father hate her so much? She pulled the blanket up over her head and shut her eyes. If only the blanket could shield her from thinking about her dad.

If only she could bury herself deeper, bury down to someplace safe, bury down to rest and rest some more. If only things were different – like how she'd once hoped that someday Dad would want to be part of her life. Fat chance of that happening now.

Last year she thought she had it all worked out. School was good. Friends were great. Looking back, she had been so naïve. She'd taken it all for granted until the move. She regretted cutting herself. How could she have been so stupid? The last thing she wanted was to die. Now more than ever, Gillie wanted her old man to see her walk away happy and without him.

She pulled back the covers and listened to the small pocket of safety surrounding her. The wind was blowing outside and a piece of metal was creaking somewhere. Inside it was quiet. It sounded as if everyone was still asleep. They had gotten back to the trailer just after four in the morning and everyone was toast.

The carwash. The van blowing up. MacAbee's office. Gillie would have thought it all a dream if her elbow and swollen lip didn't hurt so much. She felt her mouth and thought yesterday had been the longest day of her life.

She hated that Brock had invaded her home. It was just wrong. Even worse was knowing who had sent him.

Dad had never been a candidate for a Father's Day award, but if her friends had asked her last year if he'd actually send gunman out to kill her, she would have laughed her butt off and said they were nuts. In her wildest dreams she didn't think he was that bad until now. For a fleeting moment she wished he would change. She knew that wasn't likely and that Walter was right – it had come down to him or them.

Gillie stretched out. Her hair felt gross. Suddenly a long hot shower sounded really good.

One of her arms dangled off the mattress. She felt a mass of fur and peeked over the edge to see who she was petting. Both dogs were on the floor next to the bed. Her fingers were intwined in the soft fur around Cody's neck. Shadow stretched. Thankfully the dogs liked each other. Her poor pooch had endured enough last night.

Cody rose from the floor and flopped his head on her pillow. She moved his cold nose away from her neck and whispered to him. "You were my hero last night." Almost inaudibly he cooed to her as he soaked up the affection.

Gillie kicked the blanket off her legs.

Her mother moved slightly and started to snore, but then buried her head back into the pillow. She'd slept in her tank top and underwear. Gillie looked at the freckles sprinkled over her mother's shoulder and her reddish-blonde hair flowing over the pillowcase. The fragrance of her mother's shampoo brought back happy memories. It was a smell she'd almost forgotten.

With her mother's face now turned toward Gillie, she saw the awful bruise had turned a deep purple, almost black. Gillie grimaced. Mom worked so hard and had risked so much to protect her. *Why did I ever complain about doing the stupid dishes or emptying the trash?*

She wouldn't complain again. She couldn't. Not after last night. Even Cody had risked his life to protect her. She'd never complain about cleaning up after him again either.

Gillie squinted at the sunshine bouncing off the walls. She had slept all she could and her back was getting stiff from the bumpy old mattress that sagged in the middle. As she swung her legs over the edge of the bed she nearly clocked Shadow in the face. "Sorry, girl."

She slipped on her jeans and crept out to the living room, nearly stumbling over a pair of flip-flops that had been left by the kitchen. After stretching her arms and yawning she found Kip in the recliner. His wide open mouth and soft snore made her giggle. Across the room Deter, was asleep on the couch, still barefoot and still in that coat he never took off.

Walter was the only one awake.

He was absorbed by the world just outside the window, keeping watch just like he always did. His eyes scanned the junkyard. The gratitude she felt was overwhelming. No one in the world had ever made her feel so safe.

"Good morning, sleepyhead," he said without moving.

Gillie put her head on his shoulder. "What? No blueberry pancakes?"

"Gil, what have I gotten us into?"

Her face was against the soft flannel of his plaid shirt. She felt his shoulders move when he sighed. "Did you get any sleep?"

"Deter and I took turns on watch." Walter's head snapped around, his body tensed slightly, but it was only a cat exploring the yard.

Gillie wrapped her arms around his biceps. "Walter, I've been meaning to thank you. You're awesome. Helen was lucky to have you."

"It's hard to face my children after allowing YorkCare to let her die."

"That's YorkCare's bad, not yours. You did more than most people would do."

"My kids still lost their mother."

Gillie hid part of her face in his arm. "The truth is I'm a little jealous of your kids. I always wanted a dad like you. You're amazing."

Walter turned from the window, his brown eyes studied her. "You're the one that's amazing." He leaned his head against hers.

She loved the way he made her feel like he would take care of everything. Then he straightened up and returned to looking out the window.

"Today is Friday. I had wanted to go to a party with my friends tonight, but my dad just had to say *no*. That's when all of this started."

"Well, then it's time we end it – don't cha think?"

She nodded. "He should be away from the office tonight. In my dad's emails with MacAbee it said his fancy gala starts around dinner time. He is supposed to give some big speech."

"I heard. Deter's partner is happier than a kid with a new puppy. Those emails are gonna keep him busy for a while. Now, if we can get those spreadsheets, that will make a pretty damning package of evidence for the DA."

◆

Walter turned away from his view of the junkyard to find Cody sitting next to his leg and staring out the window as if he understood their mission. "Good boy," said Walter while scratching his back. He'd forgotten the pleasures of having a dog around. They were always so faithful and eager to please. Too bad Curtis never had a dog. If he had, the animal might have taught him a thing or two.

Walter watched the weary crew beginning to wake and move around. The shower was a big hit. Everyone took turns.

After cleaning up, Deter dabbed antibiotic ointment on his foot and took a cup of coffee from Lyn. She joined him, but hadn't taken her eyes off Gillie.

The kids were playing some sort of board game and sharing some granola bars. Gillie's laughter filled the room. Walter couldn't help smiling, but just under the surface worry nipped at him. How was he possibly going to protect all of them?

He thought about going after Curtis on his own, but then Deter wasn't going to stand for that. Someone had to stay with Gillie and her family and defend them against Brock and whatever fresh hot guns he had in store for today. Like it or not, it was safer to stay together.

Walter's aching body reminded him that he was too old for a mind-numbing, body-racking marathon like yesterday. Maybe today would be better. At least the rest helped.

While watching Gillie making her next move, Lyn sipping her mug of coffee, and Deter draped over the couch, popping ibuprofen, Walter felt things he hadn't felt in a long time. When someone would laugh, they all smiled. That alone told the tale.

The stress of being hunted had a strange way of forging unexpected bonds between people. Survival was a primal motivator and something no one understood quite as clearly as those who'd experienced it first hand.

In the middle of it all sat Gil with her eyes sparkling in delighted at the game and the people surrounding her. It had been like this back in the day when Helen and his dog, Duke, were alive and his rambunctious kids had gathered together in the living room. Just when Walter thought his heart was broken beyond all repair, there was Gillie who made him want to laugh again and take long hikes with a good dog.

Speaking of living, it was time to check his sugars. Walter went into the bathroom and put his meter to good use. Adjusting his insulin levels was a routine prick that had become little more than a nuisance.

Upon returning to the living room, he rubbed his sore thigh and settled into a seat next to Deter. They talked quietly about the details of their next move. Walter liked working with the guy. He was a character for sure, but dedicated and he didn't pull any punches. After being drugged, shot at, nearly blown up, and slugged in the face, Deter was still in the fight.

"I can't believe you're still hanging in there. Most guys would have thrown in the towel by now."

Deter felt his sore cheek. "Price of doing business, I guess."

"How come people like you and me always charge into mayhem, when everyone else is running the other direction?"

Deter chuckled. "JPN, my friend. Just plain nuts."

Walter rubbed his chin. "It's worth the fight, isn't it?"

"Hell, yes."

They both watched Gillie and her mother and smiled.

Walter saw himself and Deter as a couple of seasoned warriors who understood why it mattered. Part of it was just their nature, the other part was a bad experience that had turned them both into guard dogs. Walter assumed that for Deter the loss of his son probably had a lot to do with it, and if he knew him better he would just bet there was something else back there when the detective was a kid.

For Walter it was his dad's "hunting accident." Growing up, Walter had been a thoughtful kid with a soft spot for the underdog. He hardened up when an asshole with a rifle had tracked his dad's hunting party and fired at them from a ridge. He was Gil's age and still remembered standing in that clearing while the men in their group frantically put a tourniquet on his dad's shattered leg. While his father was hustled in a harrowing six-hour race to the nearest hospital, Walter and twenty-two year old Joey Dickson tracked down the shooter.

It was the look on his father's face that drove him on that day. He'd used everything his dad and uncle had taught him to track the man down. When Walter found the shooter pulling a motorcycle out of the bush to get away, he made certain that didn't happen. Dad lost his leg, but survived. The shooter went to jail and never told anyone the motive for the assault. And Walter went into the army with few illusions about those who kill.

Walter's bull-dog determination had waned since Helen's death. It was as if this experience with Gillie had jumpstarted his will and reminded him of why he'd wanted to make a difference. Each person in this room mattered. His only worry beyond surviving was that Gillie had a heart like his – that of a warrior. Only time could tell what she'd do with it.

Out of the corner of his eye, Walter caught a glimpse of Lyn watching Deter like a cat who was curious, but not willing to get too close. Walter chuckled to himself and figured she couldn't do much better. The detective was a good man.

Deter looked over at Walter. "You know you are out of your fucking mind if you break into Curtis's office?"

"Hell, we already know that," said Walter with a big grin, "but I think our plan will work."

"How are you going to get past the security?"

"I'll show you. At sixteen-thirty we need to get moving."

Lyn frowned at her watch. Her head nodded as her mouth silently counted. "That means four-thirty, right?"

Walter gave Deter a hand, pulling him upright. "Let's go, but first you need something on your feet."

The kids had finished their game. Kip grabbed the flip-flops by the kitchen and tossed them to Deter. "Sorry, they're the only thing I can find. At least they look like they're close to your size. My boots are too small or I'd give them to you."

Deter rolled his eyes and dropped the sandals to the floor.

"If the shoe fits," said Walter. He clamped his lips together and tried to hold it in, but a belly laugh was more than he could contain. He wasn't sure which looked more ridiculous – a barefoot cop or one in orange flip-flops.

"At least they don't have those giant flowers on the toes," said Kip, who was cracking up too.

Walter laughed even harder.

Deter pushed Kip sideways. He shoved back and they horsed around until Gillie said, "I have no clue what time sixteen whatever you said is, but my phone says it's gonna be five before we get out of here. Let's do this."

Lyn wrapped her arms around Gillie with a pained expression that made it clear she understood what needed to happen next. "Are you sure you still want to do this?"

"Let's get it done," said Gillie. "Mom, it's gonna be okay."

While everyone piled back into the Crown Victoria with Walter behind the wheel, Kip let the dogs out to roam the fenced enclosure of the junkyard. Gillie gave them some fresh water and then jumped into the passenger seat.

En route to the YorkCare building in Concord, Deter sat on his coat and Walter sunk deep into his own thoughts. He could taste the familiar mood in the car. It wasn't much different from his days in the army. In transport to a mission there had always been a moment when everyone became silent. Each soul looked inward. Some thought about loved ones back home. Others kissed a medal or prayed or tied their shoes in a certain way for good luck. Everyone wrestled their nerves into submission and steeled themselves for what was ahead. That was exactly what this felt like now.

The big difference, of course, was that back then he was with men who were well trained and psychologically prepared for such things. It was their job. Walter looked around at his passengers and sighed. They had no business getting in the middle of what would surely be a firefight.

Sure, Deter was trained for investigation and apprehension, but was he up to full-scale combat? Curtis would pull out all the stops to protect himself tonight. Walter feared what they might be walking into, not for himself, but for them.

He watched the rush-hour traffic and thought about Gillie. He loved that kid's spunk, but damn that girl, she was so stubborn. She wasn't going to hear *no*. She would go in with or without him. That was like sending a dog into a tiger's den. Without him, they didn't have a chance against someone like Curtis and his hitmen. What choice did he have but to go in and lead the charge? If he could field most of it with Deter's help, they at least had a chance.

Twenty-five minutes passed in near silence. Shopping centers and trees whizzed by as they traveled north. Walter drove into a small parking area adjacent to the ten-story YorkCare building.

They waited as the sun settled toward the horizon and threw streamers of oranges and golds into the clouds. Nearly all the staff had left when Walter pointed to the last remaining car. "That's probably the office manager's."

Seven minutes later, a young man in a dark suit emerged from the front of the building with a huge set of keys. He set the alarm, locked up, and drove away. Once he was out of sight, Walter moved everyone out of the car and into place, making sure they were well concealed on the wooded hillside surrounding the YorkCare parking lot.

From their higher position behind tall timbers, granite boulders, and wild berry vines, they could see the front and back of the building and the closest side door. Walter checked with Deter low tech style – he walked over and hunkered down next to him. "I put Gillie's mom and Kip higher up as lookouts. Call me if you see anything. I'm going to try something."

Crouching down, Walter then went back to Gillie. "Stay in the bushes. If anything goes wrong, run. Don't stop. Don't hesitate. Go to any place where there are a lot of people and call the police."

She mumbled something about spiders and didn't look happy about being in the bushes, but she followed his instructions and dug herself in behind a leafy magnolia. Walter checked for poison ivy and to see that everyone was out of sight before he began his recon.

Walter started by standing stock-still and combing every square inch of the facility with his eyes. The lights were on motion sensors. Cameras covered the front of the building and the parking area, but not the back. That was stupid, in his humble opinion. Fifty feet from him was the door to what he expected was their maintenance room. Walter adjusted his vest and silently slipped out of the foliage. Within a few strides he was at the entrance to the maintenance room.

To give them some credit, the door was set with an alarm – it just didn't look like a very good one. Time to improvise. Walter ran his Citi credit card very slowly above and below the door handle. A bead of sweat rose up on his lip. Inch by inch he felt his way.

His fingers confirmed what he suspected. The stickers and warning signs were for show because this wasn't a heavy duty system anywhere near what he'd seen in military installations.

Walter pulled out his Leatherman and snapped open the folding knife. The tip of the blade slipped into the latch and the door popped open. An alarm sounded.

Next he picked a business card off a cork board and quickly added to the noise level by igniting it with his lighter and holding the smokey flame up near a hardwired smoke detector. Once that started screeching, Walter carefully stepped out, locked the door, and returned to the woods.

"Kip. Time how long it takes for the fire department to get here," said Walter.

Meanwhile, they waited.

Thirty-One

YorkCare Building, 5:48 p.m.

Deter glanced down at the underbrush poking his battered toes and wondered how people had protected their feet before the invention of shoes. Whatever they had made, it must have been better than these damn things. No wonder they were called flip-flops.

His phone buzzed with an incoming call from Carl. At least he wasn't getting an eyeful of Deter's new footwear. He'd never let Deter live this one down.

"I found something interesting," said Carl. "A friend did me a favor and spent most of the night with his head in the cold cases and missing persons database. He came up with a file for a missing girl, a Rebecca A. Curtis. They called her Becky."

"Did you get a look at it?"

"Only the summary. It said that the girl just vanished. Her younger brother Michael, who was home at the time, claimed he was asleep in his room. A friend said Becky would often miss work and later she'd show up with bruises, but she would never talk about it. After the girl went missing, a local church group said they'd found a young woman, who had been badly beaten, trying to get a coat out of their donation bin. She called herself Becky. When they tried to call for help the girl begged them not to. She said her brother would kill her. Sister Mary Elizabeth retold Becky's accounting of her brother using a baseball bat on her after he'd forced her to take drugs. Of course, the nun reported it and a couple of days later a young man with dark hair and blue eyes came around asking questions, but Becky was gone. The girl was never seen again."

"Sounds to me like Curtis had everyone believing that he was the poor abused little brother when actually he was the real aggressor. My guess is that his quest to control people started with her. He likely had something on all of his family. According to the way Lyn talked, Curtis's brother, Neil, surely knows more than he's willing to tell. I wouldn't be surprised if he knows what happened to Becky or if she is still alive. Carl, that was good work."

After talking with Carl, Deter felt a little edgy as he quietly shifted to keep his knee from getting stiff and wondered what had happened to Becky. She could be living in another part of the country and have three kids by now. While his mind ruminated on what could have made Curtis into such a cold bastard, he found himself fascinated watching Walter in action.

The man's patience was remarkable and age certainly didn't seem to slow him down. The guy was a one-man tactical surveillance team. The thing he liked most about him was that he only used his weapon when he had no other choice. Deter admired how Walter was so self sufficient. The guy was even his own medic.

Deter saw the scene play out as if he were at a football game with the darkening sky and rising moon as a backdrop. Maybe fifty yards from him, Walter leaned against a trunk in a clump of trees. From time to time, he'd check his watch or look over at Kip. Walter kept Gillie close. Every time she turned her head, he knew about it.

A siren could now be heard in the background. A sports car rocketed into the front parking lot and slammed to a stop. That caught Deter's attention. He looked between the branches and eagerly waited to see what would happen next. The vehicle's door opened. Out stepped the same young man they'd seen earlier, only now he was without his tie and jacket.

Moments later a cruiser showed up just ahead of a hook and ladder. The fire department piled out in their insulated bunker gear with the neon yellow reflective tape. Deter felt a tug of regret for wasting their time. One guy had an ax in hand and they all had on their helmets.

While the manager talked with the cop, the fire personnel encircled the building. They conversed with each other on radios, checked every window, and felt the doors and walls. After a few more minutes the manager unlocked the front door and disarmed the security system.

The troop of fire fighters stormed inside with a meter Deter assumed was a carbon-monoxide sensor. Meanwhile the manager chewed his nails and kept looking at his phone. Deter figured the guy had a hot date or tickets to a game – he sure looked antsy. His hands were shoved deep in his pockets most of the time as he paced back and forth. As the minutes drug on, the manager kicked the gravel and paced in tighter circles.

Deter smiled to himself when the fireman with the meter emerged from the building and spoke with the manager as the rest of the unit boarded the fire engine. He felt bad for the manager. The emergency guys must have thought he was a putz. After the squad car and fire engine left, the manager stood alone in the parking lot, shook his head, and locked up again. As the manager's car peeled out of the parking lot it was obvious to Deter that Walter had this poor schmo pegged.

Looking over at Kip and Gillie, Deter saw them impatiently watching Walter, who sat there in the growing darkness like a big cat tracking prey with two cubs watching from the bush. Not one muscle twitched.

Deter was ready to wrap this up and get the hell out of there. Instead, another twenty minutes went by and Walter did the whole damn thing over again. The dutiful manager showed up, only this time he was without the fire department and the PD. He took a flashlight and stomped partway around the building.

Walter's silhouette didn't budge. Deter couldn't see much in the woods because of the low light, but he'd bet last weeks paycheck that Walter was wearing a sly grin. *Son of a bitch.*

The now pissed-off manager stood under a light and made a call while animatedly throwing one arm up in the air. Deter felt sorry for the poor guy. Then suddenly the manager nodded and he put away his phone. Pulling out a bundle of keys, he opened the main entrance and fiddled with the alarm panel before locking up and leaving.

Walter was one clever man. Deter could see where this was going.

◆

GILLIE THOUGHT THE COMING and going of the manager was interesting – the poor dude looked like the butt of a joke. The novelty tanked as the next thirty minutes passed way too slowly. The sun had gone down an hour ago. It was dark and even worse – she was cold. Gillie bit her nails, anxious to get this over with.

Walter suddenly turned and motioned for her to come. Looking around, Gillie could see everyone's faces popping out from the branches, but they stayed in the woods while she and Walter hustle out of the brush and entered the maintenance door. This time no alarms went off. Walter's trick worked.

"What did I tell you? Patience pays off," said Walter.

Gillie rubbed her shivering arms. "So does getting over the finish line first."

Walter just gave her one of his harrumphs that cracked her up. They entered the first hall. Even with him by her side the office still seemed daunting. It looked the same as always, except it was empty and dark. She peered around the corner and turned right. The long hallway to her dad's division felt creepy enough to be a great location for one of those paranormal flicks. She half expected a zombie janitor to leap out at her from one of the offices and someone else to film it on a jumpy camera.

The sad part was that behind those doors things much more scary than movies really did happen. This was the place where a faceless corporation decided who got care and who didn't – who lived and who died. Gillie felt her nerve waning until she thought of the smile Helen had worn as she posed for her wedding picture. That changed everything.

Gillie led the way to the entrance to her dad's division at the end of the corridor with renewed determination. On the wall next to the door, a red light on the keypad blinked to show the security system was armed. Gillie pulled out her phone, found the passcode, and entered the numbers on the keypad. The blinking LED light turned to a solid green and the lock clicked open just like she'd hoped it would.

Once inside, they both saw the large room filled with cubicles for all of Dad's workers. Just beyond them was a core of offices in a ring around his ginormous conference room. The contrast between the hallway and her dad's division was pretty startling. It even smelled different – his of fresh cut flowers and furniture wax while the rest of the offices smelled like copy machine toner and Lysol. Each of their steps sank into the soft sage-green carpeting. The front wall of Mr. Big Shot's office was all glass instead of drywall. It was her father's bullshit world. Untouchable by ordinary folks. He could have artwork and tall vases of exotic flowers that cost a fortune, but his customers couldn't have a stupid bottle of pills that could save their lives. The whole thing was so bogus. Gillie wanted to pick up a chair and bash it all into a pile of rubble.

Her head turned toward the empty chairs, Gillie couldn't help wondering how many of them knew what was really going on. If they did, what would they think? Beverly had seemed like a nice lady. Pictures of her grandkids were lined up on her side desk. Could she really go home to them knowing the company she worked for was deliberately letting people die?

She was pretty pumped by the time she used the key to open the sleek door to her father's office. Walter found a chair and sat down to watch the doors while she made herself at home behind the huge desk. *Okay, asshole, it's payback time.* Her fingers went to work. As she was waiting for the computer to boot up the vibration of her phone made her jump.

It was Deter. "Let me talk with Walter."

Gillie handed over the phone. Walter listened. "OK," he said before hanging up.

"Do you know where Beverly's desk is?"

Gillie frowned at him and pointed. "It's that one. Why?"

Walter wandered over to the secretary's file drawer. It was locked, but not for long. It cracked her up how he could pop open a lock with his Leatherman as easily as if he had a key. He pulled out a file, tucked it into his vest, and returned to the chair in her dad's office.

"What was that all about?" Gillie asked.

"Deter wanted me to retrieve this." Walter patted his vest. "Apparently your dad destroyed my file and wasn't aware that a second folder was kept in his secretary's desk. So, I just borrowed it."

Her father's twenty-seven-inch computer screen lit up and drew her attention to the login box. Gillie placed her notebook on the desk and rubbed her hands together. One by one, her slender fingers entered the numbers. It didn't take long to find his spreadsheet and related folders – Dr. Doofus kept them right on his desktop.

She couldn't break the code to get into his email, but when she clicked on the "write" button it allowed her to send out a new message. Gillie giggled to herself and quickly emailed a copy of everything to Deter, herself, and Walter – just in case. As she waited for confirmation she got another call from Deter.

"Get the hell out of there! Curtis just showed up."

"What? My dad is here?"

Walter jumped to his feet.

"But..." Her stomach went into a knot.

"Never mind. He's already in the building. Hide!"

Gillie did a hard shutdown. "My dad is on his way up here."

Walter turned off the lights and grabbed Gillie's notebook. "You have to re-set the alarm or he'll know someone is here."

Gillie quickly locked his office door and ran to the division entrance while fumbling with her phone.

Walter's head pivoted between the hallway and Gillie's trembling hands. "What about the building alarm, won't he notice it isn't set?"

"I doubt it. When the alarm doesn't go off, he'll think it's because he swiped his passcard."

They both could hear a voice and footsteps coming from the elevator. "Oh crap, here he comes."

Walter's head was next to her ear. "Just take a deep breath."

She did and her fingers steadied just enough that she could quickly punch in the numbers and push the door closed.

As soon as she'd finished, she turned off her phone and followed Walter to the other end of the room, as far away from her dad's office as they could get. She could hear her father just outside the door when they ducked down inside a corner cubicle.

There was an electronic *CLICK* and the door opened.

"Brock, I don't give a shit what your problems are – you are the damn professional. I want Lovett dead. Now. Make it happen."

Gillie put her hand over her mouth and stared at Walter. He cradled her head in his shoulder. The feel of his big arm wrapped around her was reassuring, but she was more concerned about what he must be feeling. They had known Dad was after Walter, but actually hearing him say it was just freakin' rank.

The question now was what her father intended to do with her. She still had one last secret hope that someday he'd change. Gillie knew it was silly, but maybe her dad was after Walter because he didn't understand and thought Walter was just a kidnapper. She had pissed off Brock pretty bad. Maybe he was the one that wanted her dead, not her dad. Her father was still a crook who should pay for what he'd done, but could he really have his own kid murdered? She listened as he started talking again.

"I get that Lovett has some kind of special skills, but Gillian?" Her dad snorted as if the idea of her having any kind of talent or ability was just plain stupid. Gillie's jaw tightened. "All I asked you to do was to take her down and make it look like the old guy did it. Are you seriously telling me you can't shoot straight enough to hit a hundred-pound girl? Or did she suddenly develop some magical powers too? For Christ's sake, we aren't dealing with wizards and super natural beings – just an old man and an asinine teenager."

There it was. Gillie had heard it with her own ears. She felt suddenly numb. The coldness in his voice was like an ice dagger.

It was as if her lungs suddenly had forgotten how to breathe. Walter hugged her tightly and whispered in her ear. "Don't listen to him. He's wrong. You are someone very special."

Gillie heard her father's footsteps and suddenly realized she had forgotten to delete the copies of her emails in the "sent file." It felt like her heart was climbing up her throat.

What if Dad had come here to check his email? What if he saw what I did?

If he even touched the monitor, the warmth would make him realize someone had just been in his office and they'd never get out of there alive. Each second seemed like decades. Gillie prayed he wouldn't go near his computer.

There was the sound of shuffling papers and then she heard the fax machine's distinctive chirp and her dad's voice. "Hey, Reynolds. You have a fax coming through that you will want to pick up personally. Read it very carefully. I'll be there early tonight to discuss it with you."

Her father hummed cheerfully as he turned off the lights and left the office. The door latch closed and the alarm buzzed as he reset it. After a few moments, she breathed a huge sigh of relief.

"I just can't believe it," she said.

"Gil, he is wrong about you and about everything. He is to be pitied. The guy has no idea what he is missing by not being a good dad."

Once again, Walter was patting her hand. His big bear paws made her hands look so small. If she clung to him, she knew he wouldn't let go. He'd protect her or die trying. That alone made her remember the people who cared about her, even if Dad didn't. Walter was right. Dad was wrong.

Walter stood and made her keep her head down. He was the first one to look around. Once he signaled her, they both left the corner. Back in her dad's office, she printed out the report confirming that the fax had been sent and received. And with it popped out the first page of the faxed document. Her dad had said this feature was something the legal department had insisted up on. And now, that one page was all she needed. It said "Press Release" at the top.

"Walter? Do you know who Tim Reynolds is?" Gillie handed him the message. "I don't get this."

Walter read the transmission carefully. "This is what you call blackmail."

Thirty-Two

Hotel Millennium Marquee, 8:35 p.m.

MIKE CAUGHT A GLIMPSE of himself in one of the hotel's many mirrored panels. He straightened his tie and brushed one hand through his fresh haircut.

A satisfied smile stretched across his whiter-than-white teeth as he turned to face a very perturbed Tim Reynolds.

Normally when two adversaries faced off, nerves tingled on both sides, but for Mike it was just another day of business as usual. His confidence came from learning a long time ago to deal from a position of strength. Losing wasn't an option, at least not in his rule book.

Reynolds stood there in one of those ill-fitting, two-for-one suits. His complexion had blanched to the color of his shirt. His eyes narrowed. He was glaring at Mike with his mouth set in a thin line.

It was the look of a man who had been cornered. Mike had seen it many times before.

He just wished he'd seen the first blush of shock and the stunned look of disbelief as Reynolds' had read the fax. Oh, well, waving another copy in front of his nose would have to do.

Reynolds' mouth tightened to a slit. "You don't care who you hurt, do you?"

"Tim, it's time to be reasonable. I'm not asking for your soul. All I want is your support. We both know YorkCare is the best choice anyway."

"Perhaps for you, but I doubt that is true for our servicemen and women. They deserve better than a company that resorts to blackmail and lies to win a contract."

"Don't take it so personally. I'm just doing my job and protecting my company's interests."

"What happened to that oath you took when you got your medical license – the one about not causing harm?"

"Oh, Tim, come on. Sacrifices have to be made. Vets know that."

"They've already made their sacrifices. Now it's up to us to hold up our end of the bargain and give them the care we promised. Not that you'd understand."

"The only thing I care about is keeping our board happy." Mike admired his reflection again. Damn. His new suit turned out better than he'd expected. Trim. Dark. And stylish.

When Mike turned around, Reynolds was gone. The door was just swinging back in place. It didn't matter. Mike had seen his eyes – he had the man in his pocket and they both knew it. Tim Reynolds had made it clear he didn't like Mike's tactics, but the only other option was a very public scandal that would play havoc with both his personal and professional life. Hell, Mike wasn't even worried about Reynolds going to the authorities with the fax because the information on that sheet was so damning.

As Mike confidently strolled toward the ballroom stage he called in to ensure Brock and his team were in place.

"Where are you?"

At first Mike didn't understand Brock and made him repeat himself. "We 'ave men covering da parking lot and lobby. I'm backstage. They're finishing up their desserts and are dust about ready for you to deliver your presentation."

Mike assumed the slow, slurred sound in Brock's voice was nasopharyngitis, commonly known as a head cold. He didn't give a crap about how the guy felt, but at least he was on point. Mike dropped his phone into the slim pocket of his Armani suit and transformed his smirk into an understated smile.

It was showtime.

Mike strolled on stage. The crowd cheered as the panel stood. Gerry Blakely eagerly shook Mike's hand and grandly directed him to the podium. With the thump of a switch the lights dimmed. An electronic crackle popped and the white hot circle lit up center stage. Mike tapped the microphone a few times and feigned shyness at being thrust into the spotlight. In truth he relished every second of it.

He could barely see Reynolds in the back with his arms folded and whispering to a man at his side. He'd love to be a fly on the wall and hear that conversation, but for now his engines were running. He was ready to give the audience what they had come to see.

Every word, every pause, every inflection had already been rehearsed. There was no need to pull the notes from his pocket. Instead he reached out a long arm and wrapped his manicured fingers over the edge of the podium. The enormous ring from his prestigious medical school glinted in the light. The room grew silent in expectation.

Mike glowed in the brilliant spot light while everyone else waited expectantly in the dark – this was just how he liked it.

He leaned forward, plying the audience with the boyish good looks that had gotten people to trust him. Raised eyebrows and warm smiles spread over the crowd like a wave at a football game. His mojo was working. Even Janice Winslow, the reporter, stepped a few paces closer in response. Her camera operator trailed her every move, angling for the best footage. This was it – Michael J. Curtis's moment. He took a deep breath and opened his mouth to speak.

BAM. The double doors of the ballroom flung open and slammed against the doorstops. The sound reverberated off the richly paneled walls, giving the hall the feeling of being an enormous cave. Heads turned. All eyes followed the noise. A low rumble of questioning voices dissipated the mood Mike had so artfully created.

Up the main aisle walked a disheveled girl and an older man.

◆

Gillie couldn't care less about all the linen-covered tables with the tall vases of lavender orchids, nor did she care about all the people in black dresses and fancy suits. What she did care about was exposing the man directly in front of her. More than anything she wanted them to know what her dad was really made of – like a stinkbug pinned to a piece of styrofoam for all to see.

"So killing off your customers wasn't enough? You sent gunmen to take out your own daughter? Nice touch, Dad."

Gillie heard a man next to the aisle say, "What the hell?"

"Don't even bother to deny it," Gillie screamed. "I heard you give the order yourself."

Gasps echoed around her.

Her father was wearing that fake smile she had hated for as long as she could remember. "I'm a little busy at the moment, sweetheart. Perhaps I could speak with you later?"

"Perhaps you could tell the truth for a change." Gillie wasn't going to run away ever again. He was going to listen to her this time.

"Forgive the interruption. I'm afraid my daughter has some unfortunate psychological issues."

"You're the one committing mass murder and *I'm the one* with issues! That's a good one, Pops."

Her father's voice lowered to a frightening hiss. "Don't ever call me that again."

The crowd gasped and then grew silent.

She pointed to a spot behind her father. "If you don't believe me, then who is the guy packing heat on the right side of the stage?" Gillie could see heads turning toward the heavy-velvet curtain behind the podium. "That jerk's name is Brock. He has a pistol under his jacket because he's my dad's hired assassin. His face is all messed up because he took a few hits yesterday when he tried to kill me and my mom, and some others – including a police detective."

"This is ridiculous – a delusional fantasy."

Several people in the audience pointed as Brock slipped back behind the curtain and disappeared from sight.

Gillie looked around at the crowd. "Your big shot medical director is killing YorkCare's customers. He delays their care so he can keep the money that was supposed to pay for their medical treatment."

"Someone call security," said Dad, acting like he was still the boss calling the shots. Wrong. Gillie swallowed and braced herself. She wasn't going to let him get her flustered. Many in the crowd were gawking at her with their mouths hanging open.

Walter stepped up next to Gillie. "She's right. Curtis is rationing care. He lets people die and then takes the money that should have been used for their care to pump up your bottom line. I know, he stood by and let my wife die. He delayed authorization of her treatment until it was too late to save her."

"And he has done this with hundreds of other people," said Gillie.

A rush of red flushed over her dad's neck. "This is outrageous!"

"No. Your selfishness is what's outrageous," she said, turning back to the crowd. "I have proof."

"So do I." Walter held up the folder from his vest.

"Dad, why don't you tell everyone about your clever spreadsheet and how that cute little algorithm works?"

"I don't know what you're talking about." Her dad's eyes were starting to bulge as he looked around for security.

"Jeez, I must have paid more attention in math than you realized because I understood your stupid calculations. The young healthy ones get their claims paid so your stats look good. Isn't that right? And what happens to all the unfortunate people you label in red? I'm sure everyone here will be really interested in how that works, because by the looks of it most of the people in this room fall into your red zone. Bet they'd be really surprised to learn that after paying into your system for years, you do everything possible to keep them from getting the care their doctors ordered."

The sweat on her dad's upper lip shined in the spot light. "Where is the goddamn security? Someone grab her." Her dad was yelling at Brock.

Gillie pushed her voice to boom louder. "Let me get this straight – your customers pay for their health insurance, but you pull out all your tricks so they can't use it. And if you're not paying doctors' bills like you promised, where's all that money really going? Does everyone here know about your three-million-dollar bonus? Oops. We found at least some of it. I just want to know how you can stand there in your fancy suit that your customers paid for with their lives."

"Me too," said a man who bravely stood in the back. "I'm Dr. Josiah Weir and I was forced out of practice because I couldn't run my office on your lowered payment schedule."

A dignified woman with silver hair stood. "I'm Dr. Keller. Last year your paperwork round-robin delayed the care my patients needed. Three died as a result. And don't think we haven't noticed that our payments go down when we do what's right to treat our patients." Wow, Gillie was getting more of a reaction than she'd expected.

The people around her began to mumble loudly to each other. Some picked up their things and started to leave. Others were telling each other their own stories.

There up on stage was Dad with that stupid scowl, only this time he couldn't point a sponge at her and make her feel like she was a worthless piece of shit contaminating his mansion.

Deter's voice caught Gillie by surprise. "Dr. MacAbee, you are under arrest," he said loudly.

All eyes turned toward the corner table where a startled Dr. Daniel MacAbee had tried to excuse himself before Deter had firmly planted him back in his seat and cuffed him to the table.

Gerry Blakely jumped to his feet and cut the microphones. He stomped over to the podium. Gillie could only catch a few words of what Mr. Blakely was saying – stuff like 'how the hell' and 'this is your fault' were just some of the phrases flying between them. One thing was obvious: he was pissed. His mouth was moving rapidly and his face was all red.

The outraged audience was on its feet, shouting questions and calling for an investigation.

Gillie wasn't sure what would happen next. Only that she was no longer the one on the run. Dad pushed Mr. Blakely out of the way and darted off the stage. On his way out, he pulled Brock from behind the curtain and yelled something at him.

Walter ran after him, quickly followed by Deter.

Gillie stood in the aisle not sure what to do.

Her mother rubbed her shoulders. "You did a good job, sweetie, but I think we need to get out of here."

"Mom, I can't miss this. Walter is gonna kick Dad's butt."

Thirty-Three

Banquet Service's Back Halls, 9:25 p.m.

It was like old times, except instead of a jungle to navigate Walter was chasing hostiles through long corridors and banquet rooms while staff were running to get out of their way. Up ahead he could see Curtis glancing over his shoulder as he made the corner.

Walter stopped behind a large shelf of table cloths and caught his breath. He ripped an evacuation map off the wall next to his head, scanned it briefly, and shoved it into a pocket. The fisheye mirror up by the ceiling showed him all he needed to see, at least for the moment. Curtis was running down the hall toward the kitchen. Between them was Brock with his back plastered against the wall. His one good eye was flashing between the mirror and the kitchen.

Brock was a long way from the best Walter had seen, but the bugger sure was persistent. The problem was how to get around him to get his hands on Curtis. Just as Walter was about to take a bold approach, a cook departed from the kitchen with a large tureen of soup on a linen-covered cart. Brock turned his head away, listening to something Curtis said and Walter descended on the scene with the quickness of a snap.

The startled cook jumped back. Walter hurled the hot soup at Brock. It must have stung because Brock was swinging his arms around and swearing like a soldier stuck with latrine duty. He raised his gun and Walter slapped his hand away.

Walter saw the cook running toward the kitchen. "Get down."

The cook didn't listen. His hat flew off as he scrambled to get away from Brock. Walter kicked the gunman in the back of the knee causing one leg to buckle. Before Brock could regain his balance, Walter hauled him onto the cart and ran down to the end of the corridor toward the stairwell. There he launched the cart and one very vocal Brock down the steps. The cart and the cursing stopped abruptly.

Walter charged back into the kitchen looking for Curtis and took cover.

"Please, sir. Let me go. I don't have anything you want. I'm just a cook."

"Shut up," said Curtis.

Walter took a quick glance. Curtis had taken the hapless cook hostage with a chef's knife that still had shreds of lettuce hanging from the blade. It was clear to Walter that Curtis was way out of his league. The guy might have been a master behind the scenes, but he didn't play well on the front lines.

In a flash, Walter snapped his Colt into position and nailed the hanging sauté pan next to Curtis's head. A giant wet spot bloomed in the front of the cook's black and white checkered pants. He screamed and dived to the floor. The sound of the blast startled Curtis. He fumbled and dropped the knife. The blade sliced through his fancy trousers, leaving a slit in the flesh beneath. Drops of red dribbled onto the floor.

"I hope you have good health insurance," Walter yelled as Curtis ran around the corner.

◆

DETER DODGED PEOPLE in maroon uniforms rushing by him in a panic. The hall was bounding with screams and stampeding feet. A young woman with large brown eyes stared at Deter as she ran past him. They all looked so terrified, he felt bad for them – at least most of them.

A big guy who looked like a gangbanger in an apron swaggered up to Deter and eyed his feet. Apparently this dude was too cool to run like everyone else. The detective flipped open his coat, put his hands on his hips, and let the guy get a good look at his badge and his weapon. "Buddy. You got a problem?" The guy threw up his hands and backed away to join the last stragglers getting the hell out of there.

Deter hadn't worn flip-flops since he was a kid. He'd forgotten how hard they were to run in – and that damn *FLIPPITY-FLOP* sound.

As he turned the corner, he heard Walter and Curtis yelling back and forth at each other. He slowed down to calm the flapping sounds. He must be close to a kitchen because the sweet and savory aromas drifting through the air were making his stomach growl.

The yelling was coming from a large prep area just off the kitchen. Deter peeked into the room with his piece drawn. A mixer as tall as a man was beating some concoction into submission and a long stainless steel table was an assembly line for fancy desserts. He couldn't see Curtis or Walter, but he sure could hear them.

Trying to ignore the buttery sweet smells, Deter stayed by the door and listened. Just as he crept a little closer, a woman with a large tub of frosting came out of a walk-in refrigerator. She screamed, dropped the frosting, and ran.

Curtis's head popped up. He grabbed a tall rolling shelf filled with clear plastic tubs of something white in a milky liquid. Pushing the shelf in front of him, Curtis charged at Deter.

He couldn't find a clear shot. The cart picked up speed and came directly at him. Deter tried to jump out of the way, but tripped on a doorstop just as the cart slammed into him. One of the tubs jettisoned into the air and crash-landed next to him. At least the twenty-pounds of raw squid was on the floor – instead of his lap. Deter got to his feet, but moving was a different matter. If he thought running on carpet in these damn things was a bitch, it was nothing like trying to get traction on floor tiles covered in raw calamari.

Curtis darted past him.

Walter appeared from around a rack of seared steaks and pulled Deter beyond the slick floor. Once again on carpet, he and Walter chased after Curtis.

They picked up the pace when they heard yelling up ahead in the main hallway. The moment they recognized Gillie's voice, Walter's legs pumped harder. Deter ignored the pain in his knee and raced to stay up with him. It didn't quite work. It took everything he had just to stay on Walter's heels. They charged around the corner, one after the other, like a couple of quarter horses going for the last stretch, and came to a dead stop. Walter spun out of sight, but Deter's momentum and the slippery flip-flops forced him to fall to one knee.

"Shit." He couldn't believe the ghastly sight before him. Brock's face was blistered and a long string of dirty tape was hanging off one cheek. His blood-clotted nose was forcing him to breathe through his mouth. This time he had two men with him, who were armed to the teeth. And in their grip was Gillie. Her shirt was pulled up above her navel by the knot of fabric in one man's fist. Brock's arm wrapped around her white torso. It looked as if the men were about to pull her in two.

Everyone froze except Curtis, who resembled a rat looking for a way off a sinking ship. Deter figured the doc would be an easy target if it weren't for the Beretta pointed at Gillie's head and the two AK47s aimed at his own chest.

In a nasally voice that made him sound like he had a horrific cold, Brock said, "Put yo weapon dow."

"Take it easy, Brock," said Deter, putting his Glock on the floor.

"Kick it into da stairwell."

Deter didn't much care for letting go of a pistol – especially one that didn't have a safety – and started to back away, but the blood vessels on Brock's forehead bulged out when he screamed and his head jerked sideways in a tick. *This guy is seriously messed up.*

"Kick it now or I blow her fucking head off."

"Fine. I'll do it. Just relax, will ya?" said Deter. *Goddamn it, I hate that bastard.*

Deter couldn't help staring at the red-ringed iris of Brock's one eye as he kicked the Glock into the open stairwell. Deter held his hands where Brock could see them. Hopefully, the asshole didn't notice his ankle holster.

"Let go of me," said Gillie. Brock only tightened his grip and pressed the barrel of his gun against her temple with more force. She screamed at Curtis, who was backing toward the kitchen. "Daddy, how can you let him do this?"

"Michael! Make them put the guns down or I swear to God I'll shoot you myself." Lyn's voice startled everyone – especially Deter. In a glance he realized that she had come out of the stairwell holding his gun. He could see she had a clear shot. Her hands were a bit shaky, but –*my God* – her resolve was solid granite. Kip was right behind her holding a broomstick.

One of the gunmen pivoted his weapon in her direction, but then a shot came over Deter's shoulder and took the guy out. Gillie flinched and covered her face. Lyn hit the floor. Meanwhile, Deter grabbed the Baby Glock from his ankle holster and rolled out of the way.

Brock clung to Gillie while the remaining gunman sent shots zinging down the hallway.

Crouching behind a bin of sour smelling linens, Deter fired back and missed, but the shot threw the rifleman off balance. Walter charged ahead and tackled him. Before the man could regain control of his weapon, Walter walloped his elbow smack into the side of the man's face so hard his head rebounded off the floor. Deter winced. "He'll be out for a while."

Brock was still clinging to Gillie and moving closer to the kitchen. Using her as a shield, he yanked her roughly backward. She went with the momentum and lunged into him – *hard*.

Stumbling a few steps, he hit the wall, but refused to let go. She swung her head backward and bashed into Brock's already mangled face. He wailed, pushed her away, and held his nose.

Walter was on his feet running. As soon as he got to Gillie he swung her behind him with one arm. With the other he drew a bead on Brock with the Colt and briskly marched backward until he could push Gillie around the corner to safety.

Brock braced himself against the wall and held his semi-automatic pointed at Walter, warning him not to move. A clear blood-tinged liquid seeped from Brock's nose as Deter slowly moved in front of Lyn. Drip by drip a damp patch on Brock's shirt got bigger.

Shoulder to shoulder, Deter and Walter trained their weapons directly at Brock. It was two to one and no one dared to blink.

◆

WALTER HEARD CURTIS yelling orders at Brock. "Leave it. I need you with me."

The man didn't move. That eyeball with the red halo remained zeroed in on them.

Curtis's head poked out from the kitchen. "Get over here – now."

Brock broke off and backed toward Curtis's voice.

Walter assumed the guy had to know how close he'd just come to getting blown away, but right now he was more concerned about Gillie.

"Are you okay?" he asked her. He checked for bleeding, alertness, and vitals. A rapid assessment of Kip and Gillie's mom showed they were all unharmed. "Gil, stay with your mother and listen to me this time, will ya?"

Walter pulled out the evacuation map and showed it to Deter. "There's two other exits in the kitchen." He scratched his head. "This is nuts. We're chasing them in circles."

"You want to split up?" said Deter.

"Yup, but first we need to determine where they are so you don't have any surprises coming up behind you. They could be anywhere by now."

He and Deter thundered down the hall, pushing ahead and ducking behind anything that would give them cover. At the entrance to the kitchen, Walter crouched down to make himself a smaller target. A long time ago he'd learned that most shooters instinctively fire straight ahead at the level of a man's torso. The trick was to keep all vital parts out of their line of sight long enough to have an opportunity to fire back. Then there was Deter, who was still standing straight-up with his feet spread and his arms braced for action. "What the hell am I going to do with you? Deter, get your head down. This isn't a goddamn shooting range."

Deter flattened himself against the wall next to an ice maker. "I gotta find Curtis and that asshole Brock."

POP-POP. Slugs zinged through the air over Walter's head.

"Found them," Deter said with a shit-eating grin. He answered. *CHINK-SNAP.* His shots ricocheted off stainless-steel equipment in the kitchen.

POP-POP. More bullets rocketed back at them. Deter looked like a TV cop in girlie sandals as he slumped against the wall and reloaded his Baby Glock.

"I told you to keep your head down." Walter checked his ammo. "You nearly got yourself shot. Look at your coat."

Deter checked his torso and held out the flaps of his overcoat. Two holes the size of a man's thumb had ripped right through the fabric at nipple height on the right side. "Damn. I liked this jacket," said Deter.

Walter ignored the detective's grumblings and moved closer to the kitchen. Just inside he could hear Curtis giving orders. "Shoot anyone who gets near us," he said to Brock. Then things grew quiet except for a dishwasher that was churning away in the midst of a steam cloud.

For the moment it seemed like a standoff until someone stumbled behind Walter. He whirled around ready to fend off an attacker only to realize it was Lyn.

Walter lowered his voice to a whisper. "Where's Gillie?"

She shrugged.

Mother of God. Walter was almost afraid to look back into the kitchen.

"Go hide and stay put. I'll find you," he told Lyn.

Deter moved over next to them. "I'm going around to the next door to cut off Curtis." Walter watched Deter and Lyn running toward the main hall.

Turning back, Walter crept into the kitchen. Over by the line of fryers, what looked like a squat stainless steel bin moved just slightly. It didn't take long for him to figure out it was on wheels. He got down low and looked under the tables and counters. Curtis and Brock were hunkered down on one side of a partition near a floor drain. On the other was Gillie, less than twenty feet from them. Right next to her was Kip, looking every bit like a kid who'd just realized he'd gotten in over his head. *Shit. She must have used one of the other entrances.*

Walter prepared himself for the worst. He'd wanted Curtis to stand before a judge and face the humiliation of a trial, but if he tried to hurt either of those kids he was a dead man.

What the hell was Gil trying to do? From his position he could now see the hefty bin had a spigot. It was one of those filtering grease buckets cooks used to clean out fryers. He guessed it was filled with hot grease and the cook had hightailed it before he'd finished the job. Gillie confirmed it was hot when she bumped her shoulder against the metal side and flinched. To catch her balance she put both hands down on the floor. Her face scrunched up in disgust as she wiped her palms on her pants. When she looked up, she saw Walter.

He motioned for her to hide. Gillie held up one finger and then opened the spigot. Hot grease poured across the floor in the direction of Curtis. It sputtered and popped when it came into contact with pockets of water. Gillie and Kip sank deeper into the shadows under the prep tables. The problem was that the kids had boxed themselves into a corner.

Suddenly a startled voice rang out. "What da hell is dis?" Brock was staring down at his feet and the floor that looked like it was undulating. "Shit." He jumped back. The soles of his black sneakers were steaming.

"It's grease, you idiot," said Curtis, as he stepped safely up onto a pile of floor mats. He ducked down to look for the source of the goo and spotted the kids. "Go get them."

"Are you shittin' me? I can't go over dere. I'm not gonna deep fry my feet."

Walter's heart was racing. This could go real bad, real fast.

Brock knelt down to take aim at the kids. Walter didn't hesitate. He popped off a shot. Brock's arm flew away from his body and his hand flopped around at an unnatural angle. His pistol skittered across some mats and landed only a few feet from Curtis.

Brock squealed like a wounded animal. His head was twitching madly as he cradled his injured hand. "I've been fucking shot." His high-pitched voice was pitiful.

Curtis hopped off the mats and picked up the gun. "Come on." He started moving toward the other door.

"Didn't you hear me? I've been shot," said Brock. Red streaks streamed down the front of his shirt and the man's nose had started to bleed again.

Curtis lowered his shoulders and heaved a sigh. He turned around and raised the gun.

"I've had enough of you," he said and pulled the trigger. *THUMP.* Brock grabbed at his chest, stumbled backward, and sunk to his knees. The grease was still hot enough to steam when his back landed on the floor with a *SPLAT*. His hands went helplessly limp. Tears streamed out of the swollen eye and the other stared wildly up at the ceiling as if the words of his own salvation were printed up there somewhere. Brock gasped just once.

Walter couldn't see Curtis, but he could hear him.

"You can sit here all you want, but I'm getting the hell out of here."

"Oh no, you don't," said Deter.

Walter charged forward, looking for a clear shot. He caught a glimpse of the detective standing in the other doorway. Curtis fired at Deter. He spun around and went down.

"Lovett, put the gun down," said Curtis as he stood and aimed Brock's Beretta right at him.

Walter took cover, but could see that Deter had taken a hit. He had no idea how badly he was injured.

Curtis picked up Deter's pistol and examined it. "My understanding is that you call this a Glock. Am I right? Cops are rather fond of these."

The guy was still trying to play the big shot, but his dirty clothes and rumbled hair made him look like a derailed senator who'd been caught with his trousers down.

With Brock's pistol in one hand, Curtis swung Deter's Baby Glock around in the other. Walter didn't know how many rounds

Curtis had to play with, but he was sure Deter's was fully loaded. The other certainty was that the kids were too close.

"Give it up, Curtis," Deter said. His voice was strained, but Walter was thrilled to hear the sound of it. He knew that if he was still yapping, the guy could breathe and had a pulse.

"Backup is downstairs." Deter grunted and caught his breath.

Why in the hell was he talking to Curtis? Then it dawned on him that Deter was handing him an opportunity by deliberately distracting the doc. Walter moved in closer. To his left, he could see that Gillie and Kip were carefully tiptoeing across the thick layer of congealing ooze covering the floor.

"By now the whole world knows what you did," said Deter, a little louder than needed. "My captain is having a field day with your emails with MacAbee. Your only way out of this building is in a body bag or a pair of cuffs."

"Considering I'm the one standing and you're the one on your ass, I think I'll take my chances." Curtis kicked Deter's leg out of the way and ran.

Deter tried to roll on his side and started to cough.

Walter descended on him and tore open his shirt. "Stay still."

The wound was close to his left shoulder, just under his collarbone. Walter grabbed a clean bar towel off a table and shoved it under his shirt. He checked the exit wound and put another towel in place. Walter positioned both towels under Deter's holster strap and adjusted the whole thing to tuck them tightly in place.

Deter spoke between gasps and grunts. "Never saw – a holster – used like that."

"Sometimes you gotta improvise." Walter smoothly snugged the strap up a bit more and hoped it would control the bleeding. So far it was working. "Call for help."

Deter moaned and showed Walter the phone in his hand. "Already did."

"Good man," said Walter. The detective was looking at him with that pleading expression he hated so much, it was one he'd seen too many times. "Hang in there for me."

Deter tried to smile, but grimaced instead. "Just get Curtis for me."

Walter reloaded his Colt. "Buddy, you can count on that one."

He hated seeing Deter down. Walter tried to make him more comfortable by helping him sit up.

Deter winced. "You're wasting time. Go."

Walter gave him one last look and moved down the hall. The first two doors were locked, but the one on the left was half open. The sign said "The Crystal Room." He slipped into the dark room and waited until his eyes adjusted. Round tables and carts filled with stacks of banquet chairs started to appear out of the darkness. It was a dining room.

The moment he moved next to a folded round top he heard the click of a pistol ready to fire.

Thirty-Four

The Hotel's Kitchen, 10:30 p.m.

GILLIE TRIED NOT TO LOOK at Brock's body as she made her way out of the kitchen, but she couldn't block the nasty smell of burnt hair. The image of Kentucky fried – still with feathers – zipped through her brain and turned her stomach. *That's just gross.*

She found Deter on the ground. "Are you okay? What can I do?"

He shifted to look up at her, but it was obvious that he was in a lot of pain. "I'll be fine."

The corner of her mouth pulled into a smurk, she wasn't convinced. Nodding toward the kitchen she said, "He's dead, isn't he?"

Deter looked. "I'd say so."

Gillie slid her back down the wall to sit next to him. "We need to get you help."

"Already made the call."

While they waited Gillie tried to figure out what to do next. Kip plopped down next to her and wrapped his long fingers around her hand. At least they were together. She clung to him, amazed that he was still at her side after all this. "How can you sit this close? I'm soaked in grease. It's totally disgusting."

"Shut up," he said with a smile.

Mom's voice came from around a corner. "Gillie, is that you?"

Gillie waved for her mom to join them. "Deter's been shot."

"Oh my Lord." Mom scampered down the hall with Deter's service pistol still in hand. The sight of her packing heat would have been hysterically funny on any other day but not today. She knelt next to Deter and put his gun on the ground. "Who did this?"

"*Dad*," said Gillie. Totally disgusted, she shook her head and went back to picking at her nail polish. Gillie glanced up. Mom was hacked. She could tell by her eyes.

Deter's right hand felt his shoulder. "I'm okay, at least for now. Walter is a damn good medic."

Mom was just about to check out the kitchen when Gillie and Deter blurted out – "Don't look" – at nearly the same time.

"Mom, a dead guy's in there, the one in the Mountain Dew shirt, and it ain't pretty."

"Did your father shoot him too?"

"Roger that," Deter said.

Gillie caught a glimpse of the pistol on the floor. For some crazy reason she just couldn't take her eyes off it. "Dad ordered Brock to kill Kip and me, but Walter stopped him and shot the gun out of his hand. Then Dad just picked it up and blasted Deter with it. If it weren't for him and Walter, Kip and I –" Gillie's voice faded to nothing. "– never mind."

She watched her mom rub the side of her face like she always did when she was pissed and couldn't do anything about it. "I can't believe this," she said while holding Deter's hand.

"At the office I heard Dad tell Brock he wanted me dead. He was dissing Brock, saying he was too bad of a shot to take out an 'asinine teenager.'"

Kip looked away, but his hand squeezed tighter.

"Honey, I'm so sorry. I've tried to protect you from him. He wasn't cut out to be a father, but I never thought he would hurt you."

"I tried to think of one stinkin' time when he'd said something, anything, nice to me, but I couldn't. I know we don't have pictures of us together. Walter has tons of pictures with his kids." Gillie felt something starting to rise in her that was beyond anything she'd ever felt before.

Mom looked down at her hands folded in her lap. "This is not your fault."

"Was he ever nice to me?" She had to know.

Mom just shook her head and wiped her eyes.

Gillie nodded. She was beyond crying and looked over at Deter and continued to stare at the pistol lying next to his leg. "Where did Walter go?"

"He's in the room down the hall. I expect he plans on having a 'come to Jesus meeting' with your father. Backup is working their way up from the Lobby." Deter coughed a few times, turning his shirt red. "I hope they get here soon."

"Mom, Walter says you have to put pressure on wounds and get them up higher than the heart. You better do it."

Kip helped get Deter into a sitting position. While Mom put pressure on the wound, Gillie scooped up the pistol and stood. "How many shots are in this thing?"

"Five," said Deter. "Careful, it doesn't have a safety."

"Gillie, put that down," said Mom as only a mom could do.

Gillie backed up a few steps. "And what if Dad comes out of that door? Are we gonna just sit here and let him shoot us too?"

Her mom started to get up.

"Stop, you have to keep pressure on that wound or he's gonna bleed to death."

"Sweetie, please. Put the gun down. Don't do this."

◆

WALTER STAYED STILL and let his eyes adjust to the low light inside the room. Even though Curtis had two pistols, he was unschooled in navigating in the dark and Walter knew it. He and the darkness had become comfortable with each other a long time ago. For him such spaces were a protective cover, but for people like Curtis, it was a strange and unnerving blindfold. The man hadn't learned to trust his other senses.

Point taken – Walter heard Curtis bump into a table near the far wall. The guy just gave away his position. Clearly, the doctor knew political tactics, but not urban maneuvers. Cornering him wasn't going to be that difficult, provided Walter continued moving slowly and kept backlight from turning him into a silhouette.

Walter was about to home in on Curtis when a sound came from an unexpected location. Walter stopped and listened. It had to be footsteps, but they were light, hesitant, but clearly there. Just when he was about to investigate, the fluorescents flickered and bathed the room in a harsh white light. He squinted at the door. Kip was by the light switch. Much to his horror Gillie stood right in the middle of the dance floor.

Curtis's head popped up on the other side of the room.

She cautiously put herself between him and her father and changed the game for all of them.

"Gil, no!" said Walter.

She ignored him and held out her hands as if she were walking a tightrope. He found himself captivated by her delicate white fingers that flared out almost featherlike. With his heart pounding in his chest, Walter scrambled to find a path to head her off.

Curtis moved to a closer vantage point.

Gillie stopped.

Her father took a long look and then ducked out of sight.

"Dude. You can pretend you're all that with everyone else, but I know who you really are."

"Shut up," said Curtis.

"How dare you go off on me after what you've done."

"You don't get it – "

"Really? I get that you've never even tried to get to know me."

"I couldn't."

"Oh, right. Was pampering your ego taking up too much of your time? Or are you so in love with yourself, you didn't have time for anyone else?"

Curtis moved closer. "It wasn't like that. I worked like hell. I had to prove I was worth something more, something better. You don't know what happened to me. I had to make it on my own. No one looked out for me. No one ever had time for me."

Gillie's looked down at her shoes. "I would have, if you'd given me a chance."

Walter was stunned at what he was witnessing.

Curtis stared at her. "How would you know anything about pain? You've had everything."

"Everything except a father." At first her voice was soft. "I can tell you about pain. It's looking for your Dad – the one person you want to see more than anything in the whole world – only to have him never show up – all the other kids' dads came, but not you." Damp streaks were running down her face. "Not at track meets, our band performances, or even one single freakin' birthday." Gil was now screaming at him with a force that grabbed Walter by the throat. "Never! You never did anything with me."

Curtis looked at the guns in his hands and shrugged. "It's too late."

"No, it's not." Gillie reached out one hand. "Daddy, *please*. Can't you give me just one chance?"

Curtis winced. "I can't." His hoarsely croaked reply and sad expression made him look like a lost kid about to cry.

"Why not?" said Gillie. Walter could tell her chin was trembling.

"You can't trust people, they only let you down."

Gillie's hand fell limp to her side. She stepped back. "Like you? You're the poster boy for letting people down."

"Shut up." Curtis howled at her. "You have no idea what its like to have your father abandon you to monsters or never having your mother around to protect you."

"Are you blind or something? Can't you see – that's exactly what you've done to me? You sent hitmen to kill me – that is about as close to monsters as you can get – and you filed a restraining order to keep me from seeing my mother. *Hello*?"

Curtis looked confused. "That was different."

"Like hell it is." Gillie cut him off. She held her hand high in the air like a crossing guard. "Talk to the hand, asshole, cuz I ain't listening anymore. I've heard enough crap out of you. If you shot everyone you didn't like, you'd be the only person left on the planet."

"I said, shut the fuck up."

"Or what, Dr. Big Shot? You gonna put a bullet in me too? And just how is that going to change the truth?"

Walter inched closer. Even without seeing her face, he knew she had that brave but hurt look in her eyes that twisted his heart into a knot.

Gillie's voice boomed across the room. "I heard you tell Brock to kill me. How could you? I'm not just some 'asinine teenager' – well, maybe sometimes, but –"

Walter bit his lip. *God I love that kid.*

"– I'm figuring out this growing up stuff just like everyone else. And I'm a real person. And a damn good one."

Walter was shaken by the guts it took to dress-down her father like that.

"At least to him, I was just another mark, but I'm *your daughter*."

Curtis's hands rose slightly. Walter jumped into action, running for Gillie as Curtis aimed Brock's semi-automatic it at her chest.

"Lovett, put the gun down or you'll be wearing Gillian's brains."

Walter froze just a few feet behind her and held both hands in the air. "OK, Curtis. You win. Leave her alone – I'm the one you want anyway."

"Lovett. Put the damn gun down."

Everything in him wanted to jump in front of Gillie. If only he could get three more paces forward before Curtis fired.

"Now," said Curtis.

Walter set the Colt on the floor. As he stood back up he realized that Gillie had stuffed Deter's service pistol into the waistband at the hollow of her back. Walter eased just a bit closer and gently pulled it free.

"Kick your gun toward me," said Curtis, keeping Brock's pistol pointed directly at Gillie's chest.

"Dad. Stop it!" She extended her arms like a point guard, making it difficult for Walter to get around her. "Look at what you're doing." Gillie's voice became more insistent as she stepped back, moving Walter back with her. "Is this really what you want? Do you hate me that much?"

Curtis's eyes pivoted between Walter and Gillie. She stepped forward with her hands balled into fists.

"What's wrong with you?" Gillie screamed at him, full force. "*Parents are supposed to protect their children!*"

Her words stopped Curtis cold. For just the briefest moment he stared into Gillie's eyes. His pistol drifted lower and his hands trembled.

Walter took the opportunity. He wrapped one arm around Gillie and pulled her behind him.

Curtis stood there looking lost. Walter aimed, but before he could fire, Gillie pulled down his arm and Walter let her. He didn't want to kill Curtis anyway – especially in front of her. With the gun lowered, two loud *POPS* echoed in the room as Walter took out one of Curtis's legs.

Gillie jumped. Curtis dropped one of his weapons. As he crumpled to the ground, he peppered the ceiling in a spray of bullets with the remaining pistol.

Walter pulled Gillie behind a cart of stacked chairs. On one knee he hugged her to his chest. "I'm so sorry," he said as a lump rose in his throat. "No father should put his kid through what you just saw."

Her hand gripped the fabric of his sleeve and he kissed the top of her head. "Thank you for not killing him," she said.

Walter covered her ears and rocked her in his big arms while Curtis wailed like a wounded animal. Seconds later, they heard footsteps and voices. Walter saw Kip pointing into the room. "They're in here," he said.

Walter peeked around the chairs. Curtis stopped hollering abruptly when he realized someone was standing over him with a rifle barrel pointed directly at his face. He immediately dropped the remaining pistol.

"You want another one, asshole?" said a cop who identified himself as Officer Carl Blackburn. "Don't move. You're under arrest."

Carl went to kick Curtis's weapons aside when Gillie screamed, "Look out!"

Right behind Carl was the guy Walter had knocked out with his elbow. He was standing in the far doorway with his rifle pointed at Carl's head.

THUD-UMP. Walter discharged two rounds, this time going for a kill shot. Both bullets entered the man's forehead. The back of his head exploded, sending an aerosol of red over the polished wood-panels behind him.

Gillie covered her eyes. *FLUMP* – the body hit the floor.

Shouts from the hall and the sound of boots stampeded into the room. One by one, officers in bullet-proof vests swarmed the dining room. Carl was calling out orders as Walter pulled Gillie to her feet.

"Girl, you scared the crap outta me, but you did a damn fine job. I'm so proud of you," he said as he engulfed her in a bear hug and wished he could remove this horrible event from her memory.

He searched her sweet face, terrified that he'd find a wound, but all he found was a big smile and sobs of relief.

"We did it," she said.

"What's this 'we' shit?" said Walter. "You did it. That was a neat trick with Deter's pistol."

While two officers finished cuffing Curtis, Walter retrieved his Colt from Carl. "We need a medic," said Walter.

Carl looked at him squarely. "Where's Deter."

"Follow me." Walter trotted out the door and down the hall. Up ahead, Deter was slumped against the wall with Lyn's hands frantically holding pressure on the red soaked towels.

Walter started barking orders in his military voice. "Get a medic over here. Now."

The detective tried to smile, but his eyes didn't lie. Walter knew he was in pain and sent Lyn to a table just inside the kitchen to get more towels.

"Don't even think about giving up on me now, you pain in the ass," said Walter, while putting more pressure on the wound.

"Just for the record, you're the worst goddamn kidnapper –" Deter grunted. "– I've ever met."

Walter chuckled, but he could see Deter's skin had gone clammy and pale. "Well, considering your footwear of late, you're not gonna win the best-dressed cop award this year."

Deter started to laugh, but went into a fit of coughing instead.

Lyn had returned with a stack of clean bar towels. Walter put a fresh one over each of the soaked ones. She turned her head away while Walter pressed down hard.

"Ouch. Shit," said Deter. He was starting to shake.

"We need a blanket and O_2 over here." Walter held Deter's shoulder. "Hang in there, pal. I know this hurts like a son of a bitch."

"The EMTs are here," said Carl, clearing the way. "Make room."

"Where's Gillie?" asked Walter.

Lyn nodded toward the end of the hallway. On the other side of the people processing the scene, Walter could just see Gillie standing next to Kip near the doorway. He pulled one of the blankets off the gurney as it passed by and wrapped it around her. Then he pulled her close. The boy hesitated for just a moment, his mouth was less than a inch from hers.

The two kids were oblivious to the cops bustling around them. Their lips met and Gillie giggled.

SIX MONTHS LATER
Saturday, April 20

Thirty-Five

Goffstown High School, 11:00 p.m.

*P*OP-POP. Two loud noises echoed in the dance hall. Months had passed and Gillie still jumped even though she knew the sound was only balloons.

Goffstown High School's prom was in full swing. Gillie and Kip danced, surrounded by a throng of their classmates. The gym was transformed with streamers, balloons, and a large sign that spelled out this year's theme – "The Sky's the Limit."

For Gillie it felt like the world had finally stopped spinning out of control, except that those three days had changed everything. She felt like the same person, only different. Simple stuff like riding the bus or eating dinner with her mom were things she'd never take for granted again. So much had changed. Now she preferred the sounds of her friends laughing and talking to being plugged into her tunes.

Tonight was magical. The lights twinkled. The music rocked. The friends meant everything. She took in every moment of it. Kip still bought her gummy bears, but he'd changed too. They both had.

Since the kidnapping they'd grown so much closer. No one understood what they'd been through like each other. When she would jump at loud noises or just wanted to sit on the porch with Cody and listen to the wind in the trees, he got it.

More than what they'd been through, it seemed as if they had both grown up. There on the dance floor in his black tux, he even looked older. She never imagined he'd look *that* good dressed up.

Gillie wore a simple long gown in a peach satin that mimicked the glamor of Hollywood back in the forties. The retro look was kinda fun. She'd had a blast shopping for it with her mom.

As the crowd cheered for the newly elected prom king and queen, Kip excused himself, saying, "Don't move. I'll be right back."

She was a bit surprised and crazy curious. It was more than the impish gleam in his eyes. She knew something was up when he went on stage and tapped on the microphone.

"Cool night isn't it?" Kip said. The crowd clapped and cheered. "Well, it's about to get even better because tonight we have a special award."

Gillie's curiosity was driving her nuts. She bit her nails and tried to remember which awards hadn't been handed out yet. They had already done everything – best athletes, brainiest, funniest, best smile, best dressed, cutest couple. *What else could there be?*

One of Gillie's friends, the student council president, handed Kip a silver envelope. He held it with both hands and looked out at the students. That amazing smile of his was dope. The crowd anxiously held their breath.

Gillie could see his fingers tremble as he opened it. "The student voted by her peers as the person most likely to change the world is – Miss Gillian Curtis."

She felt her chin drop. *Oh My God!* "You have to be kidding me." The words *voted by her peers* stuck in her head. *They'd do that for me?*

A roaring wave of hoots and hollers erupted all around her. Kip looked as if he barely noticed – his eyes were stuck on her. He waved for her to come to the stage.

As she made her way through the cheering crowd she felt her face turn all warm and flushed. Even her ears were hot. With each awkward step up the stairs, she held her skirt and prayed she wouldn't trip. *Oh, my, God. Everyone's looking at me.*

From up on the stage she could see everyone's faces. If only they knew how much they all meant to her. Even the huddle of bullies didn't scare her. After Brock, even the worst bad boys were like comic book characters.

She shook her head and laughed as the clapping went on and on.

Kip nudged Gillie and pointed to the other end of the dance floor. Her mother had snuck in and was standing against the back wall in a simple black dress. Right next to her was Deter, who was sporting a new coat.

Gillie laughed. "I'm gonna kick your butt for this one," she whispered.

Kip looked at her sideways with that stupid grin he got when he beat her at checkers. "And we have a special guest to present the award. Would you please give it up for Master Sergeant Walter Lovett."

Gillie's head was flying back and forth looking for Walter until Deter opened the door. A tall stately man with silver hair marched into the back of the room. She barely recognized him in full uniform.

Walter removed his beret and neatly tucked it under his belt. The uniform made him look so imposing. As he walked forward the crowd parted and sounds of kids saying "whoa" followed him. All eyes were on him as he marched up and onto the stage.

Kip handed him the shiny medal hanging by a maroon and white striped ribbon. Walter's deep voice boomed over the sound system. "It is my pleasure to bestow this award upon Gillian Curtis. I have no doubt she will change the world. She surely changed mine."

Gillie couldn't believe the sight before her. The plaid shirt and the rumpled vest and that old hat were gone. Walter's shoulders were squared and his head held high. His big hands slipped the ribbon over her head. A lump rose in her throat and she tried to wipe her eyes without ruining the eye makeup.

For the first time in her life, Gillie was completely and utterly speechless.

She looked at the floor and shook her head, but the words just wouldn't come. So she did the only thing she could think of – she stood tall and saluted Walter. He chuckled and wrapped her in one of those hugs that made her feel like nothing would ever hurt her again. By now even Kip was clapping and three guys on the dance floor yelled, "*HOORAH*."

When the noise died down, Gillie managed to say a heartfelt *thank you* into the microphone. The music started up again and Walter held out his hand. "May I have this dance?"

"Sure, if I don't fall on my face getting down those steps."

"I'll catch you."

Gillie could not get over this night. Even the girl who had teased her mercilessly in her freshman gym class was smiling and waving.

Once they reached the middle of the dance floor, Walter put her hand on his solid shoulder and held her other hand up high in the warm palm of his hand. It was liked she was a star on one of those dance shows.

"I didn't know you knew how to do this."

"Helen loved to dance. I was kind of forced into it."

He nearly lifted her off her feet as he whirled her through the crowd like a princess. That's when it hit her just how much he meant to her.

"How are you doing?" he asked.

"Good." Gillie smiled, but looked away.

"But?"

"I just wish I had a family that was normal, like everyone else's. It's weird answering kids' questions and having to explain why my dad is in jail."

"Gil, sometimes we are born in a family, sometimes we choose our own."

"Does that mean I get to keep you?"

Walter laughed out loud and kissed her forehead. She thought it was the first time he'd really looked happy since those photographs she'd seen in the hall.

"Oh, I nearly forgot." Walter stopped dancing and dug his fingers into his breast pocket. He pulled out a delicate silver necklace. "This is for you. It was Helen's. I think she'd like you to have it."

For the second time in her life, she was without words.

Walter put it around her neck and snapped the clasp. "Might be a little easier to wear than that big medal."

Gillie touched the pendant that looked like a bird soaring through the sky. "Thank you so much and –" Gillie fought with her throat to get the words out. "– thank you for caring about me."

Walter nodded. "Actually, I'm the one that needs to thank you."

Gillie wanted to stay in his arms forever.

"You look beautiful tonight."

"So do you. I mean, you look handsome." Gillie scanned Walter's chest looking at all the medals and giggled. "You look like a teddy bear who packs heat."

"Too much?"

Gillie shook her head. "No. You look amazing."

Kip stepped up next to them. Walter patted him on the back, then he simply kissed the back of her hand and let Kip step in.

Gillie put her head on Kip's shoulder and watched Walter disappear back into the crowded dance floor. Still holding the necklace with one hand, she kissed the pendant and smiled.

TWO YEARS LATER
October, 23

Epilogue

Gillie's Journal Entry for October 23

LOOKING BACK on the last two years, I can say that Walter still cracks me up, but I'm not sure if I really did or ever will change the world. Things are better in a lot of ways. Kip and I are still together, College is pretty cool, and my eighteenth birthday was the best ever. Even so, I sometimes sit on my porch with Cody and wish I could forget some of the things that happened.

Deter said I played a key role in their investigation of my dad and all the stupid things he'd done. I still can't get over that my own father killed people. If I hadn't seen him with the gun, I would never have believed it. I guess sometimes people fool you.

During Dad's trial, my picture was in the papers and on the news. The reporters made it sound like I was a hero or something. If they only knew how embarrassed I was to even be related to my dad after all the things he did. Walter helped me through it all. The good news is that they gave Walter full immunity in return for his testimony. That was pretty great.

Captain Morrison had a party for Walter to thank him for saving two of his detectives. Walter told me that Deter got his car back after they repaired it and that his partner gave him the keys on a key chain he'd made with one of the orange flip-flops. Walter thought that was pretty funny and is still teasing him about it. He and Deter hang out sometimes either at the shooting range or just sittin' around swappin' stories and having a couple of brews.

Deter also hangs out with Mom over at the coffee shop. She is doing great, especially after getting her job back at the library. The divorce worked out better than she expected and they gave her most of Dad's assets instead of alimony. It wasn't like he was going to be able to send her anything from behind bars.

No surprise to anyone, Dad was found guilty of a bunch of charges: murder, attempted murder – that one was for what he did to me – blackmail, and a lot of other stuff. They nailed him on all of it. I still can't picture him wearing an orange jumpsuit and working in the prison laundry, but that's where he ended up. He won't be pointing guns or soggy sponges at me or anyone else again.

MacAbee and the people on my dad's committee all got busted too. I read in the paper that YorkCare lost one of the largest class action suits ever filed and then went bankrupt. Get this – the penalties were so big and the public outcry so loud that it forced the Senate to have hearings on the state of the health insurance industry. They found out that companies all across the nation were doing the same kinds of dirty tricks. For once, Congress went bipartisan and pushed for new accountability measures in health insurance, but like anything else, it will probably take a long time to fix it all.

We've gotten back to normal, except for Deter, who is still looking for his son Ryan. I hope someday he finds him.

I see Walter a lot. Either he is at our house fixing something or Kip and I go over to get some of his grilled cheese sandwiches, which are still the bomb. I got Walter a puppy for his birthday and named him DJ – short for Duke Junior. Thanks to the puppy, Pookie now stays on his own lawn. Mrs. J is still making her chocolate-chip hockey pucks and she still thinks I'm Walter's granddaughter. Oh well, I guess some things don't change – and maybe that's okay too.

…Gillie Curtis

What about Deter's son, Ryan?

One lost boy who knows too much. One grieving father—
and a day that will change everything.

TORN APART 2
Finding Ryan

Twitterbe

Boston bank programmer, Madison Stone, discovers a software anomaly that lands her in the crosshairs of the FBI's most illusive cyberterrorist as he infiltrates the banking industry with a cyber assault that will send the entire US economy into a death spiral—and he sets her up to take the blame.

2013 Releases

About the Author

MARTA SPROUT is nearly as fast paced as her thrillers. Outside of writing you'll see her kiteboarding, skiing, and scuba diving or you just might catch her rescuing sea turtles or sharing her latte addiction with her detective, firefighting, paramedic, and professional writing friends.

The serious side of her has long been an advocate for people, especially in her jobs as Ski Patrol and medical management. Marta has written many published works and now writes full-time. She grew up surfing the waves off Southern California beaches, but today she lives in Corpus Christi, Texas with her family and her beloved dog, Nina.

Find her at:

www.martasprout.com
Goodreads
Twitter
Facebook Fan Page
Linkedin
Google+

StormRider Publishing
www.stormriderpublishing.com